Dusklight at Noon

Dusklight at Noon

A Novel by

Damodar Khadse

Translated by

Sewak Nayyar

AUTHORSPRESS

Worldwide Circulation through Authorspress Global Network
First Published in 2021
by
Authorspress
Q-2A Hauz Khas Enclave, New Delhi-110 016 (India)
Phone: (0) 9818049852
E-mail: authorspressgroup@gmail.com
Website: www.authorspressbooks.com

Dusklight at Noon
(A Novel)
ISBN 978-93-91314-80-4

Translated in English by Sewak Nayyar

Printed in India at Thomson Press (India) Limited

Remembering the women
who braved all odds in life
tore apart shackles
achieved their dreams and desires
and rose to rare glory

Preface

Dusklight at Noon, the English translation (Sewak Nayyar) of Damodar Khadse's Hindi novel *Badal Raag*, is a story of love, longings and self-assessment; a celebration of a woman's dreams, desires, and intellectual faculties. It's an enticing journey leading to the beautiful protagonist Sunidhi's social and financial empowerment and her sexual liberation, culminating into that priceless moment of her self-realization.

The story is a compelling one, tearing apart the shackles of tradition and male dominance, leading to the protagonist breaking free of the corporate glass ceiling, discovering herself, her inherent potentials and her desires. It is the tale of two individuals, forlorn in their own spheres of life, facing existential dilemmas, bonding with each other while trying to shove away the gathering dust and decay in the daily grind of life and living. They find each other alluring, irresistible and indispensable. Walking down the path of human follies and foibles, of desires and cravings – the trappings and loopholes which often make the strongest and the worthiest buckle – this singular companionship blooms into a rare partnership.

The English translation is crisp and taut. The art of storytelling creates an aura of mystery and thrill around everyday affairs, builds a foaming sea of intense love and passion, holds the reader in rapt attention and magically balances the sweeping tides of windy romance and the mundane moorings which anchor life.

Published by the Bhartiya Jnanpith, Delhi, (2017), the Hindi original Badal Raag has recently been awarded the Goenka Literary Award, 2021.

1

Somehow, Vikas reached Delhi airport. It was four in the afternoon, but already dark outside and bitterly cold. The sun had not risen since morning. He had come to the airport straight after attending the meeting and having lunch at Vigyan Bhawan. His Air India flight was at five. He was in a rush and hadn't even managed to enquire if the flight was on time. The only thoughts crowding his mind on the way to the airport were the complex issues discussed at the meeting. The well-lit roads of Delhi enhanced its stature of a capital city. His car moved fast along the wide roads. But as it approached Lodhi Road, the traffic suddenly worsened, becoming chaotic like in any other city in the country.

There were long queues at petrol pumps. Perhaps the petrol prices were rising after midnight. As his car crossed Lodhi Road, he started riding on a series of flyovers. Vikas was deeply impressed and wondered if he was in India or a foreign country. The Commonwealth Games had certainly brought about a lot of development in Delhi, but he conjectured if the tallest leaders of our polity also got embroiled in acts of corruption, then who could be trusted any more.

Vikas was visiting Delhi after two years or so. And Delhi had undergone a sea change in between, particularly in areas connected with the organisation of the Games. Vikas was a general manager in a national bank. He had seen 'administration' closely. He thus viewed everything from an administrator's eye. His approach was not that of an investigative journalist or a disgruntled politician. He knew very well how bureaucrats and leaders handled development works. His car sped across the flyovers and he felt assured that he would reach the airport on time. The crazy and haphazard movement of cars on the meandering roads resembled the racing cars in a video game. He noticed that very few Maruti 800 cars were left to be seen on the roads. Most of the cars were now big, somewhat reflecting, the level of the country's affluence.

His car had just crossed a flyover and was about to ascend the next, when it suddenly jerked to a halt. There was a terrible traffic jam. All drivers looked confounded. In spite of the biting cold outside, they had rolled down the window panes of their cars to see what had happened. And then, finding a slight movement in the traffic, they didn't hesitate in barging ahead.

Nobody seemed to know what had caused the jam. This was a snag in the one-way system. As no vehicle came from the opposite side, you didn't have any means to learn what the impasse was.

Vikas felt his heart sink. He asked the driver what the problem was. He even reminded him about the time of his flight.

'Don't know sir, but must be something serious. Such a traffic-jam is generally not seen this side', he said propping his head out of the window. He was trying to take stock of the situation. Soon the traffic started moving. The driver said,

'A serious accident, sir. A car has hit a biker badly....They drive so recklessly. Tend to push their way through from nowhere. And they speed up so much. He has lost his life, sir....!'

Vikas looked out and saw a man lying in a pool of blood on the road. A few minutes ago, he was alive. But dead now. What could be the cause... speed and flyovers... or mighty hurry to meet a target...or carelessness...or destiny! Whatever it was, Vikas felt completely shaken. He was dumb-founded for a while. How ephemeral was human life, he thought! Suddenly, his car picked up pace. He looked at his watch, forgot what had happened on the road and started thinking about his flight.

'Oh, where are you going? I have to catch a domestic flight. You should have taken right...' Vikas chided the driver.

'No sir, I am going the right way. These days, all flights leaving Delhi take off from the international airport'. It didn't take long for the driver to tell that Vikas was visiting Delhi after a long time.

Vikas felt relieved that he was going in the right direction. The bank had hired the car from a trusted agency; else the taxiwala would have fleeced him and even caused avoidable delay. He was, however, still worried about the flight.

They soon arrived at a big terminus and the driver stopped the car. 'Sir, from here you have to go in a bus', he said pointing towards a bus.

Vikas tipped fifty rupees to the driver. He carried his bag to the bus. The bus left immediately and reached the airport in no time. He stood in front of a massive structure exactly at four. He was flabbergasted to see it. At once he thought of the Washington airport. He had visited the United States ten years ago and wondered when and how would India have such airports. He was convinced that we had come a long way in ten years. But something still agitated his mind. Had all our resources been honestly and rightfully utilized on development, we could have progressed much faster! He was already inside the airport building. There was a huge electronic board in front. It displayed flight information in quick succession. He took some time to spot the flight going to Pune. It was delayed by five hours!

He was lost for a while; he didn't know how to spend these five hours. He checked if another airline was flying to Pune in the next couple of hours. There was none. He even weighed the option of travelling via Mumbai. But it didn't make any sense. It would have taken the same time to reach Pune and the journey would have been more cumbersome. He felt stranded and didn't know what to do. He looked at the electronic board again. By now, a large number of people had gathered under it. All wore the same look of dejection. A thick layer of fog had delayed the departures of all flights!

The airport lobby was about a kilometer long, from one end to the other. There were countless check-in counters of so many airlines and a whole street of restaurants and eateries flashing sign-boards of many international food-giants. He was a little overwhelmed by so much hustle and bustle all around. Amidst all this, his gaze suddenly fell upon a woman, standing at a distant check-in counter. Her back was towards the lobby. She wore a beautiful silk saree with a sleeveless blouse. Sunidhi, he thought wishfully. She looked so much like her from the back. He grew curious to see her. Dragging his bag on wheels, he walked faster to quickly reach that counter.

'Sunidhi', he wanted to yell! But his voice wouldn't reach her in such a din. He was the general manager of a bank. He couldn't have been running like a common man. However, he increased his pace.

While his gaze was still fixed on that figure standing at a distant check-in counter, he almost jammed into a man rushing from the other side of the lobby, ferrying a fully laden trolley. He said 'sorry' and moved on. But in this commotion, Vikas lost sight of 'Sunidhi'. Upon walking a little further ahead, he discovered she was not there. She had left the counter and disappeared.

He felt sad and sorry for himself and consoled his heart that it was not Sunidhi at all. How could she have been there! He didn't even know where she lived these days and how she was doing. There had been no contact between them for the last two years. It would have been wonderful if the lady had been Sunidhi! Five long hours of waiting for the flight would have shrunk into five short minutes. But how could it be Sunidhi… if it was not she! He continued to console himself and walked up to a tea and coffee stall.

Vikas had a cup of tea and paid fifty rupees for it. Inflation was skyrocketing and really high, particularly at the airport. Anyway, he thought he would check-in, go inside and get some sleep. But as he crossed the security-checkpoint, he discovered an all new dazzling world! There was a large market-place. Was it a shopping mall with shops, shops and more shops? Shops selling garments, toys and lovely items for gifts; there was even a pharmacy. Looked like a wonderland! He was flabbergasted. Such a big change in two years! He entered a book shop and bought a copy of India Today. Would flip its pages later, he thought. He walked around for a while. Then he moved ahead. There were more shops and stalls of eatables. He was hungry. He stopped at one shop, bought a coupon for a dosa and waited for his turn.

He opened India Today and started flipping its pages, casually. After a while, he lifted his eyes and looked around. There was no sign of sleep in his eyes. India Today was not engaging him. Even the dosa was making him wait. He remembered he had not checked his mail for a couple of days. He took his lap-top out, inserted the internet stick and focused on the screen. The inbox was full. He started checking the mails, one by one. He even sent a reply where needed. He noticed the dosa being placed on the table, but preferred to finish with the mails first.

Suddenly, he was aware of someone removing the plate of dosa from his table. There was no one at the table in front. People at the neighboring tables were busy eating their own food. Nobody was watching others. Vikas was the only one looking around. In his quest to know who had removed his dosa plate, he turned around. Lo and behold! It was Sunidhi .... in her pale green silk saree and sleeveless blouse, smiling in her familiar style, holding the dosa plate in her hands.

Vikas felt a sudden flush of romance. A strange current ran through his body. He was dumbstruck! He couldn't believe his eyes. At the same time, he couldn't take them off Sunidhi. Two long years of separation had just vanished in a moment! Sunidhi placed the dosa plate on the table and stretched her right hand out. He came back to his senses, as if waking up from a dream. He raised both hands and threw them wide open towards her. Immediately, they were caught in a warm and tight embrace. People sitting around watched them with a sense of amusement.

But Vikas and Sunidhi were totally unmindful of the public gaze. Even when they disengaged and took their seats, their eyes were still fixed on each other, as if trying to make up for the long gap of two years!

It was only when they had had enough of looking at each other, that Vikas broke the ice as usual and spoke.

'Strange, isn't it? Oh … my god! But tell me first, what will you have?'

'Nothing', replied Sunidhi, chewing imli lozenges. Her eyes were still on Vikas. They didn't know how and when they started eating dosa from the same plate!

Vikas was about to say something when Sunidhi interrupted, 'Yes, it's really strange! …Sorry, you were about to say something?'

'Strange it is! I saw you about an hour ago … '

'Where?'

'At a check-in counter. I almost ran to catch you … but suddenly I hit a man with a trolley and you were gone'.

'As usual', said Sunidhi before Vikas could complete the sentence. They laughed! Their eyes were still fixed on each other. 'You look much prettier than before,' said Vikas. 'Your style of drapping the saree is the same and this one looks so nice on you. There's only one change …'

'What?' asked Sunidhi, impatiently.

'Do you really want to know?'

'Yes …'

'Sleeveless …!'

'Oh!' she blushed in her own unique way and started covering her arms with the loose end of her saree.

'I didn't mean that. Your bare arms look beautiful. Strong and …' Sunidhi blushed, her cheeks turning red. She felt a tingle in her body. She could only manage to mumble, 'Enough of that … let's talk of something else!'

There was an announcement on the public address system. 'Jet Airlines Flight Number 9W0272 is ready to go to Mumbai. Passengers travelling on this flight are requested to proceed towards Gate Number 48 to board the plane.'

Sunidhi looked at her watch and mumbled, 'Oh my God, its 5.40 already. Didn't realise how quickly time passed. I should be leaving now.' She took out her visiting card from her bag and gave it to Vikas.

Vikas took the card with both hands, looked at it and started reading it out loudly, Sunidhi Joshi … Joint Vice President. He even read out the address and said with a heavy heart,

'Sunidhi, how fast did the time pass! We just met a while ago and you are leaving already!' He started closing his lap-top. But before he did that, he turned towards Sunidhi. There was a certain glow in his eyes. Sunidhi sensed he was up to something. Vikas turned the lap-top screen towards her …

'A picture!'

'What for …!'

'A sweet memory …!'

'Will you be able to keep it … '

'Why not? There's no problem now …!'

Sunidhi looked into the lap-top screen, smiling. Vikas pressed a button and captured her in his lap-top. He then shut it and put it in the bag. 'Now, say something …'

'You say … we are meeting after so long! Maybe two years …! How have you been, all this time?' said Sunidhi, looking at her watch.

'It was hardly a meeting. We just struggled against time! Though it helped us refresh our contacts,' Vikas said giving his visiting card to Sunidhi.

Neither of them wanted this meeting to end! But there were repeated announcements about Sunidhi's flight. They rose with a heavy heart and started walking towards the escalator. There was a grand corridor on the first floor with departure gates, positioned on the right and left. The flight announcements had now started naming Sunidhi.

A Jet Airlines staff, holding a walkie-talkie in his hand, was even personally looking for Sunidhi. When he noticed Vikas and Sunidhi, hurrying towards the departure gates, he accosted Sunidhi. She nodded in approval. He beckoned her to get out of the flat escalator and ride a battery car, which was coming from behind. 'Please hurry up, Ma'm, the flight is getting late.'

They got into the battery car. It left for Gate Number 48, in a flurry. Their hands soon clutched each other's, their fingers impatient to tie a passionate knot, which would get tighter as the car fled. The air-conditioning in the corridor was quite effective, but they were still feeling hot and flushed.

Sunidhi was afraid she might miss the flight. Vikas was criticising his stars, not allowing him to spend enough time with Sunidhi! At times, the grip of their hands would become unbearably tight and cause pain. They would look into each other's eyes, yearning to immortalise the moment. Their minds were overwhelmed with nostalgic memories of the past, flashing quicker than the speed of light and sound.

They seemed to forget that there was a flight to be caught and the boarding gate was not far away. Notwithstanding his declining age of 55, Vikas experienced additional energy flowing into his whole body, through his hands, which were still held by Sunidhi. Their trance was suddenly broken when the driver announced, 'Gate Number 48'.

Alighting from the car, they passionately shook hands and hugged each other warmly. The airline staff manning the gate had been impatiently waiting for Sunidhi. They looked at them with indignation. Then a female staff member of the airlines took charge of the situation and came up to Sunidhi. She had noticed an unusual bond between them. Realizing the tenderness of their situation, she smiled and softly told Sunidhi, 'Please hurry up, Ma'm … the flight is getting late.'

Sunidhi took long strides towards the plane and vanished in its open jaws. As she entered the plane, she felt she wasn't a welcome guest. Everyone was staring her, as if to nail her for the delay. All overhead compartments were full. So she kept her bag under the seat in front of her. Of late, Sunidhi had taken a fancy for aisle seats in aeroplanes. She found it convenient to move around with ease, without disturbing others. The PA system had started making announcements about tying of seat-belts and safety regulations.

There was a buzz on her phone and she knew it was a message from Vikas. 'Good bye,' he had wished her. She smiled and typed 'Good bye'.

Then she turned the phone off. Holding it in her hands, she closed her eyes. Her mind was racing. The memory of the beautiful moments spent with Vikas, even though far too few than desired, created strange ripples in her heart. She was experiencing a sweeping bliss after, god knows, how long! It was beyond belief and description. She wondered if it was a coincidence or a chance or destiny or the fulfillment of her heart's long-cherished desire! Whatever it was, it had happened for the first time in her life. She was overwhelmed. The images appearing on the panorama of her mind were so romantic and soothing! She had not even cared to see who were sitting beside her. She sometimes smiled, as if under the influence of a spell, until an air-hostess shook her out of it and brought her back to reality.

'Excuse me,' said the air-hostess, 'a drink for you?' She handed over a small bottle of Nimboos to Sunidhi and moved on. Sunidhi put the mobile phone inside her wallet and put the wallet in the pocket in the front. She opened the bottle of Nimboos and started sipping .... She was still trying hard to assimilate and re-live all that had happened today, during the chance meeting with Vikas. She didn't know for how long she enjoyed sipping the drink. It was only when she sipped it hard, that she realised, it was over.

She woke up from her dream and hoped nobody had noticed her sipping an empty bottle! People all around had already fallen asleep. Sunidhi put the empty bottle in the pocket in front of her and took out the flight magazine. It's normally picked up to flip pages and look only at the pictures. But she didn't even feel like doing so …! She just opened it, put it in her lap and readied herself for another memory trip. Then she lifted both her palms. They were still sufficiently warm, radiating the intoxicating aroma of Vikas's hands. She softly rubbed them around her face, pushed her seat behind and closed her eyes.

Vikas sat on a recliner outside Gate Number 48 for a while. He then lowered its back, preparing to lie down. There were mobile phone charger points in front of him. He put his mobile phone on charging. Some kind of charging seemed to be going on even inside him. He met Sunidhi only because his flight got delayed by five hours. It was a blessing in disguise, in a way.

His mind was totally relaxed. His body felt light. He removed his shoes and kept them aside. He folded his arms and put them under his head as a pillow. He felt his palms were unusually warm, as if they had also been charged with an eerie current! He closed his eyes and started rewinding the day's events in his mind. After check-in, he was to go to Gate Number 27. But there was still time for the flight. So he started loitering and ultimately landed at a dosa place!

When the present and the future both shut their doors on you, you tend to repose in the past. You always hold its keys and nothing on earth can take them away from you. Not even time! So, Vikas took a plunge into the past, going back ten years, along with Sunidhi!

❖❖❖

2

Vikas was busy in his cabin. His phone rang every now and then. A fax or two were also received in between. An officer of the planning department stood at the door seeking permission to come inside. Vikas was too engrossed in a file. Suddenly, he heard a knock at the door. It was the same officer waiting for his permission to enter. Vikas looked at him and politely said, 'Come in'.

Jayesh was an officer in the planning department in Vikas's office. Hard-working and well-conversant with his job, he knew Vikas well. Vikas also had a lot of respect for him. The competition amongst the banks was increasing day by day. Vikas had nearly sixty branches under him. His Regional Office, where he sat had more than fifty employees. His cabin was situated at the far end of a big hall. You had to cut across all employees to reach him. Jayesh briefed Vikas every morning about the activities of the region. He had come to Vikas to show him a fax message received from the Central Office.

Vikas went through the message and got a little worried. How could they expect him to furnish information pertaining to all branches in such a short time? The anxiety on his face clearly belied his disapproval of the Central Office trying to exert unnecessary pressure on the subordinate offices. Jayesh read his mind and took charge of the situation:

'Don't worry, sir. We'll try.'

'I know that. But how is it possible, in such a short time?'

'We'll try, sir. I have already compiled some information. As you were away on tour, I didn't bother you', added Jayesh. Vikas looked a bit relieved. He knew Jayesh was a capable officer; intelligent as well as resourceful. He could always read what went on in Vikas's mind, anticipated his decisions and followed his approach. Vikas smiled at Jayesh and asked him to order some tea.

Jayesh pressed a button under the table on his side. The peon came in. 'Two cups of tea. One green tea with lemon and one regular for Jayesh'. Vikas's table was so big that he could hold a meeting with ten people without moving from his chair. So he had had a call bell fixed at the front of the table as well, to be used when required.

The table top had a big glass placed over it, with a fairly large map of Maharashtra placed in between. It showed the location of all branches under Vikas's region, marked in red circles. During usual discussions, he generally focused his attention on the map as though he was in virtual control of the branches.

They drank tea and also discussed all pending work. Vikas was convinced of Jayesh's common sense, administrative acumen and far-sightedness. He knew that Jayesh had played a major role in his winning over the Chairman's confidence. They had a good rapport and a smooth working relationship between themselves.

When they had finished discussing all important matters, Jayesh rose to leave. He looked into Vikas's eyes as if to confirm that they hadn't left anything out. Then he remembered something and sat down again.

'The Central Office has made a fresh appointment of twelve officers. Ten of them have already joined. Two of them have been allotted to us. One has not joined due to some family problems and has requested for his retention in Pune. The other joined yesterday and wanted to see you, if you so permit... It's a lady officer.'

'Not right now... let me clear the pending files first. You go out for a day and so much work gets accumulated,' said Vikas, looking around the room. 'Send her in at four...by the way, who is she going to work with?' Vikas asked casually.

'Haven't decided yet. We were waiting for you to come back. For now, I have put her in the HR department.'

'HR is already full of officers...anyhow, we'll see later... at four...may be,' said Vikas and he started opening the Dak received from the Central Office. He preferred to personally open the Dak received from the Central Office. He read each and every letter carefully, duly marked it and put it aside in a tray.

As Jayesh left the cabin, Vikas thought he should have called in the new officer right away. A brief meeting wouldn't have taken long. He didn't know why he had pushed it to four? For a moment, he even felt strongly inclined to see her right away... but...!

As the day progressed, Vikas got extremely busy with work. There were many meetings with clients. Many heads of sections came in to discuss official matters. Time flew when he was in office. At lunch time, Preeti invariably called to confirm if he had had his food. Vikas also enquired if Garima had come back from school. Garima was seven years old.

Vikas was a very caring person, extremely attached to his family. He had his own views about life. He had always wanted to have one child and that too, a girl child, so that he could give her the best upbringing. He liked to maintain a healthy balance between his work and family commitments. So he took exceptional care of his parents. He had great affection for his younger sister. He tried to be at his best on all domestic fronts.

Vikas commanded a lot of respect in his office. He didn't believe in putting undue pressure on the employees. They too had the highest regard for him and his orders. He knew who all were shirkers at work but front-runners for availing privileges; who the ones given to gossip and rumour-mongering. He knew how to handle them all. His subordinates simply loved him. They knew he was always standing by them through thick and thin, lending support. He attended all their family functions. Even his wife Preeti accompanied him at such occasions. He motivated their children to do well at their studies and rewarded those who achieved academic excellence. He even got their achievements published in the house journal of the bank. Everyone was sure that he would be at the top of the list when it came to promotions for the next rank.

Like Vikas, Jayesh too had a good reputation in the office. He was Vikas's blue-eyed boy, held in high esteem. He had the delegated authority to directly deal with the regional heads. Many officers felt envious of the power and position he held, but lacked the guts to say anything to anyone.

Jayesh had placed the lady officer's dossier on Vikas's table in the morning. He wanted him to go through it before he met her. But Vikas had had no time to even look at it. First he thought he would see it later and then it got dumped in the heap of files.

The lady officer came to Jayesh's cabin exactly at ten to four. People had been talking about her since yesterday. It was a custom in this office. Moreover, females in the office were already more in number than males. So employing yet another lady officer was bound to give rise to speculation and discussions.

This office had many oddities. Whenever a young employee joined, everyone wanted to know his or her marital status. If the new recruit was unmarried, it caused a rift in the staff. The not-so-young ones spotted an opportunity for a probable liaison with their younger brothers, sisters, nephews or nieces whereas the young saw an opportunity for themselves. Those who didn't belong to either of these categories simply behaved as bystanders.

Another specialty of this office was its cohesiveness. There was hardly any rift or discord amongst the staff. In case of a young man joining office, all young ladies watched him slyly and evaluated his personality during lunch break. He would be rated out of hundred marks. The criteria to judge him included his personality, dress sense, mannerisms, body language and the way he spoke, etc. No credit was given for his proficiency in work.

Today, it was the male employees' turn to rate the new lady probationary officer. Many of them had already given up on her after noticing a delicate but highly suggestive mangalsutra dangle around her beautiful neck. Many others were happy to see it as it dissuaded rumour-mongers fabricate any scandals around her.

All the same, the young ones did talk about her during lunch time. Many gave her very high marks, sometimes a score of ninety out of a hundred. Her beauty, sartorial sense, choice of colours, her dark green silk saree, the cut of her blouse, the way she carried herself were all discussed and admired. She was neither outspoken nor withdrawn. Though she knew that people were watching her, she neither became self-conscious nor indifferent. She was highly balanced! There was a strange sweetness in her voice and a bewitching attraction in her dreamy eyes. Her hairstyle was unique, coiffeured all by herself. The light brown colour of her hair heightened the charm of her face. She was slim and when she walked, she took very measured and balanced steps. She had already won the hearts of many. A few even admired her footwear. Her nimble fingers, well shaped nails and the shade of her nail polish were all topics of discussion. The light pink hue of her lipstick was bound to be talked about. One of them went to the extent of saying:

'She is Rekha of our times.'

'But for her mangal-sutra!'

At this time, Vikas entered the office through the main gate. Lunch time was almost over. His gaze was on the ground. He was probably thinking about something. He walked straight into his cabin, without looking at anyone. That was how he generally entered the office.

Jayesh was busy preparing a report for the Central Office. It was only when he saw the lady officer enter his cabin that he recollected that Vikas had called her at four. Since she had not so far been assigned any desk, she had spent the day meeting other female employees, introducing herself and learning about them. When she came to Jayesh, she kept standing till she was beckoned to take a seat. And as she did so, her presence permeated the air with a special aroma. Jayesh looked at her intently.

Usually, a man finds it hard to hide his excitement while meeting a beautiful lady for the first time. It shows in the movement of his eyes and his facial expression. And it doesn't take the lady much time to notice it. She, in fact, makes it a benchmark to evaluate her effect on the man. It makes her even more conscious of her charm. Jayesh looked at this lady intently and turning his eyes away, he called the peon.

'See, who is inside.'

'Some clients are there, sir …!'

'We want to go inside. Tell me when they are gone.'

'It may take some time. Sir has ordered tea for them…', said the peon, without being asked. Jayesh didn't like it. 'It's okay. Tell me when they are gone,' he replied curtly.

'Yes, sir,' said the peon and left.

Jayesh tried to get back to work, but he couldn't. He wasn't able to obviate her presence. She sat there in front of him, slyly observing his actions. He picked up the phone and as if to camouflage his uneasiness, he started shouting at a manager.

'In case I don't get the report by this evening', he threatened. 'You may then have to explain to the regional manager.' In between he would steal a glance at her and then increase his chiding.

It was four thirty. The lady officer said softly, 'May I sit on the sofa there? I am unnecessarily disturbing you.'

'No, no, nothing like that. We'll go inside as soon as the RM is free.'

It was clear that Jayesh would also go inside along with her. Soon the peon announced that the clients had left. Jayesh got up without losing a moment and went to Vikas's cabin. The peon opened the door. Jayesh knocked at it before entering, but Vikas didn't respond. He was going through a file. Without raising his head, he said, 'Come in …'

Both of them entered the cabin. Vikas was still engrossed in the file. Once again, without raising his head, he pointed towards the chairs on other side of his table and said, 'Please be seated.' They sat down. Vikas was still lost in the file and said, 'Give me a moment please…' He raised his head and passingly glanced at the lady officer. It was obvious that he was still not mentally free and had probably not noticed her properly. After some time, he closed the file, looked at them and said, 'Yes, please.'

'Sir, I had spoken to you in the morning about…a new officer in our office…she is Sunidhi Joshi, Probationary Officer.' Vikas looked at Sunidhi and then at Jayesh and again at Sunidhi.

'Sir, I had left her dossier with you in the morning,' Jayesh said trying to remind Vikas.

'Oh, yes… I know. But I have been extremely busy today,' said Vikas, shaking his head. He didn't even seem to recollect where he had kept the dossier. Jayesh rose, picked up some files from a heap and picked out Sunidhi's dossier. He placed it in front of Vikas.

Vikas went through Sunidhi's dossier very carefully. He looked at her photo in the file and then, inadvertently, he looked at her. No word was spoken for some time. Jayesh too was silent. While Vikas flipped the pages of Sunidhi's dossier, she stealthily looked around the cabin, quietly appreciating its huge size. There were big boards and some graphs displayed on the walls. She also noticed Vikas's pictures with the chairman of the bank, a few trophies and shields, probably earned by him!

Suddenly she heard him say, 'Why did you leave the previous job?'

'I was a teacher. There was hardly any scope of progress. Besides, I have had great interest in banking. So I left the previous job,' Sunidhi replied as if sitting at an interview.

Vikas abruptly looked at Jayesh. Jayesh said, 'Excuse me,' and came out of the cabin.

Vikas had a long formal talk with Sunidhi. He told her that workload in the banks was increasing day by day due to severe competition. Sunidhi actively participated in the conversation and assured him of playing a constructive role. At this time another officer came inside with a file which contained lots of loose papers. He picked them up one by one and Vikas kept signing them blindly. Sunidhi wasn't familiar with the administrative work. Therefore, it disturbed her to see Vikas signing the papers even without reading them. Sometimes, he asked something from that officer and then looked at Sunidhi in the passing. When the work was completed, the officer went out with the file. There was silence for a while.

'May I leave, sir?'

'No, not like that. Let me offer you a cup of tea, at least. It's your first time in my office.'

'Sir, I have already been offered tea, when I came here.'

'Doesn't matter. Have another one with me.'

Vikas rang the call bell. The peon appeared.

'Four cups of tea. One for me and...please send in Jayesh and the HR Manager as well.'

Vikas resumed his talk, 'We have a very cordial atmosphere in this office. If all of us put our hearts and souls in the work, we can do wonders. The staff is very cooperative. You'll not have any problem. But you shouldn't be wanting in work...'

Jayesh and the HR Manager were already in before Vikas could complete the sentence. He beckoned them to take seats. Tea was brought. Sipping his tea, Vikas remarked that they should start training Sunidhi on work. The HR Manager looked at Jayesh. Vikas clarified that Sunidhi would work in the planning department under Jayesh. He told the HR to immediately issue a formal order to that effect. Both of them uttered 'Yes, Sir', got up and left.

Sunidhi had finished her tea. Preliminary briefing was also over. She was about to get up when Vikas asked, 'Who all are there in your family?'

'My husband and in-laws…' So saying, Sunidhi lowered her gaze and started looking down. She felt a bit embarrassed. She wasn't expecting it. Vikas too realized that it was unwarranted and hadn't been liked by her.

'Any children…?' He couldn't resist asking.

'No… I've been married for three years but… nothing yet,' said Sunidhi. She seemed to be lost somewhere.

'Well, there may be good news, soon. A new guest with a new job…!' Vikas looked at Sunidhi and realized that his remark had not pleased her at all. He changed the topic. He told her that she would enjoy working in the planning department. Jayesh was a good officer and he would train her well.

'Thank you, sir…', said Sunidhi.

'Should you still have a problem, come to me.'

'Thank you, sir…'

Sunidhi thought they had discussed everything. She was back to normal now. She got up to take leave. She felt a lot of respect for Vikas. She thought there was more grandeur in his conduct than was there in his cabin. She was impressed with him. Before she could leave, Vikas wished her 'All the best!'

'Thank you, sir…' uttered Sunidhi and looked at Vikas, informally, for the first time maybe. So far she had covertly set her eyes on him only when he signed the papers or conversed with other officers. When he spoke to her, she just said a word or two and then looked aside. That was the traditional custom, her *sanskar*. But now when she looked at him informally, she saw the real Vikas. She had a good feeling and liked him. Even

Vikas sensed it and became self-conscious. He corrected his posture and feigned to look into a file.

Sunidhi slowly got out of the chair. Vikas was slyly watching her. He noticed the elasticity of her body and then his gaze rolled up towards her face. Sunidhi turned back. She bowed a little as if to express her gratitude. Vikas was moved by this gesture. She knew how to carry herself. As she walked out, Vikas's gaze fell on her back. She was moving towards the door. Each stride she took, exuded loads of self-confidence. She had an exquisite style of draping her saree; very neatly pleated, smart and attractive! Its dark green colour made it look fabulous on her. Her supple body bloomed in this silk attire. Her blouse had a broad cut at the back, enhancing the beauty of the lush white complexion of her body. She had a novel style of doing her hair. As he watched her moving towards the door, Vikas felt a strange sensation within him. He was not the kind to get carried away by a woman's physical charms. He enjoyed an excellent reputation in the office. His conduct with the female staff was always above board and praiseworthy. He had complete control over his emotions and was never found lacking in his respect for the fairer sex. But he didn't know what was happening today!

Sunidhi covered the cut in her blouse with the loose end of her saree, as if she had a premonition of being watched from behind. Vikas quickly turned his eyes away from her. As she stepped out of the room, she turned her head and looked back! By now Vikas was already lost in the files. Vikas raised his head only after the sound of the closing door had confirmed her exit. And then he kept looking at the closed door for quite a while. A file lay open in front of him. But he was not there. Suddenly there was a knock at the door. It was Jayesh…

Vikas took charge of himself. While he said, 'Come in', his eyes were still fixed on the door, unmindful of the file which lay open in front of him. Jayesh observed it with surprise as he had never seen Vikas in such a state of mind.

❖❖❖

3

Sunidhi felt fresh after a long time. On her way back home, there was no commotion in her mind. She was fully at peace with herself. She didn't even know where she was headed to. She had probably asked the rickshaw-driver to take her home.

On the way, she only thought about the new job, the people she had met and the novel environment. She had left office around eight. She found it strange to see that almost all officers worked till late. Most of them wound up their table only after Vikas had left. Sunidhi had been sitting opposite Jayesh. Suddenly she noticed him rise from his seat. She turned around and saw Vikas coming out of his cabin. He just waved at people sitting in the hall and left.

'Sir has left. You may also go now.'

'It's okay…you are still working. Many others are also there, replied Sunidhi, confidently.

'Banks have fixed time to come but no predetermined time to leave…now, you see, sir has to submit a report tomorrow about the position of loans in all branches under him,' said Jayesh. There was a phone call from a branch and he started noting down some details. When the call was over, he again addressed Sunidhi,

'You may leave. I'll have to sit for some more time.' Sunidhi didn't say anything.

'You'll slowly learn the ways of working in this office. Tomorrow, I'll have a table and chair put up for you, next to mine. And then you start the work…!' Jayesh started telling her about the routine chores for the next day.

Sunidhi found Jayesh to be an efficient officer. He commanded good respect in the office and was close to Vikas. She had picked up her bag to go, when another lady officer came up to her.

'Let's go now. After some time, you'll also have to sit till late.' Sunidhi looked at her. Then she looked at Jayesh, as if seeking his permission to leave. He nodded in positive. Going down in the lift, the lady officer asked Sunidhi, 'Where do you live?'

'Navjeevan Society… on the University Road.'

'Oh, I thought you lived somewhere near Karve Nagar. I could have dropped you there...'

'It's okay. I'll take a rickshaw.'

Getting out of the lift, they just looked at each other and parted ways. They didn't indulge in any conversation. Neither did Sunidhi show any inquisitiveness to know about the new place, nor did the lady exhibit any interest in knowing anything about Sunidhi. This perhaps was typical of the metropolitan culture which held its people back from easily opening up with others!

All along the way, Sunidhi kept comparing her new job in the bank with the previous one. Although she liked teaching small children, she had always felt that she was being cheated by the management. They appointed her only for a year at a time and didn't even pay full salary. She signed the pay-bill as per government rules, but received only half the amount she had signed for! So she really needed a good job. And today she was happy, she had got one. She felt satisfied and elated.

Sunidhi was happy that the anxiety about getting a good job was finally over. But would it end her woes? Would this slight ray of hope fight and eradicate all the gloom from her life? Suddenly, she thought of her home. It made her feel terribly helpless, like a bird whose wings had been clipped. The very thought of the dark and gloomy environs of her home was enough to exterminate all hope and happiness from her life.

Sitting in the rickshaw, she wished she didn't have to go home! And as she thought so, the rickshaw came to a grinding halt. There was a traffic jam ahead. Uff, there was so much of smoke and pollution–everyone in a great hurry to get back home. Home was something which had never brought peace in Sunidhi's life. But this killer traffic...one suffering compared to another. But life is not led by logic, you live it through emotions. It's the mind, however, which, riding the horses of logic, wants to control the reins of life.

'Where exactly should I stop...madam?'

'Er...have we reached Navjeevan?'

'Yes, madam.'

Sunidhi lowered her neck to look outside.

'Oh, yes, it's Navjeevan.' Somewhere in her mind, she wondered, 'So soon?'

The rickshaw stopped near the main gate of the building.

'Forty-eight rupees...' said the rickshawdriver.

Sunidhi handed a fifty rupees bill to him. He took it and put his hand in the pocket to hunt for a two-rupee coin.

'It's ok', said Sunidhi and started walking towards the building.

Her flat was on the third floor. There was no lift in the building. As she moved towards it, she felt her steps become heavy and fatigued. They had been so light and fresh during the day. Climbing the stairs, she wondered why had she come there at all? She should have gone to her mother's house instead. But... she was already there. She put her finger on the doorbell but felt almost paralysed. It stayed there for a while, before the bell could be pressed!

Having rung the doorbell, she waited for the door to open. It was 9.00 pm. She heard the sound of footsteps inside. It could be Nandan. She felt depressed. Nandan was her husband. The door opened. Thank god, it was her mother-in-law!

❖❖❖

4

Everyone at home waited for Nandan till 9.30, but he was nowhere to be seen. She didn't know why but the fact he was not home made her happy! Then she sat at the table along with her in-laws to eat dinner. The three of them did not usually talk much when they were together. And when Alok, her father-in-law, was there at the table, the conversation would be further reduced to naught. Even if they did speak, they talked only about food.

'Pass me the salt', said Alok. Both Sunidhi and Yashodhara stretched their hands to reach the tiny vial of salt. Yashodhara got it first and passed it on to Alok. Sunidhi looked at her with a smile. Yashodhara liked it. She often wished Sunidhi would handle her son's life too with such a smile!

'What are you thinking of, Mom!' asked Sunidhi, in an effort to bring her back from her reverie. She knew what Yashodhara was thinking about. She was waiting for her son, her eyes glued to the door. Nandan was still not back. She missed him. She was a mother after all. Even Sunidhi could feel the anguish of a mother having a son like Nandan! She was not totally devoid of compassion! She understood what motherhood was, though she hadn't had the pleasure of becoming a mother herself. She was stressed and unhappy on this account and it showed on her face, many a time. Even Yashodhara empathised with her for this void in her life. But she had not given up hope!

Alok had finished his meal. He got up to go downstairs for a stroll. Sometimes Yashodhara also went along with him. At such times, they usually talked about Nandan and Sunidhi. Tonight, Alok went out alone. He was feeling very lonely and was withdrawn. Was it because Sunidhi had joined a new job?

Yashodhara sat at the table till Sunidhi had finished eating. Then she got up, cleaned the table and dumped the utensils in the sink. Tonight, Sunidhi also helped her. On other days, she would be absolutely lost in her thoughts. Or that is what Yashodhara thought. Being a woman, she could feel the pain Sunidhi was going through. But Nandan was her son, her only son. Tonight, she was happy to notice a positive change in Sunidhi. She looked much better and had even extended a helping hand to Yashodhara.

Yashodhara was the chief manager of a bank. But she was a perfect homemaker as well, extremely affectionate, caring and devoted to her family. She was indeed a wonderful human being. This was probably why, in spite of unfavorable and unsavoury conditions in her marital home, Sunidhi had continued to respect her and stay with her.

'How was your first day at the new job?' asked Yashodhara, settling down on the sofa.

'Superb!'

Sunidhi's eyes brightened up. Though a bit late, Yashodhara had touched the right chord. She wanted to share a lot of things about the boss, other officers, female colleagues, the office premises and the new job itself. But she couldn't have said anything of her own. She switched on the television. They both sat quietly for some time. Then the doorbell rang. Sunidhi wanted to get up, but she didn't. She picked up the TV remote and started tossing it in her hands. Yashodhara opened the door. It was Alok. Sunidhi placed the remote on the side-table.

'How was your first day, dear...?' Alok asked Sunidhi looking into her eyes. She knew it was coming. She got up and touched Alok's feet as a mark of respect.

'Stay blessed always ...!' murmured Alok, patting her on the head. It was this upbringing and culture of Sunidhi's which had enamoured them for marriage with their son. They had overlooked the social and financial status of her parents, as a compensation of her *sanskaars*–the traditions that she was steeped in. But later on, the situation had taken a sad turn. Their own son had let them down. He had failed to prove himself equal to Sunidhi!

It was quiet for a while. Then Sunidhi got up and left for her room. Alok and Yashodhara kept talking…

Before her marriage, Sunidhi had developed a fondness for books. She had even brought them along to her in-laws' house. But she hadn't read them for a long time. These were dumped in a corner of her room. One of these books was titled *The Fountainhead*. Shirish had presented it to her when she was in the final year of college. He had already read it and told her,

'This will always enliven you whenever you feel low…'

Tonight, she suddenly thought of Shirish and the book he had presented. She didn't know where he presently was, but remembered him all the same. Was it because it was a landmark day in her life? She had started a new job and saw lot of possibilities in it.

It was eleven o'clock in the night and time for her favourite television show *Bela Ke Phool*. She lay in the bed. The space beside her was empty. Nandan had not come back yet. But, did it really make any difference to her whether he was there or not? She didn't know. She also didn't know why she felt so relaxed and light tonight. Was it due to the accumulated fatigue of a hectic day or the excitement of getting a new job or was it something else…? She didn't know. But she felt buoyant, as if she had no body, no weight, no baggage!

She fell asleep and the sub-conscious mind got working…

'Why did you do it to me, Nandan?'

'What?'

'You know what I am talking about?'

Sunidhi felt her beautiful eyes were flooded. The deluge was incessantly falling over Nandan, dissolving him like a piece of clay. He soon vanished into nothingness. Yashodhara also stood there, watching her son, in awe, transfixed like a statue of stone…

'My Nandan is not a bad sort, Sunidhi. He is ill. Putting on weight. Suffers from high BP. So he tries to run away from worldly affairs. We had hoped that with your charm and intellect, you would be able to bring him around…. and things would work out ….'

'But it's I who got cheated in the bargain. It's me who is suffering. It's my life which is ruined… don't know what to do? But I can't even blame you. It's my own father who pushed me into this mess, knowing everything very well!'

'It's not like that, my child. He had your good in mind, as we had our son's…'

'But what good has it done to me…and what good has it done to you…?

Yashodhara didn't have any answer. She empathised with Sunidhi as a woman. But she felt differently as a mother. She had set high hopes on her!

Sunidhi woke up all of a sudden. It was a shrieking sound in the radio which had disturbed her sleep. It was two thirty in the morning. The space beside her still lay empty. But she could hear somebody snore heavily…in the room. She rubbed her eyes and got down from the bed. It was Nandan. He lay sleeping on the floor, covering himself with a sheet. As usual, he had probably had too much to drink. The rancid smell hung in the room. He mumbled in his sleep, "You moved after seeing my cards. You cheated on me. I'll never play with you…" Sunidhi immediately knew he had lost money in gambling.

Sunidhi was dumbfounded for a while. The ticking of the wall clock caused tremors in her mind. She felt very uneasy. She looked at Nandan and then at the ticking clock and at Nandan again. Time nibbled at her soul and ate her heart away while Nandan pushed her deeper into a swampy quagmire. She knew she'd have to do something to get herself out of this mess.

Sunidhi picked up Meena Kumari's book of poems and went into the living room. Her eyes fell upon Nandan's shoes lying upside down near the sofa. She had desired to relish Meena Kumari's poetry...but did not any longer. The sight of Nandan's shoes had put her mood off. She didn't know what to do! She switched off the light, went near the door and just stood there like a statue. She watched the door intently. Nandan had just shut it and forgotten to lock. What if somebody had entered the house? But who would do so? And what would he steal? She had nothing left with her! She put the latch in place and bolted the door from inside. Then she scornfully looked at Nandan's shoes, picked them up and placed them on the shoe-rack. She headed towards the basin to wash her hands. But there too, she confronted an ugly sight. Nandan had filled the basin with paan saliva and there was tobacco spitted all over it. Its disgusting stink just drove her mad. She cursed herself for having come out of bed at this hour. Had she stayed there, she wouldn't have suffered all of this. She would have tossed and turned for a while and gone to sleep.

For a while, she stood near the basin undecided. Then she opened the tap. Water gushed out forcefully and washed away the pan saliva. Some drops of it splashed over her saree. She stepped back. The basin kept getting cleaned itself. Then she closed the tap. As she did so, she realised that the snoring sound inside her room had become louder. She didn't feel like going back to bed.

She came to the living room again and dumped herself on the sofa. The remote was lying on the side table. She switched on the television. It was a news channel Alok must have been watching before going to bed. It was repeatedly showing some ugly scenes of commotion in the Parliament over inflation; an ultimatum by Anna Hazare for undertaking another hunger strike; a minister slapping a subordinate. She felt irritated. She didn't feel the need of changing the channel and simply switched it off.

She picked up Meena Kumari's book of poetry and kept looking at her beautiful picture on the cover. Some pictures looked awesome in black and white. When she opened the book, she realised a ray of light was streaming in from the front, falling directly on her eyes. It was a minor thing, but it disturbed her. Suddenly she started rewinding all that had been unfavourable in her life. She thought she would make a compromise. She turned herself to the other side. The problem was solved. The ray of light was now falling directly on the book. Gulzar had edited this book. She opened it and her mind was immediately transported to Chandigarh...

On one of the last few days of their college, most of the students had gathered in Sector 17-C in Chandigarh. Most of them were there to buy clothes and sweaters. Some had gone to the theatre to watch the film *Dil Chahta Hai*. Even Sunidhi and Shirish had watched it for a while. Then Sunidhi had asked him–

'Shirish, what, according to you, is love?'

'Er...'

Clearly Shirish's mind was somewhere else. They were surely out on a romantic trip. But he was not inclined to philosophically ponder over the definition of love. He felt bewildered and just uttered whatever came to his mind, 'Love is respect for each other, taking care of each other, knowing each other's mind...'

They looked into each other's eyes. It was pitch dark in the theatre, but they saw so much in each other. Certain things were beyond the boundaries of definition. They both held high moral values. In spite of their being so young and so close to each other, they had not crossed the barriers of decency. Sunidhi asked–

'Have you seen *Gadar*...?'

'Yes!'

'It's showing in the other theatre.'

'Have you seen it?'

'No… not yet!'

'Then let's go and watch it!'

They both got up. People sitting around were surprised to see them leave. The show of *Gadar* had already started more than an hour ago. The ticket window had also been shut. Disappointed they settled on a solitary bench in the theatre itself. Then Shirish told her that there was a bookstore close by and suggested that they go there.

Sunidhi was very fond of Meena Kumari's acting. Whenever her films were telecast she tried to watch them. She observed an artistic expression of suffering in Meena Kumari's performance. Looking at the shelves in the bookstore, she hit upon a book titled, *Meena Kumari Ki Shayari*. She picked it up and casually flipped through its pages. She decided she would buy two copies of this book, one for herself and the other for Shirish. Right then Shirish had come to present her a copy of Ayn Rand's book *The Fountainhead*'.

'It's for you. You must read it. It will enliven you if you ever feel low… in life,' he said.

For a moment Sunidhi didn't know what to do. All that came to her mind was the thought that presenting Meena Kumari's book to Shirish at this stage would only belittle its value. It would make it look like a give-and-take. So she accepted Shirish's gift, looked into his eyes and lovingly thanked him. He was too overwhelmed to reply. Sunidhi too was nervous and looked right and left when Shirish actually stood in front of her! After a moment, he said,

'Want to have coffee…?'

'Why, shall we not watch the rest of *Dil Chahta Hai*?

'No, I don't feel like it.'

'Then let's go for coffee.'

They went to the Indian Coffee House, which was not far. Some of their friends were already there. Out of formality, they sat with them. One of them picked up the books Sunidhi had placed on the table. He opened them, turned a few pages and remarked, 'Good, very good.'

Sunidhi feared he had seen something Shirish had written in the book he had presented! She didn't even know what he had written. So she wondered about it while sipping her coffee. When she reached home, she opened the book and found that there was nothing written by Shirish!

All these years, she had kept both these books with her. They had been very close to her heart and she had read both and never lent them to anyone. Tonight, she flipped the pages of Meena Kumari's book in the middle of a dreary night. Even in the days she had purchased the book, she felt that Meena Kumari's anguish was not simply her own. Tonight, she was convinced that it was her suffering, being expressed in Meena Kumari's poems.

She wondered where Shirish could be then! How would he be doing at present? With the open book lying on her chest, she tried to transcend time and peep into the unknown...!

The clang and clink of utensils in the kitchen woke her up in a flurry. It was morning, and already! Someone had covered her with a sheet, while she slept on the sofa. The light had also been switched off. Yashodhara must have done it. She felt a bit awkward, having gone to sleep like that.

Yashodhara emerged from the kitchen with a broad smile on her face, asking Sunidhi, 'Would you like to have tea?'

Sunidhi quickly took charge of herself. She picked up the book, folded the sheet and looked into Yashodhara's eyes. There was a lot of compassion there for Sunidhi. She felt sorry for having slept like this on the sofa. Alok normally passed through the living room for his morning walk. He must have seen her lying like this. God knew what would he be thinking..!

❖❖❖

5

The way Sunidhi entered Vikas's cabin had since changed. She had completed six months in the office. Now she neither knocked at the door nor sought his permission to enter. She just walked in. And God knows how, Vikas always knew about her coming. He had just brushed his hair, set his clothes right and corrected his posture when she stepped in. Sunidhi usually wore a special perfume. She also preferred to wear a saree. It looked so elegant on her. Even today she was in a light blue saree.

She would enter his cabin with a file or two in her hand, a smile on her face and a gaze fixed on Vikas. He, on his part, welcomed her with a gesture of his eyes. She would invariably occupy the chair in front, without any formality. Irrespective of the position of the red light on the door, nobody entered the cabin without prior notice when Sunidhi was in. Meanwhile, Jayesh had been promoted and transferred to Baroda as chief manager and his charge had been handed over to Sunidhi.

'Good morning,' said Vikas, with a friendly smile. 'Good morning!' responded Sunidhi, equally warmly. It may have been a formal way of greeting each other, but between the two of them, it was much more than that. It confirmed their general well-being and conveyed some of their intimate sentiments for each other.

'Is there anything in the file too?' asked Vikas, rotating both ends of a pencil with his fingers.

'Yes, a lot!' said Sunidhi taking out several newspaper clippings from the file. Vikas looked more at Sunidhi's fingers than the press clippings. He couldn't hold himself.

'Your fingers are so pretty!'

'Thanks,' said Sunidhi, as a formality. His remark had kindled some romance inside her. Nobody had ever perceived her so minutely and complimented her so generously. Her fingers quivered, exposing her bashfulness and the essentially feminine moral values. The press clippings fell out of her hands. Vikas stretched himself out to catch them and in the process his fingers touched Sunidhi's.

'Excellent...I am so glad. The opening of our new branch in Aurangabad has been covered so well by the press. We have never received such a wide and comprehensive coverage'.

Sunidhi was still struggling to get back to normal.

'See this one? It looks so lively due to this picture over here. Who is this beautiful lady standing behind the Chairman?' asked Vikas playfully, handing over the clippings to Sunidhi.

'Come on...' said Sunidhi, lowering her eyes coyly. Vikas was asking about her standing just behind the Chairman.

'By the way, where are you in the picture?' she asked, taking out some other clippings.

'Just behind you...that is where I would always like to be', said Vikas, readily. He was going through each clipping very carefully. 'We have received good publicity. Aurangabad is a tourist centre. People come there from various parts of the country and abroad to visit the Ajanta and Ellora caves. We must run and maintain this branch well. Your planning has shown excellent results, Congrats...'

'Thank you...' replied Sunidhi laughing heartily. She had smartly applied a lipstick of dark chocolate shade on her beautiful lips. It looked more charming when she laughed and showed her snow-white teeth. Vikas felt she must have carefully viewed herself in the mirror before entering his cabin.

Vikas picked up the intercom and asked for two cups of tea. Sunidhi tried to dissuade him, but he didn't listen. 'None of our programs has ever received such a grand coverage. You'll have to share a cup of tea with me.' He wondered why Sunidhi was hesitating to have tea; was it because it could spoil the look of her carefully applied lipstick?

'Sunidhi, tell me about your family and the other members.'

'Err…!' Sunidhi was not ready for this question.

'Sorry, I shouldn't have asked about your personal matters,' Vikas apologised. Picking up a file he threw a glance at Sunidhi. Her eyes were gradually losing their lustre and lowered, with her gaze fixed somewhere on the table. She managed to mumble, 'In-laws and husband….'

The way she had mentioned husband after the in-laws, set Vikas's mind rolling. Naturally, he asked, 'How many years have you been married?'

'Three years…', replied Sunidhi. Her gaze was still fixed somewhere on the table. She was conversing, all right, but each question Vikas was asking was piercing her heart. Soon tea arrived, breathing in some relief. She felt some relief. Vikas had sensed the awkwardness of the situation and he didn't want the peon to be around.

'We'll help ourselves,' he said, asking him to leave,

When Sunidhi raised her head, she found Vikas watching her intently. She couldn't contain herself and burst into tears. Vikas was nonplussed. If somebody entered the cabin at this time…what would he think! There was a staff of fifty people. Anybody could have come in. Vikas switched on the red light on the door. People outside would think that they wanted to have their tea in peace! There was a stoic silence for a while as Sunidhi wiped away her tears and tried to compose herself. Then Vikas broke the ice.

'Any child?'

Sunidhi's eyes had become moistened and welled up once more. She was on the verge of crying again. 'Please…', said Vikas, lifting his cup of tea. 'Sorry, I didn't want to hurt you. That was never the intention. I think, I shouldn't have asked you about the child…'

Sunidhi was all the more perturbed. She raised her head and stared at Vikas. Her eyes were wet, her cheeks were soggy and a major share of the lipstick had already been smudged by the handkerchief. She felt paralysed. She couldn't have gone out in this condition. And it was becoming difficult for her to continue sitting. Vikas understood her predicament. He had finished his tea. He told her, 'Why don't you have tea, Sunidhi...you'll feel better.'

Sunidhi picked up her cup, following Vikas's advice.

'We have been together on so many tours, but…never got a chance to talk about these things,' Vikas said, trying to bring about some normalcy in the situation. By now, Sunidhi was feeling better.

'You have such a jovial nature…and an excellent knack to handle work with ease but…there is so much turmoil inside you? I can't believe it! But your silence in the matter only suggests that it's not a planned step, at least…', said Vikas, still prodding her. He knew he would never want to talk about it again.

'These days, there are so many treatments available for it… you shouldn't lose heart,' said Vikas, trying to console Sunidhi.

She looked at Vikas. He appeared to be genuinely serious. His concern, curiosity and sympathy were not fake. But she wondered how anyone could help her in such a personal matter?

'No treatment can help...'

'What's your husband's name?' asked Vikas, as if that had anything to do with the problem. Sunidhi didn't say anything. She felt like a badly wounded deer, trying hard to wriggle out of the situation.

By now, everything was crystal clear to Vikas. He didn't need to know anything else. Sunidhi was also more or less normal. The press clippings lay quietly on the large table top. The files were silent. The discourse was going on within. Sunidhi was constantly trying to take her mind off the door behind her. But it kept going back there. The door kept opening, again and again, within her mind. She wanted to leave only in a fully normal condition.

Vikas again took the pencil in his fingers and started rotating both its ends. He didn't easily get disheartened in the face of adversity, howsoever difficult it might be. He always fought it bravely and invariably found a way out. Even in official matters, he treaded cautiously and wisely. He didn't like looking back. He never exerted any undue pressure on his employees. Still they held him in the highest esteem. It was also because of the human side of his personality. He not only looked after their professional difficulties but also took good care of their personal problems. He always stood by them through thick and thin. But he never allowed anyone to make any compromise at work. He was their ideal and a great leader. Sunidhi's predicament lay bare before him.

Sunidhi was almost back to normal. Her tears had dried up. Her demeanour wasn't a very happy one, but it wasn't gloomy either. Vikas's penetrating enquiries had hurt her a lot, but now she felt that they had actually given her much respite. They helped her undergo a much needed catharsis. She felt light and so much the better. Nobody had so far evinced any interest in her problems and thought of getting her out of the mess she was in. She felt grateful to Vikas. She wanted to turn around to look at the door behind, when Vikas said, 'Don't mind if....'

'If ...what?' Sunidhi was fully alert, now.

'Have you watched *Astitva*?'

'Yes.'

'What do you think about it?'

'I don't endorse the man's point of view.'

There was a knock at the door. Vikas immediately lowered his head and feigned to be busy with a file. Sunidhi started collecting press clippings, which lay scattered all over the table.

'Come in,' said Vikas without raising his head.

Sunidhi got up holding the file in her arm.

'Sir, there is an urgent message from the Central Office. The credit department has sent a fax.' It was Vikas's PA.

Vikas turned his revolving chair towards the fax machine. There were a few papers lying over there. He picked them up. He took out the one received from credit department and started reading it.

'May I leave, sir?' Sunidhi asked.

'Yes, you may,' replied Vikas, without looking at her.

Sunidhi turned around to leave when Vikas asked her, 'Hope you have got all clippings in the file. It's a very nice coverage.'

'Yes, sir. I've got all.'

'Good. Send them to the Chairman's Secretariat, with a forwarding letter. They should also know we can get such publicity for the bank without spending a penny. Also send a copy to the planning department of the Central Office. And yes, please issue an appreciation letter to the manager of Aurangabad branch. He and his team have done well and it's them who have to run the office.'

'Yes, sir!' said Sunidhi and left the cabin. She felt as if all eyes were fixed on her. She didn't look at anyone, quietly headed towards her table and started typing a letter on her computer.

❖❖❖

6

When Sunidhi left office, everything about her seemed to have changed. She felt least excited to go home. She had never liked the place. But today, her dislike for it was at an all time high. The closer she got to home, the more she loathed going there. She missed the office and more so, Vikas. It was such bliss to be there! Vikas had completely overpowered her consciousness. She wished he was always there with her!

Yashodhara had been noticing a change in Sunidhi, ever since she had joined the new job. One day, she decided to probe her.

'How is your new job going?'

'It's good.'

'You have to work late hours?'

'Yes... sometimes...'

'Working in banks is getting difficult these days. There is a lot of work pressure. Then there are responsibilities too. The teaching line is much better.'

'May be. But you need a PhD to get a proper teaching job.'

'That's no issue. You are so intelligent and studious. You can easily do it in a couple of years. Then there'll be no late hours, no transfers, no problems.'

'But I find it better... now. The working environment in the bank is a lot better...particularly in our branch...we have a very good AGM. Very caring and...'

Yashodhara noticed that Sunidhi was conversing with so much ease. There were no signs of anxiety on her face. There was no bitterness in her voice. The way she voiced her preference for the new job showed she was well-settled there.

Yashodhara was happy to see Sunidhi in such a healthy frame of mind. She herself was a noble person. She liked giving Sunidhi her space. She wishfully thought that a positive turnaround in Sunidhi's mindset could as well lead to a positive change in her attitude towards Nandan. She had always believed that with the kind of training and maturity Sunidhi had, she could easily change Nandan's life, if she so willed! Being a hardcore optimist, she had never given up on her. Now that Sunidhi seemed to be so relaxed and receptive, she thought she would quietly give vent to her pent up feelings about her relationship with Nandan.

'Sunidhi,' said Yashodhara, 'you seem to be so well settled now. You have got a nice job. It suits your temperament and keeps you happy. May I ask you to invest some time to improve your relationship with Nandan as well?'

Sunidhi was taken aback. It came as a bit of a shock to her. She didn't know what to say. So, she gave an absolutely blank look to Yashodhara and turned towards the TV. It was playing a family drama, which nobody seemed to be watching. Sunidhi's complete indifference disturbed Yashodhara. She saw all her hopes being razed to the ground. But she was not willing to give up. She looked at Sunidhi imploringly, one last time, as if begging for her son's life.

Sunidhi was extremely quiet and tense. Her body language displayed her restlessness. The expressions on her face warned of a volcano, about to erupt! Yashodhara got terribly scared. She had never seen Sunidhi so agitated. She sincerely repented having broached the subject with her. In her zeal to mend matters, she had actually complicated them.

Sunidhi looked at Yashodhara and understood what was churning inside her. With great difficulty, she composed herself and said, 'I can understand your feelings Ma, and I expect you to understand mine.'

'I don't have a daughter, Sunidhi. And I don't want to belittle your suffering by saying that I have always looked upon you like my daughter. I wish I could bring happiness in your life. But I am helpless. I am a mother too…'

'I know that, Ma. But there's something which has been bothering me too, for quite some time. I haven't shared it with anyone, not even my mother. I'll not shower any praises on you, but I am sure you are mature enough to appreciate what I am going to say,' said Sunidhi, determinedly.

It was Yashodhara's turn to be taken aback. She didn't know how to react. She was silent. Sunidhi was silent too, for quite some time. Yashodhara knew it was a lull before the storm. She mustered some courage and said, 'Go on. Say, what's there on your mind?'

'Please excuse me for saying this, but I cannot carry on any more…as a wife…'

'What are you saying…?'

'I want a divorce…'

'But why…suddenly, after joining the new job!'

'I knew you would say so…'

'Have you thought about us…about our family?'

'Yes, I have…that's precisely why I have continued to stay here till now…but not any more…'

'But what will people say…my dear?'

'People would be saying something or the other, even now. So far, I have pulled on with this dysfunctional relationship…only for the sake of 'people'. I have never felt myself a 'wife'…' Sunidhi finally gave voice to all that had been broiling inside her for so long. And she felt so light, doing so. On the contrary, Yashodhara felt the sky was about to fall upon her!

Soon, Alok entered the room. Yashodhara looked at Sunidhi and with a gesture of her eyes, she implored her not to say anything in his presence. Alok was a man of few words. He talked only when it was required. He went into his bedroom straightaway, changed into his night clothes, had his dinner and settled down on the sofa. Sunidhi had left for her room meanwhile.

'What's the matter...you look perturbed? Anything to do with Sunidhi?' asked Alok, trying to gauge the situation.

'No, not exactly...' replied Yashodhara, without looking at him. Alok knew there was a problem. He was well aware of what was going on in the house. But he had never said anything. It was his nature not to interfere in any matter. Besides, he always chose to stay away from problems. He was one of those who would never take the bull by the horn and always consigned themselves to destiny. He believed in the eternal power of time to resolve every issue, howsoever complicated it might be. But as for Nandan, he too had given up hope.

Yashodhara knew him well. So she decided it was better to keep him away from the blow Sunidhi had just delivered.

'Would you like to come out with me for a stroll?'

'No, not tonight! I don't feel up to it...'

'All right!' said Alok and went out alone. Yashodhara quickly headed for Sunidhi's room. The door was half open. She knocked on it. There was no response.

'Sunidhi...' Yashodhara called.

There was still no response. Yashodhara slowly pushed the door open. It was dark inside. She switched on the light. Sunidhi lay in bed, sobbing miserably, with her head tucked under the pillow.

❖❖❖

7

Next weekend, which happened to be a long weekend, Sunidhi planned to go to Surat to meet her close friend Nandini, who had been transferred there for work. She had earlier been working in a bank as a clerk, but had recently been promoted to an officer. She was the one who had motivated Sunidhi to join banking service and even helped her in preparing for the examination for probationary officer.

Nandini stood on the railway platform waiting for the train to arrive from Mumbai. She had positioned herself under a signboard displaying 'Coach S-8'. Sunidhi was travelling in this coach. The train stopped close enough to the signboard, Sunidhi got off and began walking up to Nandini whom she had spotted among the multitude of people. Nandini noticed her and nearly jumped in excitement. She opened her arms wide to welcome Sunidhi and tied her in a warm hug. After a few moments she said,

'Oh, I almost forgot about the luggage. Where is it?'

'On my back...'

'That's it?'

'Yes, that's it. I haven't come here to live forever! And I believe in travelling light.'

'Okay, madam. Let's get out of here first...we'll have a plenty of time to talk at home,' said Nandini, touching Sunidhi's cheeks lovingly. They started walking towards the exit. All the way, Nandini tightly held Sunidhi's hand. She would even steal a glance at her, every now and then. She placed the bag on the back seat and started the car.

'Good you can drive', said Sunidhi.

'Can't you?'

'No', replied Sunidhi, without looking at Nandini. There was a touch of remorse and resentment in her voice.

'In a city like this, it's difficult to survive without a car. Public transport system is in a mess. And you don't want to haggle with a rickshaw-wala first thing in the morning.'

Sunidhi was quiet. Nandini realised that she was talking about something which didn't interest Sunidhi. So she changed the gear as well as the topic and asked Sunidhi, 'Should I increase the AC?'

Sunidhi was quiet. She only looked at Nandini.

Nandini wanted to talk about many things. But Sunidhi's silence put her off. She knew what was ailing Sunidhi. But she didn't want to talk about it right away. She extended her hand to change the gear and doing so, she held Sunidhi's hand in hers.

Nandini lived in Nai Basti, just outside the city limits. She drove at a good speed. She again held Sunidhi's hand and gently pressed it. This time Sunidhi gave her a lovely smile. Nandini started talking again.

'You have done two wonderful things since we met last. First, you have joined a good job.' She paused.

' And second?' asked Sunidhi, impatiently.

'You have come here...' answered Nandini, with a hearty laugh.

Soon they reached Nandini's flat. It was on the first floor. They climbed the stairs. Nandini opened the lock.

'Get fresh...we have a lot to talk about. But let me first make some tea for you,' said Nandini merrily.

'Why, won't you have it?'

'Yes, madam, I'll also have it,' said Nandini, switching on the fan. Sunidhi smiled and started opening her bag. Nandini went to the kitchen, humming a song.

Nandini had an impressive personality. She was very talkative. She had bewitching eyes and a typical style of casual talking, sprinkled with Mumbaiya slang. She was emotional to some extent, but never allowed her emotions to take control over her reason. She was quick in taking decisions and she never repented even if they proved wrong.

'Tea is ready!' she announced soon from the kitchen.

Sunidhi entered the room. Nandini offered her a cup of tea and sipping it, they started talking.

'How many months have you been at the new job? Must tell you one thing, compared to the time we met last, perhaps about a year ago, you look so much better. Lesser worries marked on the face. And beautiful you have always been...'

'Shut up...don't tease me. It's been about six months since I joined...'

'I can tell. The new job suits you. By the way, how is that Nandan of yours?' asked Nandini unwittingly. She knew somewhat about the initial period of their relationship. There was a long silence, before Nandini broke it.

'Sorry, I shouldn't have asked,' she said, apologetically.

'No, no, it's okay. In fact I have come here to talk to you about that. But I am not fast like you.'

'I think you have suffered enough. Now that you have a good job, no dependence on others, you should ...'

Sunidhi felt good. She appreciated Nandini's concern and liked her views. In fact, she needed some support and encouragement from friends to take a firm stand. But she wasn't brave like Nandini.

'Nandini, in your case...it was soon after your marriage that you disclosed everything to your husband!'

'Yes, on the very first night.... I told him everything. I told him that I had married only to please my parents and that I was in love with another guy, who lived in America, but was soon coming back to marry me. I told him that I had shared it with my parents as well, but they didn't listen to my pleadings and hurriedly arranged my marriage with him. He was shocked. He jumped out of the bed, moved towards the sofa and lit a cigarette. I didn't want to hurt him. But I also didn't want to keep him in the dark. In any case he was much older than me…thirty-five plus!

'I didn't ask him why he hadn't married till then. He was a strange guy. He puffed at his cigarette, made rings of smoke and watched me slyly through them. He didn't ask me anything, though, I felt he wanted to say something. There are many such people in the world who don't speak up but just keep everything to themselves and live in mystery…'

'Then…?'

'Well, nothing much! He chain smoked cigarette after cigarette. When he tried to confront me and 'make love', I told him clearly that he could rape me if he so desired…I wouldn't object. I told him I would also bear his child…even bring it up…but I wouldn't be able to love him ever as a wife. And I also wouldn't like to keep him in the dark.'

Sunidhi was shocked to hear all this. She didn't know what to say and how to react? She had never witnessed this aspect of Nandini's personality. She had heard that Nandini had very bravely handled her marital disharmony but after listening to the finer details she sat shell shocked.

They had finished tea, but Nandini was unstoppable.

'We lived together for a year, but never had sex. He never tried to change me nor did I ever think of doing so. Then we got divorced. He proposed it. I found him to be a good guy, though I never enquired about his past. We just lived together under a roof, for the sake of our parents' happiness. Meanwhile, I got a promotion and came here on transfer.

'Come on Sunidhi…we have to live the life we are meant to live. But we must try to break the barriers and overcome the hurdles before they get the better of us. My family raised a hue and cry for a while... they are fine now. They come to see me. But they didn't understand me then...'

'And your American friend...? What was his name?'

'Anaadi.' The mere mention of this name seemed to pump in fresh energy.

'Are you still in touch with him?'

'Yes, I am. He came here about two months ago. We chat every day. But we haven't planned anything about marriage, yet...' Nandini blurted out.

Soon, there was a call from Anaadi. Nandini rose, went to the kitchen and got busy talking to him.

Sunidhi too kept herself busy thinking of ...Vikas? Or Shirish...or was it all about herself...? She didn't know!

'Sorry...' said Nandini, finishing her call. She found Sunidhi lost in her thoughts.

'Now, you tell me. So far only I have been narrating my woes. But you know, you feel so much better and lighter, doing so, particularly with a friend. You can't discuss such matters with others.' She picked up the teacups to dump them in the kitchen. Then she came back, sat on the sofa and started looking at Sunidhi.

'I have told Nandan's mom that I can't live there any longer. She is a nice lady and I respect her for that. But as for Nandan, my partner in life...no, it's not possible to continue with him! So, I told her everything. Then I thought I should meet you and...' Sunidhi spoke very softly.

'Have you told your mom?'

'No, not yet. I haven't told her anything yet about my recent decision, though she knows everything about the background. I know what she'll say: relatives...society...neighbours... that's where her world lies. My dad is even worse.... it's very difficult!' Sunidhi really seemed to be in a fix.

'Nothing is difficult. You shouldn't be living with your in-laws or parents. Pune is a big city. There'll be many hostels there. You just have to move into one, a working women's hostel maybe… and leave the rest to time. Everything will come around and get sorted out, slowly.'

Sunidhi appreciated Nandini's attitude towards life and the problems it posed. before you.

'My in-laws are not bad, but for Nandan! They are nice and sensible people.'

'…but that doesn't help you. And you shouldn't complicate your life any more…' Nandini was trying to close the issue.

'No, I won't. I have decided to get out of this mess. Let's see…how it works out!' said Sunidhi, conveying her resolve.

'It'll surely work out well, don't worry. And I am always there…for you. Now tell me, should we order some food or go out for dinner?'

'Out…!'

'Good, I like that…a quick decision. Now nobody can stop you from taking care of yourself!'

'But these three years have just been a waste! Don't know how many more years…'

'No, Sunidhi, you shouldn't mind sacrificing a few years of your life if it can save the rest of it from going waste.' Sunidhi didn't say anything. She only listened to Nandini, preparing herself for the next challenge.

They were going out for dinner. She took out a nice salwar-kurta. Both got ready and went out. Getting into the car, Nandini asked Sunidhi, 'Where shall we go?'

'I don't know, it's your town.'

'I mean veg or non-veg…?'

'You know I am a vegetarian.'

'I know, but I thought you might have…'

'No.'

'It's okay, madam. I'll take you to a good place. Gujarat is full of good restaurants, particularly for vegetarians. By the way, I have started eating non-veg. What about some beer?'

'No thanks, not at all…'

'You are incorrigible! It's time you started enjoying a beer or a gin, occasionally at least. You enjoy it all the more when you are with friends. I have started taking everything. No taboos. Eat, drink and be merry!'

Sunidhi constantly watched Nandini. She seemed to have turned into a brave, fearless and pragmatic woman. What a drastic change! She felt bad to be so backward and old-fashioned.

Their car stopped in front of a grand restaurant. It had valet parking. Nandini wore jeans with a t-shirt. When she walked, her high-heeled sandals clip clopped fashionably on the floor. She spoke fluent English and exhibited sharp responses. She could easily impress anyone she met. But she was extremely humble…very polite and respectful to all she met, irrespective of their social status!

They discussed varied topics at the dinner table.

'Sunidhi, do you know my first job was in a co-operative bank in Ahmedabad. We had a fresh appointee as our manager. He thought he was very smart. And smart he actually was. His appearance, his brain, his heart, everything was A-One. But he was a workaholic. Many women had a crush on him…including me! But no one could succeed. He was already married and too smart for all of us. He was very polished in his behaviour and very mature for his age. He talked suavely, as if he had a lot of experience. He was a master of all trades! I was mad about him. You name any subject–marriage, friendship, right and wrong, post-marital relations…practically anything under the sun and he would speak on it eloquently. He was very efficient at work and had all the qualities of a great leader…' Nandini went on and on!

'It's alright. Enough of that! Now you are working in a multi-national bank...why are you still stuck with the memories of a co-operative bank?' Sunidhi wanted her to stop.

'Okay, sure honey. You tell me, now. How's it going? What's the news? How are your colleagues? Have you had a crush on anyone...?'

'What...? Nandini, your express train of words is unstoppable! And these things don't interest me anymore.'

'They should, if you want to stay young. Or else you'll start aging before time...'

Sunidhi knew that Nandini was absolutely right...only the way she had put it was too blunt. But she still liked it...that's why she had travelled so far to meet her. She also wished to share a few things about her office...at least those which concerned her!

'Nandini, our AGM is also very smart. He is very intelligent ...in fact a genius. Everyone respects him from the bottom of their hearts. And he also cares for all. Enjoys a very good reputation in the head office, too. And...'

'Hmm...You are opening up slowly. But you shouldn't take a boss at his face value! Their appearances are often deceptive...!'

Sunidhi lowered her visage and as if unconsciously, she murmured, 'Vikas cannot be like this...'

'What did you say...? Vikas...?'

'Yes, Vikas!'

'Hope it's not Vikas Dixit!'

'Y..."

❖❖❖

8

Sunidhi returned to Pune. She got off the train at seven in the morning and straightaway went home in an auto-rickshaw. On the way, she pondered on how Yashodhara had reacted when she had told her about her plan to go out for a couple of days.

'We can all go out for a vacation. Our bank has a holiday home in Lonavala. I can book it.'

As there was no response from Sunidhi, Yashodhara felt she shouldn't have broached this subject too. So, she tried to make amends:

'Why don't you visit your Mom, Sunidhi? It's been long since you went there…'

Sunidhi was still quiet. Then she responded,

'I haven't seen Nandini for a long time. Wish to meet her… that's all…nothing special…'

'Okay', replied Yashodhara. She didn't want to prolong the argument.

Sunidhi's auto-rickshaw stood in front of her house. She paid for it and climbed up the stairs. She was about to ring the bell, when the door opened itself. It didn't take her long to realise that Yashodhara must have been anxiously waiting for her and had probably even seen her getting down from the rickshaw.

Sunidhi looked at Yashodhara and gave her a meaningless smile. Yashodhara wanted to engage with her, talk to her and know what had transpired between Sunidhi and her friend. But Sunidhi didn't seem to be in a mood to oblige. She stood there for a moment, motionless like a rock and then walked into her room.

Yashodhara went to the kitchen, poured water in a glass and headed towards Sunidhi's room. The door was open. She went inside, kept the glass on the bedside table, looked at Sunidhi and came out.

Yashodhara had always wished Sunidhi took care of Nandan, her son. She wanted her to change his life-style. But this was not to be. She got busy in cooking. Chapatis had already been made by their part-time maid. She put dal and rice in a bowl and a plate. She generally bought chopped vegetables. They just needed to be fried and the meal would be ready. Sunidhi was a good cook. Everyone liked her cooking. She even helped Yashodhara with the household chores. If only she also took care of Nandan and changed his life!

Nandan had left home early in the morning today as he had to attend to some Union work. Alok had also gone out to meet an old friend. They had probably planned it that way to avoid meeting Sunidhi on her return. But Yashodhara had been waiting for her. She yearned to bring the household back on its rails, though she wasn't able to do anything in this regard. Even the stars didn't favour her. Things were moving from bad to worse. Sunidhi had started reacting strongly and adversely to every little thing. But could she be blamed for it, Yashodhara wondered! Nobody knew what her thoughts were; her mind was a mystery.

When Sunidhi emerged from the room, Yashodhara was waiting for her at the dining table. Today, she wore the perfume gifted by Nandini. She was highly impressed by Nandini's life-style, her courage and boldness. So the fragrance of her perfume gave her a lot of comfort. She felt so light hearted wearing it. But once out of her room, she was confronted by the mundane ennui of this house which nullified even the fragrance of Nandini's perfume. 'Come, let's have breakfast', Yashodhara's voice startled her. It wasn't Sunidhi's nature to say 'no' without a reason. So she responded to Yashodhara's call, even though she didn't want to eat anything.

Sunidhi didn't say a word and quietly walked up to the dining table. As she sat down, Yashodhara smelt her perfume. It was new. She looked at Sunidhi, from head to toe. She seemed so different; even her saree looked bright and new, which Yashodhara hadn't seen before. Yashodhara had never noticed Sunidhi so carefully and closely. 'How beautiful and well-built she is....', she thought to herself.

'Should I give you some pickle?' Sunidhi asked Yashodhara and brought her mind back to the dining table.

'Yes, a little...' She never turned down anything offered by Sunidhi. She feared it might hurt her. And she didn't want to take any such risk. She wasn't scared of Sunidhi. She only wanted to win her heart. She was convinced that Sunidhi alone could fix her household and change her son's life. Besides, she also wanted to make up for her son's shortcomings by being excessively good to Sunidhi.

Sunidhi sensed what was going on in Yashodhara's mind. In the past three years she had learnt to read Yashodhara's mind well. She knew she wasn't fake or deceitful. She only wished Sunidhi to accept her fate and continue to live with them! But...she was helpless, because of Nandan.

They sat at the table in complete silence. Yashodhara couldn't dare ask her anything. And Sunidhi had nothing to tell her. It was one of those times when a lot went on inside you but you couldn't say a word! It felt like the lull before a storm.

'Your lunch box is ready', Yashodhara broke the ice. They had finished their breakfast. Sunidhi wanted to say, 'There was no need for it. I could have eaten something from the canteen.' But she didn't reply. She simply picked up the lunch box, bade good-bye to Yashodhara with a gesture of her eyes and left.

Their offices were in different directions. They generally commuted by auto-rickshaws as the bus service was not convenient. Sitting in the auto, Sunidhi's thoughts dwelled on

Yashodhara's dilemma. She was impressed with her behaviour and appreciated her love. Yashodhara had never behaved like a typical Indian mother-in-law and always treated Sunidhi warmly, like her own daughter. She had actually been more affectionate than Sunidhi's own mother. Yashodhara was very mature, calm and composed. Even Alok was caring and non-partisan. He never found faults with Sunidhi. She wondered why her concern about Nandan's family was on the top of her mind today.

Sunidhi reached her office on time. She brushed her hair sitting inside the rickshaw and pulling out a pocket mirror from her purse she looked into it and applied her lipstick carefully. She paid the auto fare and quickly entered her office. While walking on the road, she never looked right or left. Even today, when she got off the rickshaw, Vikas had waved at her from his car. But she hadn't noticed him. Vikas felt embarrassed and awkward. He looked around to make sure nobody had noticed him, particularly any of the office staff. He took the lift and went up.

Sunidhi saw Vikas entering office and moving straight to his cabin without looking at anyone. This was routine. But today he was disturbed by his own spontaneous waving at Sunidhi. He wanted to look at her, but controlled himself with great difficulty.

❖❖❖

9

Today Sunidhi's mind was not at peace. It kept going back to the moment when Nandini had disclosed some secrets about Vikas Dixit. She and Vikas had joined that co-operative bank together as clerks. They were both new at the job. Vikas must have been around twenty-five or so. Gautami had joined the bank that same year. They were now posted in different branches, though they had been together for training.

Right from day one of their training, Vikas had started taking interest in Gautami. There were twenty-five of them in the batch. Most of them were unmarried. They were all ambitious and had big dreams. Gautami had a bewitching persona. She was very pretty. Everything about her, from her eyes, eyebrows, nose, lips, cheeks, to her hair-style was unique and attractive. She looked like Madhuri Dixit, except that her face was not as round as Madhuri's. She usually wore salwar-kurti suits. Soon she became friends with Vikas. They started dating, breaking many a heart.

Nandini had even told Sunidhi that in the beginning, she too had a crush on Vikas. She had, however, quietly withdrawn when she saw Vikas getting close to Gautami. But she never stopped praying for their separation so that Vikas could come back to her. She always felt jealous of Gautami, as Vikas didn't take interest in anyone else when Gautami was around.

Vikas wanted Gautami at any cost. She came from a rich family. She was as mature as she was beautiful. Job was not a need for her. Her father was one of the directors of the bank. She had joined the bank without any ambition. She didn't want to make it a career or have a future in banking.

Before the training came to an end, the entire batch was taken to Khandala for a picnic on the day of Holi. Vikas and Gautami got an opportunity to be together, unmindful of what others said. They weren't anxious or bothered about anything. Whether it was watching the sunset or looking down into the deep crevices in the mountains or feeding corn to the monkeys, they were always together.

By the time they left Khandala, it was already night. They were travelling back by a minibus after having a great time in Khandala-Lonavala. Back in those days, not too many good restaurants on the highway remained open after eight at night. So their bus stopped in front of a very ordinary restaurant. Even this one had already run out of food. Vikas asked the owner, 'Do you have provision? We can cook ourselves.'

The restaurant owner had plenty of provisions. So they paid for it and started cooking. Vikas always took the lead in such matters. He enjoyed working with people. Gautami made *chapattis* and served them first to Vikas, much to the chagrin of others.

Everyone was tired on the way back, but no one went to sleep. Neither did they let anyone else sleep. They played a game of *antakshari*. Vikas remembered all kinds of film songs. Co-incidently, he and Gautami were part of the same team. Vikas was a good singer. He had a great memory too. But in case he missed any words of a particular song, Gautami came to his rescue and softly whispered the song in his ears. Ultimately, Vikas's team won. Then they all slept off, one by one.

Nandini had told her that she was sitting in the rear of the bus. She wasn't feeling sleepy. How could she possibly sleep?

By the time they reached Chembur, everyone had dozed off, except Vikas and Gautami who were still talking. Nandini wondered what they could have been talking about for so long!

Upon their return, Vikas continued to be in touch with Gautami. Nandini also didn't give up. She always wanted to follow them in their relationship. Soon she learnt that Gautami had been married into a family of doctors and Vikas was awfully hurt. Then she learnt that even Vikas's marriage had been fixed. This time it was her turn to be hurt as Vikas had a special place in her heart. She had given up on him after he seemingly fell in love with Gautami, but the news of her marriage had re-kindled her hopes and feelings for Vikas.

Nandini had told Sunidhi everything about her life. She had even told her how she had come so close to Anaadi in the final year of her graduation. But before their relationship could fructify, he had left for the United States to study MBA.

Sunidhi felt a big change in herself after meeting Nandini. Since yesterday, she had only been thinking about her own life. She was also anxious to know more about Vikas.

She reached office quite early and drowned herself in work. Vikas had been away on a work tour for three days, before the long weekend. So much had happened in the past few days and Sunidhi was still in the process of gathering herself and settling down. She didn't even think of meeting Vikas. What was the matter, she wondered! Why was she hesitant to meet him today? It was the same Vikas who seemed to have become an integral part of her recent past.

'Would you not see Vikas today?' she questioned herself. The answer was no, not yet. Before she met him, she should assess the work load, to know how much and what kind of work could be taken to him. The newly acquired knowledge from Nandini about Vikas's background and his escapades seemed to hold her back from going to his cabin. She wasn't able to decide what it was, but she continued to think about him.

'Hello...please come here....'

She just heard this on the intercom and it got disconnected. It was Vikas. He had never called her privately on the intercom before; today he preferred that to ringing the bell and asking the peon to send her in. She got on to business...pondering on what she could carry to his room...And what he could ask her?

❖❖❖

10

'Tuk-tuk' she knocked at the door.

'Come in', said Vikas without looking up.

Sunidhi felt strange. Vikas told her to come inside but didn't look at her. What could be the matter? She entered the room but kept standing.

'Please take a seat', said Vikas, signalling her to sit down. He had still not looked at her. She felt awkward and out of place.

After some time, Vikas closed the file he was reading, raised his head and curtly told Sunidhi that a signal had been received from Regional Office about the sudden visit of the Chairman to their office. So, preparations had to be made quickly. The reason given for the visit was the formal 'opening' of the foreign exchange branch, which was already functioning. The Chairman had not been able to come when it started functioning, so the opening had to be formalized. Wasn't it strange? You schedule or cancel a visit whenever you wish to. Vikas was apparently vexed at the issue and gave vent to his resentment. He had even been pulled up by the Chairman at a recent meeting. So he was already upset with him.

The Chairman didn't enjoy a good reputation with his subordinates. He was known to be very rude, ill-mannered and foul-mouthed as well as extremely unpredictable and abusive. He wasn't good at banking; so he tried to hide his shortcomings by pulling others down on the slightest pretext. He threatened them with transfer, withholding promotion, departmental inquiries etc. He believed in humiliating senior officers in front of their juniors. Vikas thought of him and all his traits and frailties flashed in his mind. He was really upset on learning about his visit. Gloomily he looked at Sunidhi.

'What's to be done by my department?' asked Sunidhi.

'Credit department will be the main target', replied Vikas, opening another file lying in front of him.

'What should we keep ready?'

'We should have complete information about all good and big loans. Their contact numbers should also be readily available. If need be, we may have to arrange a meeting of some special customers...'

'Okay. All this will be ready.'

'Besides we should also have the details of all such accounts where the recoveries are not up to the mark. We may have to first meet some people. The Chairman is coming solely for this purpose. We must make his visit successful. We should try to effect immediate recoveries where possible. Where it's not possible, we must analyse the legal aspects of converting such cases into NPAs. It's the last month of the third quarter. We have to take care of the profit for the next quarter as well as the whole financial year. Do you get what I'm saying?' Vikas gave her a meaningful glance.

Sunidhi understood everything. She knew that she would now have to play the numbers game. Simultaneously, she would have to carry out recoveries, update contracts, keep ready auction notices etc.

'Most of our accounts are average except one which is really big–Sampatlal & Company.

'I know,' mumbled Vikas, his mind wandering.

'The Chairman is coming only for this. It's a bad account, but it's his. It was opened in another bank, while he was there. They fleeced that bank by over a crore of rupees through a compromise proposal. Now he has brought it to our bank.' Vikas's face turned pale and drawn.

Sunidhi quietly listened to what he spilled out. Today, Vikas seemed to be under immense pressure. Sunidhi's expectations set for this meeting had proved to be completely off track. !

Very soon, Vikas realized that he had needlessly shown too much anxiety for the Chairman's visit. He had not even properly talked to Sunidhi. He closed the file, looked at her and smiled.

'Let's have a cup of tea…', he announced, ringing the bell, and not waiting for her response.

There was a call on the phone. Vikas was about to pick up the receiver when the phone stopped ringing.

'Hmm…' he let out a sigh. He didn't know whose call it was. Sunidhi sat there quietly, her eyes downcast, stealing a glance at Vikas in between. Vikas looked at Sunidhi but his mind still wandered. Suddenly, he noticed the peon.

'Yes…'

'Sir, you called me in…'

'Oh… tea… get two cups of tea,' he ordered and went back to his reverie. The peon left.

'You look tense! Has anything out of the ordinary happened?' asked Sunidhi, trying to initiate a conversation. Vikas looked at Sunidhi but his eyes spelt out that his present worries were beyond her ken. Then the doorbell rang again. He didn't know why he had rung it. The peon entered immediately. Vikas stared at him for some time. He finally remembered,

'What happened to the tea?'

'It's coming, sir…' The peon quickly left. Vikas wanted to say something to Sunidhi when there was a knock at the door.

'Come in…' answered Vikas and found his PA standing at the door.

'What's the matter?'

'Sir, the Chairman's Secretary had called from Head Office.' The PA glanced at Sunidhi.

'May I leave?' she quickly asked.

Vikas was holding a pencil by its ends and twisting it. The PA stood waiting at the door.

'May I leave?' she repeated.

Vikas dropped the pencil on the table and looked at the PA. Sunidhi rose to go. He watched her go dispassionately. As she closed the door, Vikas got up and asked the PA what the matter was.

'Sir, the Chairman's secretary had called to say that Pande, his PA is also coming along. Here's his programme.' The PA handed over a piece of paper to Vikas.

'Why is this Pande coming? He is very shrewd. You should handle him separately… it's okay. Please send Joshi in.'

The PA left. There was a knock at the door. Joshi, a senior officer stood outside.

'Come in, Joshi…now the Chairman's PA, Pande is also coming with him…' They looked at each other. Joshi brought a mysterious smile on his lips and replied,

'Don't worry, sir. I'll handle. You leave it to me.' Vikas looked deep into Joshi's eyes and knew. A strange smile came to his lips. He was a man of few words, when it came to dealing with subordinates. He didn't like beating about the bush but right now there was an imaginary dialogue ticking in his brain.

'May I leave, sir; everything will be taken care of,' assured Joshi, rising to leave. Vikas watched him leave and wondered why this man was always so confident about himself and sure of everything.

Sunidhi noticed tea being taken inside, where Vikas was all alone at the time. Today he had appeared to be quite confused and restless. He had called for tea and forgotten that it was for her. 'Never mind,' she thought to herself. She was certain that noticing the two cups of tea now, he would remember and call her in. They had not even properly met today. Soon, Sunidhi saw the peon bringing the tea back. She was disappointed to realize that it wouldn't be possible for her to see Vikas again today!

Everyone in the office was talking about the Chairman's visit. So she also got down to work. Who knew what information could be called for and when!

The Head Office was collecting information of all types. They had asked for details of the pending work and reasons behind the delay. The Chairman is supposed to have full information about the region, when he visits a regional office. So the entire office was working under great pressure. Sunidhi decided to give up the idea of having tea with Vikas that day. But tea was just an excuse to be with him and discuss a couple of personal matters. Now it would be possible only after the Chairman's visit and she would have to wait, she thought in silent consolation to herself.

Some people in the office were busy making hotel bookings, some planned meetings with the customers, while others were busy searching suitable buildings for the new branch. The whole office was engaged only in one job–the Chairman's visit.

Sunidhi too prepared information about her accounts. Most queries were likely to be raised on her department. While she made her files ready, she eagerly wished Vikas to call her in. But it wasn't to be. Office time was drawing to a close, though during such emergency preparations, the staff hung around as long as the boss was there.

A meeting was held every day at 5.30 in the evening to review preparations for the Chairman's visit. Vikas spoke to every officer enquiring about the progress in work and probable problems. He even offered to help, if needed. They all valued his guidance and tried their best to follow it. But there were some, though negligible in number, who didn't feel concerned with whatever was going on. They behaved like silent spectators and feigned work. They would often hamper other people's work by finding faults and criticizing it. Vikas had his own way of handling such people. He never assigned them anything which was important. He even neglected them. Except a handful of such people, the rest of the office looked up to Vikas as their leader. He enjoyed their full confidence, carried them along, and was able to get every work done with ease.

Sunidhi was also busy proving her worth.

It was for the first time that she didn't feel tense going home. In fact she hardly had a moment to even think about it. All minor worries got automatically relegated in the face of a major one, she realised. They didn't quite disappear but were temporarily banished. Major worries relieved you of the minor ones. But Sunidhi's problems were not minor in nature. The present problem in the office was temporary and wouldn't last long. But her domestic problems were major and very palpable. They didn't seem to be ending soon. Nor could they be transferred to others. She alone had to face them and fight them till...a way out was found.

'Where do I stop, Madam?' The ricksaw-wala disrupted her thoughts battling in a monologue. She looked outside and found that she was already home.

Sunidhi climbed the stairs with a heavy mind. She knew that Yashodhara would again be concerned about her coming back late. Alok would be wondering how could there be so much work in an office. Nandan... uhff! Sunidhi sighed in exasperation. She slowed down while climbing up the stairs. Unmindful of who crossed her way, she reached her floor and rang the doorbell. She didn't realize how long she stood there and pressed the doorbell again. Then she casually looked at the door and found that it was locked from outside. She felt ashamed of herself, and embarrassed. Was she heading towards a mental illness? No, not at all! Such things could happen with anyone. It was quite possible. She took the house-keys out of her purse and opened the door. There was nobody at home.

❖❖❖

11

Everyone in the office was relaxed today after working hard and double shift for almost a week, preparing for the Chairman's visit, which was just over. Vikas had gone to the airport to see him off and they were waiting for him to return.

As usual, the staff was busy doing post-mortem of the events held during the visit. They discussed what went well and what did not. A lamp-lighting ceremony had been planned at the start of the programme. All senior officers had gathered around the lamp-stand. The Chairman stood in the center. The lamp was to be lit with a candle, which in turn had to be lit by a match-stick. Every time the match-stick was lit, it blew off before lighting the candle. Abhijit Naik, the officer tasked with lighting the candle, got nervous, inviting the Chairman's wrath.

'Don't you smoke?' The officer grew more nervous. He looked at the Chairman with a listless smile.

'Obviously, you don't...or else the match-stick wouldn't go off like this.'

At this time, Vikas signalled someone to switch off the fan. Both the candle and the lamp were lit. The hall resounded with the sound of claps. Only Abhijit Naik didn't clap. He was disheartened and even scared. Later on, many officers joked about the incident and advised him to start smoking before the Chairman's next visit.

They even talked about Sunidhi. She stood by the side of Vikas, holding a tray which carried a pair of scissors to be offered to the Chairman for cutting the ribbon. When the Chairman arrived, he took a special notice of her. He even enquired about the length of her service in the bank, the department she handled and her qualification. Sunidhi answered all his queries with tremendous confidence. Someone even commented sarcastically that she should now be prepared to move to the head office. Sunidhi had felt amused listening to such comments, but wisely chosen not to react.

It was 7.30 in the evening but Vikas had still not turned in. All members of the staff waited for him. Joshi had arranged a feast of sorts, some *dhokla, burfi* and wafers. Tea was to be ordered only when Vikas arrived. Joshi was adept at organizing such parties. None in the office could match his ability at this. They were tired but patiently waited for Vikas. Nobody thought it proper to call him. When Vikas arrived, he didn't go to his cabin, but pulled up a chair and sat down amongst the staff.

Vikas seemed a lot relieved. He congratulated the staff for making the Chairman's visit a huge success. He told them that the Chairman was very happy with the visit. While doing so, he slyly glanced at Sunidhi. He had a great quality of being able to keep certain things to himself, till an opportune moment came to make them public. Had the Chairman been disapproving of something in particular or unhappy with someone's work, Vikas kept it to himself without immediately disclosing it to the staff. He would convey it to the concerned staff only when he felt it was the right time to do so. Even then, he would mention it casually and without personal malice without causing pain or embarrassment.

They all had refreshments arranged by Joshi and left for the day. Vikas shook hands with each and every one of them, even with the peon. He too had worked and served tirelessly and to perfection!

Soon the bills for purchases made in connection with the Chairman's visit started pouring in. Nothing in this office remained a secret. The staff initiated a whispering campaign and things soon reached the boss. A fat bill was received from a jewellery shop. It pertained to the purchase of fifteen sets of four silver bowls each. It was said that these were purchased as gifts for some VIP customers to motivate them to increase deposits in the bank. Each set weighed four hundred grams. Similarly another bill received was for the purchase of fifteen pashmina shawls. Each shawl cost nine thousand rupees. The Chairman's PA was associated with each purchase, in order to ensure that the items were to the liking of the Chairman. Vikas wasn't involved in making any of these purchases; it was only Joshi who handled all shopping sprees.

The bills were paid but a startling fact came to Vikas's notice. All silver bowls as well as the shawls had been returned by the Chairman's PA to the respective shops in exchange of their value in cash. This explained why the PA was missing from the programme as well as the lunch. Even the Chairman didn't feel his need. It was a strange co-incidence but gradually Vikas saw through the game.

At this time, Joshi also presented a bill which had been paid by him through his credit card. He told that the Chairman's PA had requested him to buy some shirts for the Chairman and some sarees for his wife. He had bought them with his credit card. Incidentally, Vikas noticed that even Joshi was wearing a brand new expensive shirt. The bills had to be paid anyway.

Apart from this, some expensive silverware had been presented to the Chairman as a gift from the bank. Nobody had any information on what he had collected from the VIP clients! Vikas was extremely annoyed but he couldn't do much. It was a part of the game. There was also a cocktails-and-dinner party organized for important customers and prominent citizens of the town. Such events were a necessity at such occasions. Many commercial organizations often did much more. The possibility of such occasions being misused by some to make personal gains couldn't also be ruled out. Vikas knew it very well. He also knew that people like Joshi were indispensable for the management. He couldn't have been there everywhere. But the act of returning the gifts in exchange of money was really mean on the part of the Chairman. Vikas despised it from the core of his heart. He wondered what the shopkeeper would be thinking about him! Or maybe he was already privy to such deeds as they benefitted his business as well.

Vikas knew that this Chairman had two more months to go and would definitely want to complete the promotion process before he retired. He had learnt that a Regional Manager had gifted him a Ford Icon car and even arranged its delivery at the Chairman's bungalow in Delhi. Doing so, he had already ensured his promotion.

Before leaving, the Chairman had indicated the need for opening of additional branches of the bank in several areas. The license for the Dwarka branch had also to be utilized before it expired. Vikas had been corresponding with the head office for opening the branch for about the last four months. But the site approval for a new branch had not yet come from the head office. Now that only two months were left for the license to expire, there was a sudden rush.

A trader from Surat had come to see the Chairman and was introduced to Vikas too. The Chairman hadn't said anything about him at that time. But when he was sipping coffee at the airport, he told Vikas,

'Examine the proposal for premises in Surat.'

'But sir, I have sent three or four good proposals to the head office,' Vikas tried to convince the Chairman. The PA, having overheard this conversation, looked intently at Vikas. The Chairman looked at the PA and said,

'Put up the proposals before me when we go back.'

'Yes sir.'

'Sir, among the proposals submitted by me, there is one from Mr Dewan, which I like the most. It's in the market area and there's ample space for the branch. Even lockers can be put up easily. It's suitable even from the security point of view. Most importantly, there is no bank in its vicinity at this time.' Vikas stopped speaking. He noticed that the Chairman's mind was somewhere else. His gaze was fixed on the electronic board displaying information about the flights. Vikas wanted to talk about the proposal for Dwarka, when the Chairman muttered:

'Look…even the flights are not regular these days…it's late by an hour. Make some arrangement in the VIP Lounge. I feel extremely tired.'

'Yes, sir', said Vikas and asked Joshi to arrange for the VIP Lounge. It was done in no time. The Chairman settled down in the sofa and said,

'Vikas, it's already late for you. So you go ahead.'

'No sir, I'll wait. I can't leave without seeing you off…' said Vikas, flattering him.

'Hmm..' His eyes were already drowsy. Without even looking at Vikas he uttered,

'Try to get the Dwarka branch opened without delay. Put everybody on work. We shall invite the FM for the inauguration. Now I have very little time at my disposal…' He was already half asleep.

'Yes sir,' Vikas couldn't say anything else.

'That reminds me… have a look at the proposal received today from…what's his name…?'

'Manik Lal, sir…' the PA prompted him.

'Yes', he nodded 'the same…' His eyes were fully closed now. Vikas was feeling very restless. He got up and went to the washroom. Joshi sensed his discomfort, came up to him and asked,

'Any problem, sir?'

'No, just send the PA here and you stay near the Chairman. Take care if he needs anything, in case he wakes up…'

Joshi sent the PA to Vikas.

Vikas wanted to know the equation between Manik Lal and the Chairman. The PA didn't disclose much but confirmed that the Chairman was interested in Manik Lal's premises. Trying to prolong the conversation, Vikas asked,

'Any idea about the rate?'

'No sir, we don't get to know such details. Only sir would know this...' The PA was trying to wriggle out of this discussion.

Vikas looked at the Chairman. He was snoring. His eyes were shut though the mouth was wide open. A well-fed, shapeless, half-dead mass of flesh and blood was producing strange sounds!

Vikas didn't know what to do when the PA accosted him, 'Sir, a note on the Executive Promotion Process is being put up... at this board meeting,'

Vikas didn't show any anxiety. He knew that the PA was trying to play a game with him. Soon an announcement was heard on the public address system:

'Your attention please. Air India flight number IC 315 is ready to depart. Passengers are requested to proceed to Gate No. 1...'

The PA went up to the Chairman and woke him up. They immediately headed towards Gate No. 1. Reaching the gate for security check, they stopped and Vikas said,

'Wish you a very happy journey, sir...please excuse us if there was anything lacking...please overlook it, sir.'

'No, no, everything was all right...'

So saying, the Chairman meaningfully looked at Vikas, as if to remind him that he had better look into the proposal for Dwarka...Manik Lal. He went ahead with the PA and crossed security check. Vikas stood there, motionless, watching the Chairman vanish in a crowd of passengers. He was expecting that he would turn around once or twice, maybe, to look at Vikas, but he didn't. The PA did wave at him and Joshi, but Vikas couldn't raise his hand in response. Only Joshi waved at him with a lot of excitement till he too was lost in the crowd.

Vikas didn't talk about this new burden with anyone. He would look into the Manik Lal's proposal after it was received.

But upon his return from the airport, he felt a bit heavy in the heart. He was exhausted as well. Joshi read his mind and knew that something was bothering Vikas. Sitting in the car, he said,

'Hope everything went off well, sir…'

Vikas didn't say anything. He just nodded and closed his eyes. Joshi too didn't probe further. They went back in deadly silence. The evening rush of traffic had started polluting the air outside. Sitting inside an air-conditioned car, Vikas too felt something polluting his soul.

❖❖❖

12

Travelling from the airport to office and then to his home today, was a long journey for Vikas. He was feeling completely drained. He had once thought of taking his staff out for dinner, after the Chairman's visit. But today he felt he had no energy to do so. It was good that he hadn't told about it to anyone.

All his subordinates were happy on the success of the visit. Vikas too gave them their due credit. It had been a great collective effort which had made it possible. And they all knew it so well. When they were done with tea and refreshments, Vikas looked at Abhijit and gave him a meaningful smile. Abhijit felt good and obliged. Then Vikas thanked them again and they all dispersed.

Vikas opened his eyes only when the car stopped with a screech. He hadn't dozed off, but he was surely very drowsy. One moment he felt his mind was so light and relaxed, the next moment he felt he had added on to the burden. Stepping out of the car listlessly, he dragged himself up to the lift and reached the second floor. It was nine-thirty in the night. He rang the doorbell and stood there for a while.

There was a movement inside. Somebody peeped through the magic eyehole and opened the door. He wondered if it was Preeti or Khushi...it was Preeti.

'How did it go? I didn't call you deliberately. Didn't know where you would be...and doing what.'

The driver came in with the briefcase. The door had been kept open for him. Through a gesture of his eyes, Vikas told him to call it a day. As usual, he deposited the car keys in the drawer on top of the shoe-rack and left.

So far Vikas hadn't answered Preeti's query. Instead, he asked her about Garima.

'She's in her room, watching TV. She had been studying till now,' said Preeti. Then she called Garima to come out as her dad was home.

Garima came out running and sat beside her dad in the sofa. She was seven years old. She started loosening his neck-tie. Vikas felt a strange comfort in her doing all this. He kissed her on the forehead and asked her,

'What were you watching?'

'*Nemo*, an English film…it's good…you also come to my room and we'll watch it together,' said Garima holding her dad's hand.

'No, not today my child…' said Preeti. 'Dad is too tired today, let him rest…He hasn't even had his food…'

'May I leave?' asked Garima as her mind was in *Nemo*.

'Yes, you may go my dear. I'll watch a film with you some other day,' said Vikas looking at Preeti.

Garima left for her room.

'Uff….'exclaimed Vikas as he flopped down into the sofa. He put his hands behind his head and stretched his legs. He wanted to rest his feet on the tea-poy, but didn't, as he had his shoes on. He shut his eyes as if there was none in front, not even Preeti.

Preeti got up and brought a glass of water. Placing it on the tea-poy, she said,

'You freshen up. I'll get some soup for you. I have made veg clear soup today. I'll lay the table only when you are ready to eat.'

Vikas looked at Preeti with half-opened eyes and then shut them again. Preeti got up and went to the kitchen. Soon she came back with soup. She saw Vikas was still lying like that. She woke him up with a pat and said,

'Soup!'

'Oh yes...keep it over there...I'll take..."

'You should get up now. Have something to eat and then go to sleep. You'll be fine by morning.' Preeti rose to lay the table.

Given a choice, Vikas would have gone to sleep without eating anything. And he would probably have fallen asleep in the sofa. He neither had the energy nor the inclination even to walk up to the bedroom. He was dead tired. But he realised even Preeti wouldn't eat anything if he skipped his dinner.

So he opened his shoe-laces and removed his socks. Now he felt a bit better. He kept the shoes in the rack. He didn't like footwear lying here and there. He was very meticulous in such matters. He changed into kurta-pyjama, came out of the bedroom and sat in the sofa. He picked up the TV remote. He liked watching black and white channels.

Preeti came out of the kitchen and said, 'Come, dinner has been served. You watch the TV after dinner.... Oh, the soup has become cold...I'll heat it up. Please get up and move to the dining table.'

Preeti put the soup in the microwave for heating and started making chapatties. Vikas came on the dining table. Preeti placed the hot soup on the table and quickly advanced towards the tawa to flip the chapatti. She flipped it with her hand...it was very hot...she ran back to place it on Vikas's plate.

'The maid didn't come to make chapatties today?' Vikas asked, sipping the soup.

'She came...and left at ten thirty. I thought I'd serve hot chapatties to you. We have cooked *parwal* today, your favourite vegetable,' Preeti said, looking warmly at Vikas.

Vikas looked intently at Preeti. How caring she was! He had imagined the pleasure of eating parwals only yesterday and here they were, cooked and served by Preeti at dinner for him! He fought an urge to get up and kiss her.

'You also come, get your soup along...'

'I'm coming...you start eating...'

Preeti started rolling out the next chapatti. When she had made a few, she came to the dining table along with her cup of soup.

'Soup is nicely cooked. The vegetables you have added have enhanced its taste...' Vikas mentioned warmly, looking at Preeti.

They had been married for nearly ten years. But Vikas's love and attraction for Preeti hadn't faded. On her part, she had maintained herself well. She looked charming with beautiful, bewitching eyes and an infectious smile. Vikas had never found her sad or critical about anything in life. She was an excellent home-maker. She had kept the house beautifully neat and tidy and this home relieved him from all fatigue and worry once he stepped inside. She had many beautiful artifacts in the house and she kept changing their position every now and then to break monotony and bring about a feeling of freshness.

While sipping his soup, Vikas kept eyeing Preeti frequently. He was aware that she too was staring at him.

'Why are you sitting so far? Come closer, take this chair...' said Vikas, pointing at the chair next to his. Preeti picked up her plate and soup bowl and sat next to him. They both ate their dinner. Vikas didn't usually discuss official matters at home. But today he opened his heart to Preeti and told her everything about the Chairman and his visit. She kept offering her comments in between the narration.

'Oh, what kind of people are these! How shameless...!' She didn't perhaps know that she had inadvertently relieved Vikas of all his stress and strain. Tonight he looked at her so passionately that Preeti couldn't miss it. She too was thrilled to find him so warm and romantic.

By now Vikas's mind was almost free from the tension caused by the Chairman's visit. He felt much relaxed. They both went into Garima's room. She had fallen asleep. The TV screen was flashing scenes from *Nemo* while she held on to the remote. This animation film on the life of a fish was a popular show.

Preeti reduced the speed of the ceiling fan; covered Garima with a bed-sheet and switched on the Goodknight button. Vikas kissed Garima on her forehead and they both came out. The adjoining room was the master bedroom.

Stepping into the bedroom, Vikas was awestruck; it seemed he had landed in a new place altogether. The bed was covered with a pretty new bedspread, a bunch of fresh roses in the flower vase brightened up the room which was also sprayed with a lovely fragrant room freshener. He was madly in love with this aroma. Turning on the TV Vikas started watching the news he had missed during his busy day.

Preeti had expected Vikas to compliment her efforts in preparing the room, but when nothing came, she asked him,

'How did you like the room…?'

'Oh…it's so romantic!' replied Vikas. He held her hands and pulled her lovingly over to himself. Preeti blushed, staring shyly at Vikas. She turned the TV off with the remote. The room lights were still on. Generally they didn't shut their bedroom door, but tonight was different; Vikas quietly locked the door and switched off the lights. It was a full moon night. The moon was up in full splendor, its radiant glow beaming down on the spotless surface of white bedsheets. The turbulent tide of warm, loving exchanges in the bed slowly reached out for the depths of an unfathomable sea of passion….

For the first time in his life, Vikas wondered tonight, if he was being selfish in 'using' Preeti to give respite to his body and soul. However, even in these moments, extremely intimate and private as they were, he found it difficult to refrain from thinking about the events of the day. Preeti was intelligent enough to gauge his mind. So she tightened her grip and slowly lifted him from the mundane world to the realms of heavenly joy where all remnants of the Chairman's visit seemed to fade away into oblivion. But there was a strange vision which suddenly flashed upon his mind's eye and quickly vanished…

❖❖❖

13

The morning rush had started. Garima's school bus usually came at quarter past seven. It was a challenge to wake her up so early in the morning. As Vikas himself was lazy, Preeti had to take up this responsibility to send her to school single-handedly. She kept her dress ready, packed her bag and polished her shoes before going to bed, the previous night. In the morning she woke her up, gave her a simple breakfast of Bournvita-milk and an apple and saw her off, joined by Vikas, who would be up by then.

Today when Garima left for school, Preeti saw her off alone, as Vikas was still asleep. Last night, he had slept quite late. He had even turned off his phone so that he wasn't disturbed. Usually he would put the phone on silent mode so that he might see who had called him in the night. But last night was different. He was very tired and expected to receive many casual, unimportant calls.

The landline phone rang in the living room. It had an extension in the bedroom with a cordless handset. But last night, that too had been put on 'mute'. So it kept ringing till Preeti came out of the kitchen and picked it up.

'Some Patel is on the line,' she said.

'Tell him to call later in the office,' replied Vikas, half-awake. He finally got out of bed, wondering who this Patel could be. Then he recalled; it must have been the person who had accompanied the landlord from Surat, when the latter had come to meet the Chairman. It was his premises to be considered for the new branch, as wished by the Chairman.

'Tea...' Preeti stood before him, with tea poured in a brand new mug. Vikas preferred to drink his tea in a large mug, filled up to the brim. He looked at Preeti; she looked ravishing. He took the mug, placed it on the bedside table and pulled Preeti upon himself.

'Come on...drink your tea...what are you up to' asked Preeti beholding Vikas lovingly.

'Don't know...you are looking so fresh and beautiful this morning...' replied Vikas, pressing her close to himself. She quietly surrendered herself to his arms, closed her eyes and placed her head on his chest. His fingers ran through her soft luxuriant hair. Both of them were completely lost for a moment. Then she opened her eyes, coming out of her romantic trance, her eyes falling on the bedside timepiece. She looked at him and asked,

'What's the matter? It's eight thirty already...don't you want to go to office today?'

'Don't know...may be not. I'm bored with this routine. Want to be with you, today!' He tightened his embrace.

'First you drink your tea, it's getting cold.'

'We'll heat it again...'

'What's the matter today...never seen you so romantic? Office has always been your top priority!'

'Hmm....' He said nothing and started sipping his tea.

'Shall I make breakfast or you really want to stay at home today?'

'Oh no, I better not...not today at least. The Chairman could be ringing me up any moment. He wouldn't be at peace till the premises of his choice are finalized.'

'Then let me go and make breakfast...'

Willy-nilly she got out of his hug and went straight to the kitchen. Vikas saw her going but didn't stop her. He was completely at peace. The previous night had woven its magic. He switched his mobile on and picked up the newspaper. They were replete with the coverage of the Chairman's visit. It was Sunidhi's portfolio and she had handled it well. She must have burnt the midnight oil for turning the reports in. Even the pictures were nice and attractive. Each time he went through a report, he thought about her. Suddenly he smiled…he seemed to have pleasantly realized that the strange image which had, even in his most personal intimate moments of passion, flashed on his mind's eye last night and relieved him of all worries…and pushed all remnants of the Chairman's visit into oblivion, was of none else than Sunidhi's. How strange…!

His mobile rang. He put the newspapers and Sunidhi's thoughts aside to answer the call. It was Trivedi, a general manager in the head office. He immediately sensed what the call was for.

'Hello.'

'It's Trivedi here.'

'I know, sir…good morning. Please tell me…what's the order?' said Vikas. He was irritated to have received this call, but didn't let it reflect in his voice.

'The Chairman had called…'

'Sir…?'

'Regarding Surat-wala's proposal for the premises…'

'I'll examine it once I reach the office. We just met them yesterday…'

'I know Vikas, but it's my job to remind you. The Chairman is going to ask me about it, at the morning meeting.'

'I understand, sir. I'll talk to you after reaching office. However, some Patel had called me early morning. So early that…'

'Well Vikas…it was my job to remind you. And I have done that. As you know…the Chairman has a peculiar way of getting things done. Anyway, please tell me what I should tell him at the meeting?' Trivedi spoke in a manner which was free, frank and characteristic of a general manager. Vikas understood this corporate jargon quite well. So he replied,

'I'll put in my best efforts, sir.'

'Okay.' said Trivedi and hung up.

Now Vikas had lost interest in reading the rest of the press coverage. Even Sunidhi was nowhere in his thoughts. He quickly got ready and rushed off to office. There was a routine for the Chairman's secretariat to call all regional heads at ten to check if they were there in the office or not. And Vikas didn't want to be caught today.

The driver had arrived on time. He collected the briefcase and lunch-box and took the car out of the garage. Vikas left in a hurry, even without saying 'goodbye' to Preeti. She realized how the pressure of work told upon one's responses and took its toll on the normal pleasantries of life. Every day, she bade good bye to Vikas, standing in the balcony of her living room. But today, she stood there as always, but Vikas neither looked up nor said goodbye to her before stepping into his car. She felt very uncomfortable.

Alighting from the car, Vikas walked straight to the lift and pressed the button. As it took more time to come, he impatiently pressed the button again, fully aware that the button once pressed was enough to summon it. Similarly, when the liftman saluted him as usual, he didn't notice or respond. While moving towards his cabin, he would normally look at all present in the hall and exchange pleasantries with them. In case his neck-tie ever flew in the air, he used to gently press it with his hand.

But it was different today. He took long strides and walked straight to his cabin, without looking at anyone. His neck-tie flew a couple of times before it settled on his shoulder, but he didn't bother about it. Entering his cabin, he told the peon,

'Send Arvind in.'

The peon looked at Arvind's empty chair and said,

'Sir, he is not in yet.'

Arvind was Vikas's PA. He came in just about five minutes later and rushed into Vikas's cabin.

'Sir, the traffic was…'

'It's okay.'

Vikas wasn't interested in any explanation. 'Just find out if there was a call from the head office.'

As Arvind got up to go, the peon brought in some tea. It was a daily routine. Vikas wanted a cup of hot tea to start his day in office. But today, it didn't give him any pleasure to see tea arrive. Soon Arvind informed him that there had been no call from the head office. Vikas felt relieved. He looked at Arvind with a meaningful glance to tell him that he should reach office before he arrived. He lifted the cup to drink his tea.

Sipping tea, Vikas looked at the heap of files kept on his table. He picked up the one containing press-cuttings, opened it and found there were plenty of clippings on the Chairman's visit. He read each and every one, and rang the bell to call Sunidhi. He was told that she had not come to office. He checked with the HR and learnt that she was on leave today.

'Any special reason…?' Vikas asked the HR.

'I'm not aware, sir, the message is only for a day's leave.'

Vikas picked up his mobile to call her and ask what the matter was. He pondered for a while and kept it back on the table. It was just a day…!

❖❖❖

14

Sunidhi had come to her parents' place. She was quiet but her unease wasn't hidden from her mother. So she asked her,

'What's the matter, my child? You seem to be very upset...'

'You know it, Ma...what more can I tell you?' replied Sunidhi, helplessly.

'I have discussed it with your father. He says that your younger sister is yet to be married...what would be our position in the society if...' The mother feared spelling it out. She realized Sunidhi's agony, but hoped the situation to improve and get normal with the passage of time. She always wished well for Sunidhi and her family.

'But it can't get any better now...and I can't pull on like this anymore, even if I wish to...' Sunidhi was on the brink of breaking down.

'Has Nandan said anything to you?' Sunidhi's mother indulged in soul-searching.

'No, but my disgust for him is increasing day-by-day. I dread going into that house.' The mother could feel Sunidhi's pain. Yet she had pinned some hope on Yashodhara.

'Have you discussed it with Yashodhara...?'

Sunidhi gave her mother a dirty look, She didn't like her pushing her into the hell any more. Her beautiful large eyes were swollen and bloodshot with rage and remorse. Her river of life flowed perilously and was in deluge from both sides. The shores were caving in and the situation was going fast out of control. She was exploding and the muddy currents were pushing her down into the abysmal depths. Her mother's questions were piercing her already distressed heart. But what could even the mother do…she knew everything but was helpless. She only saw and feared the cracks appearing on the well-guarded walls of social values and morality.

'Yashodhara knows everything, Ma. And I have nothing against her. But…it's not in her control. I don't see much of Babuji…don't even talk with him much but even he seems upset.' Sunidhi was trying to console herself by telling all this to her mother.

'You have luckily got a good job now. You should focus on your work. There'll be many opportunities to move up…' The mother looked at Sunidhi for a moment, then fearing that she may be sounding too moralistic, she stopped talking. Mothers have the knack of feeling their children's anguish in no time. So she pondered for a while. Then she put her hand on Sunidhi's shoulder and said,

'Don't worry. Often when a particular path seems to close down several other avenues open up. Everybody has problems in life, but they do get resolved at some point!'

Sunidhi listened intently. She only wished that whatever her mother was saying could come true. But where was the guarantee that it would?

A strange silence prevailed between them for quite some time. They didn't even look at each other. Sunidhi noticed that the flowers in the balcony had started wilting in the pots. Right then, her father appeared there, watering the plants. It was his routine. They were both startled to see him emerge all of a sudden. He looked at them and noticing their wet eyes and gloomy faces, he abandoned watering. He went to the living room, switched the TV on and started watching news. Sunidhi knew that he didn't like talking about her marriage. But it didn't help her in any way. It rather made her feel more miserable.

Both of them got up and went to the kitchen. The mother got busy in cooking and Sunidhi went to her old room. She had grown up there along with her sisters. She and the one younger to her had been married, whereas the third was ready for it. The room no longer looked like her old space. It had undergone a complete change. There were fewer books on the table. It was occupied largely by a computer, a mobile phone, a charger and stuff like that. There was nothing there which really belonged to her, except her memories. Today she realized how one gets nostalgically attached to one's old belongings. She also had a sad realization that she had nothing left from the past nor did she hope to create anything in the future. All she was faced with was her bleak and dreadful present!

Sunidhi stayed at her mother's house for a day. She had wanted to confide in her all the baggage she carried in the inner recesses of her heart. She had hoped that the mother would listen to her, share it with her father and they would collectively find a solution to her problems. But when the mother was herself not amenable to her ideas, how could she expect her to convince her father? Moreover, Sunidhi hardly felt at home over there.

On her way back home, Sunidhi once thought of adopting Nandini's way of life. It could probably end all her woes. But going her way wasn't easy either, she realised. Simply trying to replicate the lifestyle and characteristics of people we admire doesn't lead to the desired results; we never turn into their clones. Besides, she wasn't independent in her decisions like Nandini. There was a sea of difference in their thoughts and nature. Unlike Nandini, Sunidhi valued relationships. She cared for other people's feelings.

Various scenes of her marriage flashed in her mind. Nandan hadn't been able to look into her eyes even when he put the *jaimala,* the garland flowers, around her neck. How woeful and unfortunate she had felt! All joyful moments born out of small and ordinary rituals of a marriage had eluded her. She had felt suffocated. Only her mother, who watched her from a distance, seemed to have understood her plight. She kept nodding as if to reassure her that things would work out. Her father had been busy looking after the guests. Her younger sisters were engrossed in exchanging pleasantries with their friends. She was the only one who failed to make it a memorable moment in her life!

On her way back home, Sunidhi made up her mind to end the uncertainty and confusion in her life. She decided to seek a divorce from Nandan. She knew it would smash the hopes of many who looked up to her for a solution. She could even see their gloomy and run-down faces. But she didn't care less. It couldn't bog her down from going ahead with her decision. She hadn't been responsible for the situation. So how could she be blamed for it? Besides, it was her life and she had the right to live it the way she liked and wanted. Nobody could expect her to sacrifice her happiness for the sake of their family honour!

The turmoil inside her was growing but the decision had been taken.

❖❖❖

15

Vikas was attending office after two days of touring. He wanted to inspect the sites available for opening the new branch. Entering office, he cast a casual glance on all employees, including Sunidhi and walked up to his cabin.

He perused the mail and talked to several officers. He wanted to talk to Sunidhi at leisure. Therefore, he hadn't called her in so far. Now, he was slightly free. But before he could send for her, the peon entered with a visiting card in his hand.

'This is some Patel…he came yesterday as well…'

'Okay. Send him in,' said Vikas, feeling slightly perturbed all of a sudden. He dropped the pencil he was holding in his hand and unthinkingly picked up a file.

'May I come in, sir…?'

It was Patel. His fox-like cunningness was fully evident in his voice and the expressions on his face. Without waiting for Vikas to react, he entered the cabin and occupied a chair.

'Tell me, what's the matter?' asked Vikas, coldly.

'Nothing, sir. I was just passing by…thought I'd say hello to you… hmm…hmm…'

'I haven't examined your file yet. You'll get a message once I do so. We may even call you to office, if needed,' explained Vikas, before Patel could have asked him about the status of his proposal for leasing his premises for the new branch.

'Our Saheb is visiting Delhi shortly. He thought he could carry the file personally….if it was cleared by you?' said Patel probing Vikas's mind.

Vikas was annoyed. He fiercely shook his head, as if trying to shed his anger and control himself. Bringing about a semblance of normalcy on his countenance, he said,

'Mr Patel, such matters take time. I have directed my staff to survey the site,' Vikas wanted to quickly get rid of him. So he picked up another file and feigned business.

'Sir, may I know as to who'll be coming for the survey...?' questioned Patel, audaciously.

An enraged Vikas didn't make any effort to hide his displeasure this time. But it had no effect on Patel's thick skin. He was, in fact, used to receiving such rebuffs at the hands of officers. So, smiling shamelessly, he asked,

'Sir, I have to convey this information to Saheb...so, if you could tell me...I'll request you too to have a look at the site yourself...you'll like it. It's an excellent location...for a bank and you'll get a lot of business over there'.

Patel was unstoppable. He had all the traits of a clever property-broker.

Vikas could easily see through the guiles of such people. He looked at him indignantly and said,

'You may come next week...I'm a bit busy today.'

Right then, there was a call from the Chairman's PA. Vikas couldn't help taking it. He just listened to the speaker, whose tone would, now and then, get really harsh. But he was not in a position to say anything more than mumbling 'Yes, sir'... 'Yes, sir'. Patel was intently looking at him and reading his mind. Vikas too cast a sly look at him in between.

Patel knew whose call it was. He got up and left.

Before Patel arrived, Vikas had a strong desire to call Sunidhi. But now he called Saxena instead. Saxena always came to Vikas's cabin, with a pen and pad in his hand. He had the reputation of being a competent and hard-working officer. He was generally very humble but turned highly vocal and forthright when it came to expressing his views on administrative matters. He never blindly toed a line. He could distinguish the right from wrong with a naked eye. Vikas respected his judgement in official matters and strongly depended on him. The department dealing with the selection of sites for new branches of the bank was handled by him.

'Saxena, what should we do with this Patel and his Sampat Lal...and the Chairman is repeatedly calling for them...!'

'Sir, I suspect a complicity in this deal...', stated Saxena fearlessly.

'I too feel so...and I think it's an open secret. Likely to blow into a scandal.' observed Vikas. He never hid his feelings from his trusted aides.

'I think we should forward a realistic and impartial report, Sir. We don't know...what may come out later...', said Saxena, expressing his honest view.

'Saxena, I suggest we identify some more premises at the said location and take their quotes. Then compare them with the rates offered by Patel and forward a comprehensive proposal to the head office,' suggested Vikas, finding a possible way out to safeguard his position.

'But it may infuriate the Chairman, sir...and lead to some other complications...' opined Saxena. He was, indirectly, cautioning Vikas about the impending promotion process, likely to take place shortly.

'Then what do we do? It's a pretty difficult decision. If we recommend Sampat Lal's proposal, fully aware that the rates quoted by him are highly exorbitant...we are inviting trouble for ourselves and if we recommend any other, we may invite the Chairman's wrath. How do we solve this?' Vikas looked at the door.

'Sir, there's a visitor...a Mr Mahajan,' announced the peon, softly, standing at the door. He was always aware of the climate inside the cabin and modulated his voice accordingly.

'Mahajan ...who? No, not today please.' Vikas never raised his voice, but today...he couldn't hold himself.

Saxena beckoned the peon to come inside, so that Vikas's voice didn't reach the people outside. Gently he told the peon,

'Tell him, sir is busy in a meeting. Won't be able to meet today.' Then he looked at Vikas and added on his behalf, 'One thing more... don't send anybody in.'

The peon left quietly.

'Who is this Mahajan?' asked Vikas, trying to figure out.

'Don't know, sir. But I have a hunch that he is a customer in our branch on MG Road. He has been visiting us for quite some time for raising the limit of his account. He had come in your absence too...in case he is the same guy...!'

Vikas called for tea. He wiped the sweat from his forehead and uttered, 'Oh, I remember, Saxena. An MLA had rung me up for him. The manager of the MG Road branch had also mentioned him. Tell me, how much pressure can one take huh? Everybody wants a favour.'

'Sir, we'll take care of him later. Let's first handle this problem created by the Chairman...it's more important. My only fear is that we may land ourselves in trouble. The promotion process is on and we have to do something about the Chairman's visit too...' said Saxena. Although his observation on the promotion process was unintentional, it added to the pressure Vikas already felt.

'There's still time for promotions, Saxena...may be a month or two. And that shouldn't be a consideration in such matters. We should work conscientiously, without bothering about the results.' Vikas tried to reassure himself about whatever was stressing him out.

Saxena seemed to agree. Vikas had heard about such testing situations being faced by many of his senior colleagues, many a times, but he never imagined being caught in one himself. Suffering on account of something you hadn't done was doubly painful. But time lent you the strength to bear it and tackle such situations. In spite of Saxena's unfailing and sincere support, Vikas had never felt so helpless in his life.

'Sir, let's report the facts. We'll add a few more proposals... genuine ones, offer our impartial views on the same and forward the proposal. We'll see what happens. There's no other way to handle it.'

Vikas observed Saxena intently while listening to his advice. He seemed to agree.

The tea was brought in.

It was seven o'clock in the evening when Saxena left the cabin. Vikas was still preoccupied with the thought of finding a way out of this mess. It had totally shaken his consciousness and disturbed his mind. He hadn't been able to do any work, ever since Patel had left his cabin.

In the meanwhile, Sunidhi had peeped several times into Vikas's cabin through the eye-hole, every time returning dejected by the grimness of the air, to her seat. Once Saxena was out of the cabin, she felt she might be able to see Vikas. So she got up and headed towards his cabin. Right then, the calling bell rang and she heard Vikas tell the peon: 'Send Sunidhi in...'

She entered the cabin without saying anything to the peon.

'So soon...were you standing at the door itself?' asked Vikas, utterly surprised at the promptness of her entry.

'Yes...I had been waiting to come in...'

Sunidhi tried to look normal, though the tempest mounting inside her was palpable.

'Just a minute...' said Vikas. He got up and rushed into the washroom attached to the cabin. Sunidhi also got a respite. Her emotions were taking control over her. She didn't know where to start from. She wondered why Vikas had called her. Her gaze repeatedly fell upon the washroom door.

❖❖❖

16

Soon Sunidhi heard the sound of the washroom door open. She turned her gaze towards the office trophies in the cabin, even though she had seen them many times before.

Vikas entered the room. Sunidhi slyly looked at him and knew that he had washed his face, combed his hair and tucked in his shirt properly. He had probably even cleansed his glasses. Now he looked quite fresh. She wondered why he took pains to do all this, though his actions had actually given her a lot of pleasure. Was it because he wanted to be more presentable without any signs of official fatigue and anxiety?

Taking his seat, Vikas looked at her as if he was getting to see her after ages. She noticed it and lowered her gaze with a blush. Vikas still kept looking at her.

'What happened…why you were on leave?' Vikas started the conversation.

'Yes, I had gone to see my mom…' replied Sunidhi, looking at her image in the glass kept on Vikas's table-top. She looked quite pulled down!

'Are you alright?'

'Yes, I am fine…"

'Then…?'

'Will talk about that later. What kept you so busy the whole day and people outside were talking about some problem you have!'

'Nothing much. Problems would always be there…as an integral part of your job. And they'll keep multiplying as you go up…the ladder of official hierarchy. Then you'll even be afraid of losing the position…' Vikas explained patiently, bringing about a fake smile on his face. He tried to trivialize the matter by offering a rather philosophical interpretation. In reality, he was trying to conceal his inner turmoil. But when he glanced at Sunidhi, he felt that her pain was much greater than his. Her eyes didn't have their usual luster; her lips were devoid of the rosy glow so remarkable of her; her saree was unkempt. She spoke in a feeble voice. Her nervousness showed in the way she kept resting and removing her arms on the glass-top of the table. She was not at peace. Obviously, her agony was much deeper than his.

'Sunidhi…' he exclaimed very softly and affectionately.

As she raised her head to confront him, her moist eyes completely gave her away. He got up from his seat, poured some water in a glass kept on the side of his table and offered it to her.

'Sunidhi, we got a wonderful coverage of the Chairman's visit… all the media reports were full of praise. Even the visit went off well. Congratulations to you! That time I got too engrossed in it…couldn't even check if you got some refreshment or not…' Vikas tried his best to divert Sunidhi's mind from whatever was troubling her. He wanted her to feel at home.

Sunidhi thanked Vikas. She felt much better and a bit more at ease now. Vikas called Saxena in and announced, 'Let nobody bring lunch from home tomorrow. We'll have a party. You set the menu as you do it so well.'

Saxena nodded in agreement and left. He was happy to see Vikas getting back to his normal self.

'Whatever is the matter…you look very disturbed today. We have shared our personal problems with each other, in the past. We can do so now too, if you wish,' Vikas was prompting Sunidhi to open up her mind.

'It's already very late today. In fact, I myself wanted to tell you all that is going on in my life…' said Sunidhi. She wanted to tell him all that she had gone through recently, but lost heart when she looked at the clock.

'Okay, let's plan...let's meet at Rasoi and have our dinner together...' proposed Vikas quickly.

It was a heavenly opportunity for Sunidhi and she grabbed it quickly, accepting the invitation. She had herself looked forward to something like this. Only she would have to invent some plausible excuse before people back home for being late, which she decided she would willingly do.

Sunidhi reached Rasoi much before the appointed time. When Vikas arrived, it didn't take him long to locate her. It was a huge restaurant with many dining areas. There was a fairly large banquet hall too. But they chose to sit beneath a tree-like umbrella. Sunidhi had already placed the order before Vikas arrived.

'I had gone to Mom's house to give her a piece of my mind. I had expected that she would understand me...and even empathize with me, but she didn't. She appreciated my predicament but wouldn't let me go my way...fearing social ignominy!'

'What did she tell you?'

'The same old advice. That... it would spoil my sister's marriage prospects...and that I should look at some other option. In a nutshell, they want me to abandon the idea of filing for divorce... and let my life go to hell so that my sis can live happily. In other words, I should sacrifice my life, my happiness for the sake of her life.'

Vikas had known Sunidhi for quite some time, but only as an officer of the bank. Today, he discovered her qualities as an individual, as a strong woman. She was so different than what he had imagined her to be. He always thought that she was exceedingly charming, even bewitching perhaps. No man could escape being drawn towards her. She had a beautiful feminine figure. She was well educated and very articulate. But what he didn't know was that she was so fearless and bold; so candid and forthright. At the same time, she was kind and big-hearted. Above all, she knew very well that she was the master of all these qualities.

The soup had arrived. Sunidhi pulled her cup, added some pepper to it and started sipping. Suddenly she stopped, realizing that she was showing an awkward hurry. Vikas was still looking at her like he had never seen her before. She felt self-conscious. Quickly she picked up the tray of sauces and moved it towards him.

'Sorry...' she said.

'"Sorry"...for what?'

'For having started to drink the soup...'

'Not to worry.' He picked up a glass of water from the table, held it high in the air and exclaimed, 'Cheers'.

Sunidhi also picked up the other glass, held it high in the air and echoed, 'Cheers'.

'Would you like a drink?'

Sunidhi looked at him keenly and replied, 'No...'

'Should I take it as real 'no' or...?'

Sunidhi smiled and lowered her face. It had already turned red with embarrassment. A moment later, she raised her head and glanced at Vikas. His eyes were filled with love... and showed a tinge of mischief too. Her lips quivered. She was about to say something, but stopped. Instead, she picked up her cup of soup, took a few sips and turned her gaze away from Vikas. She noticed a painting hung on the restaurant wall. She looked at it. There was something queer about it. She looked at it more carefully. She found that it was extremely beautiful but didn't make any sense like her own life.

'You can have a drink, if you like', she told Vikas.

'No, I don't drink alone, particularly if I am in the company of a lady...' replied Vikas and started sipping his soup.

Sunidhi felt that she was born to live alone. She liked Vikas and his company, though she wasn't sure about his feelings for her. For once she thought that he pitied her state of affairs. Then she felt that his concern for her and her problems was quite genuine.

'So, what have you decided?' Vikas broached the subject again, gingerly.

'I am sick of living in my in-laws' house… or at my parents' place. They aren't interested in empathising with me or my emotions and my problems. They can't even think about me, keeping their own interests aside.' Sunidhi had summed up her dilemma.

'But what have you decided to do?'

'Nothing…I don't know.' Her eyes looked hollow, heavy with tears about to roll down; she strove hard and held them back.

'Sunidhi, you'll have to decide early. You can't live like this for ever,' said Vikas finishing his soup.

'I have decided already…' Sunidhi replied firmly. There was a glint of resolve in her eyes.

'What have you decided?'

'To separate from them. I still don't know what to do after that nor decided on a place where I will I live.'

'But you'll continue with the job, won't you?'

'Oh certainly, why not? In fact, it's just the job for me now…everything else is lost.'

'Nothing is lost, Sunidhi. And even if it's lost, hope is not lost. It sustains forever, springs eternal in the human heart.' Vikas was sincerely trying to salvage the situation.

'But where do you propose to stay?'

'At a ladies' hostel… I am worried about my mother-in-law however…'

'Yashodhara ji?'

'Yes, I have formed a strange...emotional bond with her. She is retiring next year. It will be miserable for her...'

'And you'll make your life miserable if you continue to stay there. If you ask me I'll say that you have taken the right decision. And there should be no looking back...' Vikas was reassuring her in his own unique style.

'But I don't know how I shall break the news to her.'

'Talk directly. She must also be thinking about you as you do about her. Such matters do trouble you in the beginning but... time is a great healer.'

Sunidhi listened to Vikas very quietly. She felt that he was giving voice to her own thoughts. She was happy to see how he endorsed her decision; how he supported and counselled her...on the contrary her own people were unable to reach out to her or offer good advice and emotional support. She was convinced of his judgement and courage of conviction.

'But it won't be easy for you, Sunidhi. You'll have to single-handedly fight the entire social system; confront harsh and hostile behavior from loved ones, which could be extremely painful. You'll have to prepare yourself for all this...' said Vikas, pouring some dal on the rice in his plate.

Sunidhi noticed that no dal was left in his bowl. So she picked up the service decanter–the *donga*–and poured some dal in it. Vikas noticed this and was touched by this caring gesture!

'You also take some dal, you haven't had any.'

'I don't eat rice at dinner,' answered Sunidhi gravely.

'That's why you are so fit...and slim...' uttered Vikas hesitantly, looking at Sunidhi.

His compliment pleased Sunidhi. She lowered her eyes and blushed. She had heard that Vikas was not given to taking interest or interfere in other people's lives, particularly women. So she wondered how and why he showed particular interest in hers!

They both were quiet for quite some time. Vikas was thinking about his family and Sunidhi about hers. Suddenly they looked at their respective watches at the same moment. Taken aback at this coincidence, they realised it was ten o'clock at night.

'Shall we leave?' asked Vikas spontaneously.

'Yes', replied Sunidhi, heaving a deep sigh. But she rose to leave the next moment. She was nervous that she would be misunderstood by her in-laws for coming home so late at night. Her training in life and the values she had been taught were coming in the way of leading a life like Nandini's; yet the present circumstances provoked her to break away from all her values. Miserably caught in a weird dilemma, she followed Vikas and walked out.

'Come on...come with me...' said Vikas looking back.

Sunidhi nodded gently. With a smile on her face, she took a couple of long strides to catch up with him. She was, however, very nervous and worried about being seen with Vikas in a hotel. So she avoided looking here and there and when she came out, she felt much relieved. Nobody had seen her, she thought.

'Come, let me drop you home...' offered Vikas, opening the car door for her.

'No, I'll go myself...my house is not far.'

'I know. But I am going that way...please get into the car...'

Shyly, Sunidhi entered the car and sat beside him.

'Why are you worried, Sunidhi? Is it the fear of being seen with your boss, so late at night? Come on...I told you that you'll have to fight the system; confront its harsh and hostile diktats and these could be painful at times. So far, nobody knows anything about what you are up to, but the real test will start when things are public,' Vikas was driving the car and looking at Sunidhi in between.

Sunidhi had a habit of wrapping a corner of the loose end of her saree around her fingers, whenever she was in pensive or thoughtful mood. So when she looked at Vikas after his long discourse, she found that the tight wrap of her saree around her fingers had suddenly loosened itself. She felt comforted.

There was neither any red-light on the signals nor much traffic on the roads at half past ten in the night.

They were quiet for some time. Then Sunidhi glanced at Vikas. He was about to say something. Looking at her, he said, 'There are certain things which are bare essentials in life, like *roti*, *kapada* and *makaan*. We happily accept whatever comes our way. We eat whatever we can easily get. We sleep even if it's on a newspaper spread on the footpath. We wear whatever is available. But to enjoy our life as a human being, we need much more than bare essentials. We live within the framework of a social system. We have our ego to be fed and respected. We have our dreams to be realized; our desires to be fulfilled. And we struggle all our lives and strive to do so... I think I am being too didactic.' He stopped abruptly.

This time, when he looked at Sunidhi, he felt that she was totally lost in thoughts. She was actually worried about the possibility of being seen getting out of his car, so late at night. What would happen if somebody noticed her! How would she explain if questioned? They were approaching her house. She debated whether she'd get off the car and walk up to the house. But she couldn't bring herself up to say this.

'Sunidhi...' Vikas wanted to say something, but it was Sunidhi who spoke before him.

'We have reached my home,' she said. She realised it was actually not a 'home' but a mere 'house', as Vikas had said sometime back. He applied the brakes and the car stopped. Before opening the door, she looked up to survey the balcony on the second floor. Thankfully there was nobody waiting there.'

'Thank you...' Sunidhi said, preparing to get down. But before she could, Vikas extended his hand towards her. His fingers were cold due to the air-conditioner in the car. But he felt that Sunidhi's palms were burning hot. They were red hot. Their hands remained locked for a while. It was only when she opened the car door that Vikas let her go. Sunidhi got down from the car and waved a 'goodbye', turning towards her flat. As she unintendedly looked up, she found Alok, her father-in-law standing in the balcony, smoking a cigarette. She didn't look at Vikas again. He had hoped to step out and see her off but she had requested him to stay inside. Good she did so. Vikas waited for a moment and left.

Sunidhi walked briskly up to her flat. She didn't know whether Alok had noticed her getting off the car. She couldn't muster courage to look up again. Slowly she started climbing the stairs, one by one. She treaded so softly that even her high heels didn't make a sound. What would she say in case Alok confronted her! She climbed the stairs, carrying the burden of such thoughts and some guilt. She would admit that Vikas had come to drop her, she decided. And if he probed further? She found herself standing at the doorway before she could plan out a strategy. She pressed the doorbell with a frozen finger...she didn't know why and when her fingers turned so cold. They were not as cold when Vikas held her hand? The cold deep inside her heart had probably reached up to her fingertips. She heard the sound of footsteps inside. Her heartbeat doubled. She was uneasy, her heart sped and she could hardly stand still. She heard the sound of the latch being lifted...she lowered her head...she would face whatever came her way! The door opened and she found Yashodhara standing there.

'So late...?'

Before Sunidhi could reply she heard, 'It's okay, come in...have you had your dinner?

'Yes!'

❖❖❖

17

It was half past eleven when Vikas reached home. He rang the door-bell. Preeti opened the door. Garima, who stood behind Preeti, rushed to hug her dad.

'How come, you guys are still awake…it's so late in the night…?'

'I can't sleep without you… dad,' said Garima.

'I know…' said Vikas, giving her a tight hug and a kiss on the forehead, 'let's go and sleep now…'

'Yes, Garima, you must go to sleep now,' said Preeti.

Like a good child, Garima quietly got up and left for her room. Vikas dumped himself in the sofa and started removing his shoes. Preeti looked at him and sensed that all was not normal.

'Is everything okay', she asked, 'have you had your dinner?'

'Yes…'

'Want a glass of milk?'

'No … I am full…!'

'These days you don't look your normal self. Something is always worrying you. What's it? At the most, they'll order your transfer...or withhold a promotion. They can't do anything worse than that. Then why worry…and lose your peace of mind?' Preeti was trying to lessen his strain.

'Not that…' replied Vikas. He had removed his shoes. He put them aside, got up and walked towards the washroom.

Vikas had shared all details of the Chairman's visit with Preeti. Normally he didn't discuss official matters at home unless these were extremely complex and beyond his ability to resolve. Not that he expected Preeti to resolve them, but sharing with her always lessened his anxiety. However, he had never told her anything about Sunidhi.

Vikas found it difficult to sleep. He just restlessly tossed and turned in bed. This time when he turned his side, he found Garima's innocent face in front. She had this habit of quietly slipping into their bed in the middle of the night.

Vikas turned his side again, but there was still no sleep in his eyes. For a moment he thought he would get up and watch TV for some time. But it would have disturbed Preeti. So he dropped the idea. Then he suddenly got up and walked up to the other side of the bed where Preeti lay asleep. He found some empty space by her side and placed himself over there.

Preeti usually slept on this side of the bed and Vikas on the other. The landline phone had also been connected on her side so that it didn't disturb Vikas at night. If a late night call happened to come, she took it and passed it on to Vikas only if it was urgent. He put his mobile on silent mode at night and kept it on his side.

As Vikas lay by her side, Preeti immediately sensed that he was upset. She slept light and woke up at the slightest movement. So she turned towards him and fondly playing with his hair she asked:

'No sleep or there's a problem?'

'No sleep...'

'You unnecessarily carry the office problems in your head and bring them home I told you not to worry. We'll accept whatever comes our way. You know my needs are limited, I have never asked you for anything big,' Preeti tried to comfort Vikas.

Vikas felt good and clung to Preeti. Nobody uttered a word. It didn't take Preeti much time to understand what he was up to. They had such an amazingly good chemistry between them that everything else would get relegated to the back seat when they came together. So, even in that slender margin on the bed and fully aware that Garima lay asleep beside them, they managed to slip into the realm of joy. Though Preeti was still not fully awake, Vikas had already aroused her desires. And as for him, he was very tired and wanted some sleep; he needed some succour desperately to fall asleep quickly.

Sometimes, the laws of nature and destiny push one into a swirl of currents where emotions and the body surrender hand-in-hand. Vikas and Preeti were caught in this whirlpool. The thin rivulet of desire surged into rushing waters; its soaring waves crashing the shores. It was unaware of its own identity and merged with a big foaming river, which flowed with ease, camouflaging the violent undercurrents and turbulence deep down. Vikas realised he was caught in such a whirlpool. His eyes were shut. His body temperature was on the rise. Now the river had morphed into the blue sky and Vikas was merrily flying in it, leaving behind all his restlessness and anxiety. There were no worries…no anxieties and no concerns. Everything had faded out into oblivion...even his conscious self. What remained was just the body, the physical self…which too had become lax though!

Preeti felt that Vikas had been too generous in making love to her tonight. She was overwhelmed. She kissed him madly and cuddled his forehead with her amorous and magical touch. Vikas felt intoxicated. When he gathered himself a bit, he told Preeti,

'Let's sleep now…I am too drowsy.'

He was feeling so exhausted that he didn't even want to leave the slender edge of the bed, where he lay. Suddenly they heard a sound. Garima seemed to have woken up. With her eyes half closed, she made strange gestures with the hands as if to suggest that she wanted to lie between the two of them.

Vikas noticed it and told Garima to stay put; that he would come on her side. While doing so, he whispered into Preeti's ears, 'We should make her sleep in a different room, now.' He wasn't sure whether Preeti heard it or not, as she was already snoring loudly, but Garima was the one to respond with, 'No…no…'

Tonight, Vikas's sleep was smudged by Sunidhi's thoughts. Time and again, he wondered as to why only sensitive people like her had to undergo so much suffering in life…and who was responsible for it. He didn't know if she would act upon his advice but he genuinely felt concerned about her tears, her pulled down countenance, her nervous fingers and her overall frustration.

As he moved towards Garima, he noticed his mobile phone buzzing. It had been put on silent mode but its screen was flashing. He stretched out his arm to pick up the phone but it got disconnected. It was one o'clock. Half-awake Preeti asked, 'Who is it…calling you so late at night?'

Vikas had seen the name displayed on the screen but quickly replied, 'Wrong number.'

He knew Sunidhi was still feeling lonely.

❖❖❖

18

Sunidhi wasn't feeling sleepy at all. Nandan had still not come back yet. These days he usually stayed away from home, on the pretext of doing union work or whatever excuse he could cook up. Even when he came, he slept on the sofa in the living room. His very thought upset Sunidhi from head to toe. She had so far been fondly and merrily thinking about Vikas, her very dear boss, handsome, intelligent, well-educated, well-settled, holding such a high position in the bank, but still so humane, so down to earth and so very caring.

She switched off the light, but there was no sleep in her eyes. She tossed in the bed for some time. Then she picked up her mobile phone and thought of redialling the last number. Then she realized that half an hour more had since passed. It was 1.30 am and no time to call anybody. She put the phone down. She came out of the bed, switched on the light and picked up a magazine. Then she put it down too. She turned on the TV, but immediately turned it off. She liked watching black and white movies. She remembered she had a video CD of Dev Anand's black-and-white era film songs. Where could it be? However, she was in no mood to get up and look for it. There was still no sleep in her eyes. So she got up and started looking for the CD. Soon she found it and played it at a low volume.

She enjoyed watching Dev Anand's romantic songs for a while. Then she heard some voices outside. She lowered the volume, got up and peeped out of the door. There was nobody there. But she heard someone talk inside the adjoining room. It was Yashodhara telling something to Alok, who was listening quietly. She thought she would snoop. But she let it go. In any case, she knew they would only be talking about her. And she was in no mood to get involved in it and spoil the rest of her night.

She returned to her bed and decided to watch some more scenes of film songs. She was quite young but preferred to listen to old songs. She liked them for their lilting melody as much as the lyrics. They touched the inner chords of her heart. She felt as if they were written for her, to give vent to her suppressed feelings and emotions and her unfulfilled desires. She had hardly had any romance in her life. So she found it exciting and convenient to indulge in romantic fantasies with the help of these songs.

She felt her anxiety was gradually dissipating. She was more or less at peace with herself. She switched off the light. The TV was still on, flashing old romantic songs. She just watched them tossing in the bed. But this time she suddenly grew very conscious of the invaluable treasure of her beautiful body. It was no less than that of the yesteryear silver screen stars Madhubala or Nutan, dancing on the screen before her eyes. She felt mystified and started rubbing her hands on her body to feel herself. She fancied Dev Anand romancing with her. Slowly she lost control of herself and was fast asleep, dreaming of things which couldn't have possibly happened in real life.

She saw herself moving into a city club, escorted by Vikas, her knight-in-arms. It was a new place and nobody there seemed to know them. Nor did they know anyone there. Their minds were absolutely free and their spirits were high. They took a table in the large dining hall, which had a well-stuffed bar in a corner and an orchestra playing in the other. They ordered some drinks and snacks and started looking at each other deeply, with newfound joy.. On such occasions, it was Vikas who always took the lead, but tonight it was Sunidhi who broke the ice.

'What according to you is love…?' she asked Vikas.

Vikas was not prepared for such an abrupt question. Smiling, he took a deep sip of his drink, gently held Sunidhi's hand in his and replied, 'Love for me, is caring for each other… and what is it for you?'

'Now, that's not fair…' retorted Sunidhi shyly.

'My question thrown back to me…'

'Okay, let me put it this way. How much, do you think, is the importance of the body, the flesh, the physical aspect in love?'

'Twenty-five per cent, maybe…' replied Sunidhi even without thinking about it. Immediately she wondered if she had not been too quick to respond. Would it not appear to Vikas to be a stock reply? Would he not think that she was already prepared for it?

'Then what's the remaining seventy-five per cent about?'

'Feeling.'

'Feeling…?'

'Yes, feeling. The feeling that somebody is always there with you…for you…every moment of your life, in your thick and in thin, during the day and night… there with you when you are eating, drinking, crying or laughing…there in your sorrow, your happiness, your success and failure…your feelings, emotions, imagination … your entire existence. Somebody who is so dear to you that you can't even express your love for him when he is around…and you yearn to do so when he is gone….'

For a moment, Sunidhi wondered as to how she could express so much, so spontaneously, on a subject like this? This was not her forte, not a part of the *sanskaar* – the traditional practices – she professed. Was it then, the effect of Vikas's company which had inspired her to say what she had said?

'What do you say?' asked Sunidhi to elicit Vikas's response.

Vikas had still not absorbed what Sunidhi had said. He was still reflecting over it. He felt Sunidhi was being too idealistic in her understanding of love. He was himself extremely pragmatic in his approach towards life and very practical in his dealings. He picked up his glass and gulped down his drink.

'I think, real love cannot be realized without celebrating the body...' said Vikas. Sunidhi was amazed to hear it. She wasn't expecting such a curt and bold reply from him.

'Sunidhi, say whatever you like,' continued Vikas coolly, in an effort to dwell upon what he had just stated, 'but we cannot undermine or negate the importance of the physical quotient of love...the bare needs of the body. How can we overlook them...?'

Sunidhi seemed to be more or less convinced by what he said. But her *sanskaar* wouldn't let her transcend the limit of twenty-five per cent.... She looked at her watch. It was quite late. They paid the bill and left. Vikas dropped her back. Tossing in the bed, she joyfully relished the memory of the time spent with Vikas. Suddenly she picked up her mobile phone and speed-dialled a number.

'Hello.'

'Are you sleeping... so early?'

'Is it early...it's two o'clock in the night. Anyhow, tell me... any problem?'

'No, no no...there's no problem. Just called you to tell you that...I want to make love with you!.'

'What! Vikas was clearly taken aback.

Sunidhi hung up the phone and her dream merged with reality. She was awakened by a sudden knock on the bedroom door and her dream broke. Most hesitantly, she got out of the bed and opened the door. It was Yashodhara. She was already ready to go to work. Sunidhi looked at her watch. She felt embarrassed. It was nine in the morning.

'Are you alright...?' asked Yashodhara, her tone expressing genuine concern.

'No...!' replied Sunidhi without a thought. It was both true and false.

'I have made breakfast for you...eat it. Babu ji had to leave early today for some work. I am also getting late.... Take a crocin, if you have a fever. Call me if there's a problem. We'll go to the doctor.' So saying, Yashodhara was already out of the house and climbing down the stairs.

All that Sunidhi could say was, 'Okay...' She shut the door and threw herself down on the sofa. She felt extremely dizzy. Last night's dream was strange indeed! And what exactly did all that she had dreamt about, mean! She smiled and gently closed her eyes. She didn't know what was going on!! After a while she got up and made tea for herself. She wasn't sure if she would be able to go to office or not. She picked up her phone and was about to speed-dial a number... the same she had seen in her dream. But she held herself back. How could she directly call Vikas! She needed to call the HR to inform that she wouldn't be coming. She was busy talking to herself until she noticed that the tea had boiled over and had extinguished the gas flame.

❖❖❖

19

Sunidhi drank her tea. The newspaper lay on the table, but she didn't feel like opening it. She didn't even switch on the TV. She had already called office and taken leave for the day. Later she wondered whether she should ideally have gone to office, just to have a look at Vikas. She stood in front of the mirror and noticed a light pink bloom on her cheeks. That was after a really long time, she thought to herself! She felt she had taken the right decision in skipping office that day. She wished to spend the day as she liked...with full freedom. No office, no home, no husband, no in-laws...but was it possible, ever! A full day spent all by herself? She untied her luxuriant glossy silky hair and lay in the sofa in complete abandon. She was completely at peace with herself.

After a while she called Nandini.

'What...you are still stuck there Sunidhi? Oh, you'll never change,' Nandini retorted exasperatedly

'What do you mean?' asked Sunidhi.

'I mean I haven't seen a more foolish woman than you darling!, You are pretty, young...you can do anything you like.'

'What do mean by anything?'

'I mean anything....don't try to tell me you are so dumb that you don't realize what I mean by "anything". I am talking about that boss of yours... that guy called Vikas. He likes you, in fact he has fallen in love with you, quite hopelessly and madly. Had I been you, I would have by this time stolen him from the rest of the world. These men have many failings. You should know what are his.... It will change your life.'

‘I can’t really follow what you are saying... and I’d never want to do what you are suggesting. I admire your guts, but...my conscience wouldn’t ever let me do anything like that.’

‘Damn you and your conscience. You’ll see your beautiful youth simply fly past.... Just think over it coolly....hey, Sunidhi, are you there buddy? Are you listening?’ asked Nandini. She felt Sunidhi’s mind was somewhere else. Just to confirm that she was alright, Nandini asked her,

‘By the way, what are you doing and where are you?’

‘I am at home.’ replied Sunidhi.

‘At home...at this time of the day...what’s the matter? Are you not well?’ Nandini was worried.

‘No...there’s nothing wrong with me, I’m fine. Saw a strange dream last night.’

Sunidhi had slept soundly, till late morning when her mother-in-law knocked on her door and woke her up

‘Holy shit Sunidhi! You are still living in the world of dreams?’

Sunidhi changed the topic.

‘Don’t worry about me. Tell me what were you saying...something special...when we started talking about me and my thoughts?’ Sunidhi knew Nandini couldn’t keep anything to herself. She always blurted it out. Anybody could gauge her mind. You just had to prod her and she would divulge everything.

‘Did I tell you about Bharti?’

‘No, what about her?’

‘You know my boss isn’t in office today, so I can talk freely. Otherwise, the rogue keeps ogling at everyone. You talk on the phone for a while and he immediately realises it’s not a work call. And you hate the way he gives you a dirty look. But luckily he is not there today...’ Nandini went on and on, talking without a break.

Sunidhi looked at her watch. They had been on the phone a clean forty minutes and Nandini didn't seem to be in a mood to hang up yet. Just to put an end to this marathon talking session, Sunidhi asked Nandini,

'But what about Bharti? You were going to say something about her.'

'Oh, yes...but I can't talk any more now...that rascal boss of mine is back. Okay, bye.' Nandini hurriedly hung up. Sunidhi was relieved. She liked Nandini for many reasons. She was bold, carefree, straight-forward and a good friend, but she was extremely given to gossiping. She had seen life from many angles. She could take a firm stand in matters related to her life.

Sunidhi often wondered why she wasn't like Nandini. Why couldn't she raise her voice and stand up against something which was so blatantly wrong? Why had she been so unjust to herself and why on earth did she only have to be thoughtful and caring about others when they didn't spend a moment thinking about her needs?

There was an exception of course; Vikas did express concern. He was always worried about her life and happiness. But was it fair for her to think about him? She often questioned herself. And her mind always replied in the negative. But what could she do about her heart! It wasn't under her control and her thoughts continued to slant towards Vikas. Did he also think about her the way she thought about him? Did he really love her or was his concern just a reflection of his human nature. She was totally confused and didn't seem to have any clarity on the issues which lay along her path.

❖❖❖

20

Sunidhi had moved to her parents' house, never to return to her husband's home. It was an important decision of her life, taken solely and consciously by her. She had left behind her, a life full of uncertainties, dilemmas and self-deceit. And all she had carried with her was a suitcase, a few clothes, a couple of books and the burden of how Yashodhara would take it. She hadn't brought any of her ornaments or other valuables. She remembered how dejected and forlorn Babu ji and Yashodhara had looked when she was leaving them. But she had at least listened to a friend and not moved into a ladies hostel. She had come to her mother's house as advised by Vikas.

She wanted to talk to Vikas directly on his landline. But he hadn't been attending office for the last two days. She didn't want to call him on his mobile phone. She learnt from his PA that he and some other RMs had been called by the Chairman to discuss their Annual Plans. But her anxiety kept rising. The desire to share everything with Vikas made her restless.

Sunidhi never expected a warm welcome at her parents' house. Her father evaded her. He was a typical middle-class man with mediocre means. Long ago, he had purchased a two-bedroom flat with great difficulty. He and his wife lived in one bedroom and the other was to be shared by Sunidhi with her younger sister, who had no hesitation in conveying that she didn't quite approve of the arrangement. Her mother wanted the girls to live amicably, but Sunidhi's father simply couldn't tolerate her presence in the house. So she was soon driven to wishing that she had better move into a working women's hostel!

Sunidhi attended office after almost a week. She wasn't at peace with herself. She felt everyone was inquisitively staring at her. Where had she been all these days...didn't exhibit any change in her conduct...must have been unwell. Maybe she had had a problem with her in-laws. What did her husband do? What could husbands of such fashionable women do...? The female staff had their own set of assumptions...maybe she didn't want a child...or perhaps she wanted one but was unable to carry...all sorts of conjectures were being made. She felt restless. She could never comprehend as to why people had to unnecessarily bother about other people's lives and pry into their personal affairs!

She saw Ramesh, the peon, serving tea. She thought she would ask him if Vikas had come to office. She knew he hadn't...maybe Ramesh would know if he had come the day before. She could have learnt it from her colleague sitting next to her. It wasn't so important. But she couldn't ask anyone, as there was so much unrest and heaviness in her heart. This had propelled her to be the first one to have entered the office today.

'How are you Ramesh?' she asked. Ramesh smiled as usual and placed a cup of tea on her table.

'Since how long has the boss not been coming?'

'Four days...' replied Ramesh intently looking at Sunidhi.

Sunidhi was sipping tea when the office started filling in. It was past eleven, but many people were still not there. They probably knew that Vikas wasn't coming to the office even today. Even his PA had not yet come.

Sunidhi was taking stock of the papers scattered on her table when a lady officer came up to her and settled down on the chair lying empty in front.

'How are you... all fine?' she asked staring at Sunidhi.

'Yes...all well, thank you' replied Sunidhi, knowing fully well that her reply wouldn't satisfy the lady. Obviously it didn't and the lady went on to ask

‘What I meant was, if there is a good news…?’

‘What…? No, nothing of the sort,’ Sunidhi was visibly annoyed. She resumed arranging the papers on her table.

‘Can I get you some tea?’ asked Sunidhi. She had nothing to talk about to this lady and wanted her to leave. But the lady was in no mood to oblige. She had come to converse with Sunidhi, to have a peep into her life, both official and personal. But Sunidhi asking her about tea had put her off. So she said,

‘No thanks, no tea for me. It causes acidity. I have even given up my bed-tea.’ She kept staring at Sunidhi, meaningfully. Then she added,

‘The boss may not be coming even today. The Chairman seems to have detained him in the Head Office. They say, he is annoyed with the boss over the annual budget and his performance as well. You know, what a character the Chairman is… he must have chided the boss using strong words. Did he call you…?’

‘No…and why should he call me? Besides, I was on leave.’

‘Oh, yes. You were on leave…’

The lady sprung up saying, ‘Oh, I need to go. I have to make a report. The boss may need it on his return. Will see you at lunch. Let me know if you need anything.’

Sunidhi wondered why the PA had also not turned up in the office today. Then she started going through the mail received from the Head Office.

The unexpected appearance of Vikas in the office took everyone by surprise. They were in a complete holiday mood. But seeing him, they all got down to work. Vikas seemed to be in a rush. He also appeared a bit stressed out. A corridor had to be crossed to reach his cabin from the lift. It was made by erecting two dwarf glass walls, dividing the hall in two parts. Briskly crossing this passage, Vikas beckoned the Premises Manager to come to his cabin.

Whether he noticed Sunidhi's presence in the office or not, she had definitely sensed that he was under great pressure.

Soon, loud chiding could be heard from inside the cabin. It was very unusual of Vikas. He had never raised his voice in this manner. So what could have been the matter? His driver was carrying his briefcase into the cabin. The airlines tag on it showed that Vikas had directly come to the office from the airport. That he had not removed it after landing, as he usually did, also showed that he was under great stress and was in a rush. Sunidhi wondered as to why such a tense situation always arose whenever she needed to talk urgently to Vikas.

The Premises Manager came out of the cabin after receiving a bad beating. The peon was still inside. Vikas was almost screaming, 'What's going on...?' Everybody in the hall felt awfully worried. There was pin-drop silence. The cabin-door opened with a bang. Out came Vikas and slyly looking at Sunidhi, he walked past the hall, down the corridor heading towards the lift. The driver followed him almost at the same pace, carrying his briefcase.

❖❖❖

21

For three days in a row, Sunidhi thought she would talk to Vikas, but he wasn't there in the office. Neither did he call her. Now, she too didn't feel like asking anyone about him. She generally kept quiet and withdrawn. At lunch time, she just gulped a few morsels and returned to her table, though the unsavoury gossip doing the rounds haunted and hurt her the whole day:

'Our boss has fallen upon bad times...'

'I have learnt that the Chairman is after his blood...'

'And why not! Our boss doesn't give any importance to the Chairman's client....'

'Remember how, the other day, he made Patel wait outside his cabin for hours... finally, he left in disgust.'

'Now his transfer is for sure. And he'll be dumped in a god-forsaken branch...where it's just not possible to work.'

Sitting amongst the lady colleagues, Sunidhi quietly listened to this diatribe, every day. She anxiously waited for lunch break to end so that they all went back to work. But when this session prolonged even after lunch, she knew for sure that Vikas was not coming to the office, even that day. The rant would continue,

'He wouldn't get promotion this time...'

'Not only this time, he won't get promotion ever till this Chairman is in office.

In between, someone would sneakily cast a glance at Sunidhi and sensing her obvious discomfort, deliberately drag her into the controversy and sarcastically ask her:

'What do you say Sunidhi ji?

'What can I say...?' She would answer nervously.

'Why? Your department is the X-ray of the entire office. You only receive correspondence from the Chairman's office and send out its response. You should be aware of everything...though you may not wish to divulge it!'

Sunidhi had never expected to be assailed like this. She was dumbfounded. She lowered her head and directed her gaze at the empty lunch box lying in front. She felt myriad eyes piercing her body and soul; all her lady colleagues looking at each other with a sinister smile. She wished she could leave. But that would have only reinforced their attack on Vikas and given them an opportunity to scandalize her along with him.

There was a deafening silence for a few moments, before they started returning to their seats.

Vikas's office was losing its sheen. The hustle and bustle of earlier days was literally losing its gravity and being relegated to the past. More and more people were falling a prey to rumour-mongering. Their 'unity' was nowhere to be seen. Nobody really took interest in work. An eerie air of uncertainty, dichotomy and discord pervaded all around. Even Vikas's cabin seemed to have lost its grandeur.

One day, a strange thing happened. When everybody was packing up at five, Vikas suddenly appeared from nowhere. He was not his normal self. He looked weary and drained out. Instead of quickly walking to his cabin, which he usually did, he walked sluggishly, looking at almost everyone on both sides of the isle.

The peon, who had rushed to open the doors of the cabin wondered why the boss took so long to reach. He too realised the gravity of the changed circumstances. Vikas didn't enter the cabin immediately but turned back and looked at Sunidhi. He tried to communicate something to her through gestures, but Sunidhi wasn't looking at him. She was leafing through some papers in a file. Many others watched it and interpreted it in their own ways. Finally, Vikas told the peon, 'Send Sunidhi in…' and entered his cabin.

There was complete silence in the office.

The PA gathered his pad and pen and leaped towards the cabin. But Vikas stopped him from entering, 'Will call you later… there's nothing special!' The PA, totally confused, left the cabin, as Sunidhi entered.

'Sit down,' said Vikas, pointing towards a chair.

Sunidhi didn't say anything. She sat down looking at Vikas. She was trying to read his mind. Vikas rang the bell and asked the peon to bring two cups of tea. He also instructed him to not let anyone in without his permission. The peon gave a nod and left.

Vikas picked up a pencil and started rotating its ends between his fingers. He often did this to conceal his anxiety and nervousness. His eyes glossed over various reference papers kept beneath the glass top of his table. His mind was in a state of void…!

'Is everything okay, sir?' asked Sunidhi, bringing him back to reality. He was meeting Sunidhi after many days. It took him little time to know that she had surmounted a major problem in her life, but was worried about some others. However, he thought it proper to first reply to her question.

'No, everything is not okay, Sunidhi. Many unwanted developments have taken place in my life. The Chairman has turned hostile and he is using one of our own officers against me. Every rotten thing happening here reaches him in no time. I have a suspicion on one, but don't want to take any action right now.'

'Yes, many people tend to turn with the tide,' uttered Sunidhi feelingly.

Instantaneously, they looked into each other's eyes. Both of them were sad, tormented by their own sufferings. Both of them needed support. But none of them wanted to dwell upon their own sorrows.

'But, let's keep the office out. Tell me, how have you been doing?' asked Vikas.

'I have left home and come back to my parents' place...' said Sunidhi with a heavy heart. But these few words lightened all the burden she had been carrying for many days. How anxious she had been to share it with Vikas!

'Sunidhi...,' uttered Vikas.

Sunidhi raised her head to look at him. Her eyes were moist. Her throat choked. Her fingers were quivering.

There was a knock at the door. It was the peon. He came inside, placed tea on the table and left. They both wondered (and feared the outcome) whether he had sensed the gloom and heaviness prevailing in the room! 'Damn it...' thought Vikas.

Sunidhi suddenly broke down. Now Vikas got worried. He rose from his chair, picked up a glass of water and gave it to Sunidhi. He softly caressed her on the head and quickly returned to his seat.

For a moment, Vikas was himself surprised at doing what he had done just now. What would have been the consequence if somebody had entered the cabin at that moment and seen him giving her water or patting her head? He shivered thinking about it.

Meanwhile, the peon had peeped in a couple of times. Vikas had noticed it but declined to let him in. He had turned him away with a gesture of his eyes. Even the PA had knocked a couple of times, wanting to enter the cabin, but Vikas had stopped him.

For a moment, Sunidhi wondered if she should tell him what the staff had been discussing all morning about him...how they had been interpreting (or misinterpreting!) the problems faced by him. But on second thoughts, she was glad she didn't. It would have only added to his woes.

Sunidhi narrated each and every development of her life of late. Vikas listened very intently, fully empathizing with her. What disturbed him most was the fact that even her parents had not welcomed Sunidhi in their house. It had rather increased her grief. The more he listened to her, the more he felt involved with her life. As for Sunidhi, there couldn't have been anyone better than him for opening up her heart and solicit the much needed succour. She knew, she was not in a position to do anything to lessen his worries, but she knew that his moral support was extremely valuable for her.

Then they were quiet for a while, engrossed in their own thoughts or those of the other. Only when they looked into each other's eyes, they experienced a strange current pass through them, giving strength to both to fight it out.

It was for the first time that Vikas had kept his work aside to listen to Sunidhi for almost an hour. It hadn't been easy for him, though. In the midst of a complete silence between the two of them and the cabin-door, Sunidhi looked at Vikas. What she found in his eyes was a pillar of strength she could lean on. He was not merely her boss and she was not just an assistant to him. There was a greater bond between them...perhaps a profound one!

Sunidhi rose and asked his permission to leave. Vikas also got up and said, 'Look...if you don't feel comfortable in your house and if you think it proper, you should move into a working-women's hostel or stay somewhere as a paying guest. It's time you started thinking about yourself...'

Sunidhi didn't say anything. She just looked at him sweetly.

'And one more thing, this office may henceforth be remotely controlled by the central office. Many transfers could take place. Whatever happens...you should take good care of yourself....' Vikas left it at that and extended his hand towards Sunidhi. She also offered her hand to him. Their hands met and their eyes too. And the table between them just witnessed a splendid union of two souls drawn to each other by love. When Sunidhi turned around to leave, Vikas was still standing. She felt somebody had planted an incense stick on her palms. For the first time she realized that the touch of a man's hands could be so electrifying. Bemused, she came out of the cabin and quietly walked up to her table. She felt she had been freed from a centuries-old curse… and brought out of the murky shadow of an eclipse. Even though things had not changed even a bit, yet the geniality and warmth of Vikas's love had penetrated deep into her heart.

Vikas kept standing in his place for a while. He was constantly looking at the wall-clock. Soon there was a knock at the door. The PA was standing there with his pad and the pen and there was a senior officer with him.

'Sir, there are some important inwards…' said the PA.

The senior officer was constantly looking at Vikas, trying to gauge his mood. He wasn't sure if he should put some complicated matters before him or not. Vikas sat down in the chair, saying, 'Nothing for the day…it's already 7 o'clock. Will see it tomorrow…'

Both of them looked at each other. They wondered how Vikas had so easily put off the day's work to the next day. He had never done it before. There definitely was some problem. So, they quietly came out. When their gaze fell on Sunidhi getting ready to leave, they couldn't resist exchanging a mischievous and meaningful glance, questioning as to how could the boss have nearly two hours for talking to her and no time for them! What could have been such an important matter warranting such a long discussion with her? The senior officer had a mind to while away some time sitting with the PA, but the latter was called in by Vikas on intercom.

❖❖❖

22

These days, Sunidhi would come to office quite early. Only Suresh, the boy who served tea and the cleaning lady would be there before her. One day, Vikas also happened to come early and was surprised to see Sunidhi already working.

For a moment, he stood there silently watching Sunidhi and then beckoned her to come to his cabin.

'Right now...?'

'Yes, and why not?'

'But it's time for the staff to start coming.'

'So what?'

'Let everyone be in and the office start...?'

'Come on Sunidhi... I want you to come in right now.'

Sunidhi was speechless. She gathered herself, got up and walked behind him like a shadow. As they reached the cabin, Suresh came running to ask, 'May I get you some tea, sir...?'

'Yes.... Sure.'

Sunidhi sat down in front of Vikas, but she was constantly bothered by the fear of somebody standing at the door and peeping inside. She startled as she heard a din outside and turned around to look at the door. It was Ramesh. He had brought tea. She heaved a sigh of relief.

Today, Vikas looked much relieved and less stressed compared to the previous day. He was probably becoming more firm and decisive in his attitude, as he got more and more involved in the professional complications. Earlier he would hesitate and think twice before talking to Sunidhi in private.

However he was still not his normal self. Taking a sip of his tea, he plunged into the conversation.

'Yesterday I told you to shift to a hostel. But, on second thoughts, I feel you'd be more secure in your mother's house....'

'Probably yes, but my father doesn't like my putting up with them...even my younger sister doesn't feel comfortable with it...' replied Sunidhi quietly.

'Have your tea, it's getting cold. Look Sunidhi, when the going is not good, even small problems appear big. At such times, we should act coolly...last night my thoughts were only about you...'

'Uh...?'

'I mean, about all that you are going through...'

'It's all right. I feel better now. I have even applied to take the banking certificate exams. I leave home early so that I get some time in the office to prepare for the exams.'

'Oh that's good. It's not difficult at all. You'll clear it very easily.'

Vikas was happy to see Sunidhi getting into a positive frame of mind. She was bravely trying to come out of the mess she was in. He rose from his chair and pulled out a rather bulky book from his bookshelf on the wall.

'Keep this one. It will help you. And remember to keep taking the banking bulletin from me, every month. Those will also be very helpful...'

Sunidhi was moved by the concern Vikas showed for her. She opened the book he had given and casually started flipping its pages. Then she suddenly looked at her watch and exclaimed,

'Oh my god! It's ten thirty, sir. May I leave now?'

She hadn't been feeling comfortable in Vikas's cabin, since it was the start of the day and people outside knew that she was in.

'You take your own decision about staying wherever you want,' replied Vikas. I had suggested a hostel simply as a temporary make-doopion. Now I feel that you'll be safer with your parents. But it has to be your own decision. I only want to see you happy.'

Sunidhi not only listened quietly to Vikas, she even felt the love, concern and compassion that was evident whenever he spoke.

Sunidhi had already risen from her seat, when the PA barged into the cabin, this time even without knocking at the door. He carried a load of files and folders.

'Come, Saxena... I was about to call you. What's special?' asked Vikas, confidently.

'Sir, there are lot many letters...some are important as well. A lot of information has been sought for under the RTI Act. It seems somebody is trying to fix us,' said Saxena, putting the papers in order.

'Just leave them like that, Saxena, I'll clear them before I go home. You just tell me if there was a call from the central office, in my absence?' Vikas was probing him.

'Yes, sir. There were quite a few calls...' answered Saxena, trying in turn to gauge as to which one could be more important for the boss.

'Did any GM also call?'

'Yes, sir.'

'What was that about?'

'Sir, he spoke with the HR. He was probably enquiring about the length of stay of some people in our office.'

'But we have already sent a detailed plan to the central office. And I was there. They could have asked me...' There was a hint of indignation in his tone.

'I don't know, sir,' said Saxena, softly. He was Vikas's man, his confidante. But today his responses were totally impersonal. He was being elusive...not offering any comment from his side. He had never been like this before. Vikas could easily sense that somebody had already started drilling holes in his fort.

'Even I don't know what's going on, Saxena. My enemies have turned proactive.' Vikas hinted at some people in the central office.

After Saxena left, Vikas got busy going through his mail and other files. There were enquiries, complaints, proposals, applications for loan under new names...offers for new premises. There were orders from the central office for urgent action on hiring five premises for new branches to be opened up soon. Vikas felt he was getting badly trapped. He sent for Shah. Shah was Senior Manager, HR. Vikas had full faith in him. He always offered correct advice...he was crisis manager of sorts in the office.

'Shah, was there a call from the Central Office about our staff?'

'Yes sir. The HR from central office had called.'

'Called for what? We have already sent our annual transfer plan. Besides, I was there myself, they could have directly asked me or called me on mobile. Why did they call here?'

'Sir, I too have my doubts. They sought information only about a few particular managers in our administrative region...and some officers in our office too. Sir, they even enquired about me and Sunidhi.'

'But why Sunidhi? She has just completed her probation. She is not even due for transfer. And as for you, I have already informed the GM why we want you to be retained here at least for one more year!' Vikas seemed to be gripped by the fear of some unpleasant tidings.

'Sir, many people have put in requests seeking transfer to our branch. I think you know...' Shah didn't name anyone.

'I know... and I don't want them to land up here... whatever maybe the pressure from the union...,' said Vikas, clinching his fists.

'But sir, my sources tell me that these people have already managed the chairman...'

'This chairman is a...' Vikas's disgust for the chairman was obvious. 'But how does Sunidhi feature in all this?'

'Sir, please don't get me wrong, I have known you for such a long time. Many people are having problems in dealing with you because of your clean image and your straightforward nature.

'Sir, the present environment is not conducive to such virtues...for their own interest many people even shy away from coming close to you.'

Vikas was extremely perturbed to realise that the chairman had already sown the seeds of his doom. But he was impressed by Shah's honesty and loyalty. He liked the way he had frankly told Vikas everything he knew. Only if... he had also disclosed all that he knew about Sunidhi. But he couldn't have blamed him for that, Even he himself felt hesitant to talk to Shah about her. He wasn't sure why.

'Sir, I must also share with you another important piece of information. I have a hunch that this too is the doing of the union-walas. Whenever you don't oblige them for whatever they want, they start defaming you and you know how low they can stoop....'

'What do you mean, please be clear.'

'Sir, you know how much I respect you. But this has been bothering me a lot. Someone in the central office is plotting against you....'

Shah was still hesitant to come to the point. Judging by his nervousness and discomfort, Vikas had, however, more or less guessed what Shah was trying to convey.

'Sir they were asking a lot of things about Sunidhi. You know...I know you so well, but others...'

'It's alright Shah...I know what. It's not a crime to have sympathy with someone. I know her family conditions. We should help each other. But unfortunately, most people think that there can be only one kind of relationship between a man and a woman....'

Vikas was extremely agitated.

'Sir, it's customary for the union-walas to adopt such mean tactics to pressurize senior officers. But this time, they seem to be having a support from our own seniors.' Shah had amply clarified the situation. He wasn't among those who deserted the ship when they found it sinking.

For the first time in his life, Vikas felt miserably helpless. He knew that he had been sieged from all sides. He had exhibited the dare to stand up against the chairman and the union and it was time to face the consequences. There was dreadful silence in his cabin for a while. Then he rang the bell and told the peon, 'Two cups of tea…' That's all Vikas could say.

❖❖❖

23

Monday was usually a heavy day in the office, but Vikas always came well-prepared. He reached office half an hour earlier than the rest. When he came in today, he saw Sunidhi already working there. He looked at her. She also looked at him. Even a smile was exchanged, which exuded intimacy but no zeal. Vikas straightaway entered his cabin. Sunidhi had a hunch that he would call her in. But he didn't.

Soon, Shah entered the office in a hurry. He dumped his bag on the table and rushed towards Vikas's cabin. On the way he cast a casual glance on Sunidhi as well. He knocked at the door. Vikas thought it must be Sunidhi. But when the door opened, he saw Shah. He was almost breathless and perspiring profusely.

'What's the matter, Shah...?'

'Sir, have you seen the mail?'

'Yes, I have. Have you seen it...?'

'No sir, but I got a call from Deshpande. He is in HR in the central office. On Saturday night, we worked till ten. There was no news till then. Deshpande rang me up around 11.30. Sir, they have ordered my transfer...? My son is studying in the tenth standard and my daughter in the twelfth. It would be devastating for me and my family...'

Shah was the one who himself issued transfer orders of those working in the region. He had often come across people having problems of children's education. He had always told them to bravely face it. He had been arguing that by the time they reached a senior level in service, their children were bound to be in such classes. But today, when he was confronted with the problem of his children's education, he was extremely upset. He was literally begging for help, knowing well that Vikas wasn't in a position to help him.

Vikas's face hardened a bit.

'Sir, the plan we had sent has just been thrown into the dustbin. Sir, Sunidhi is not even due for transfer,' Shah was trying to provoke Vikas. But Vikas was absolutely calm. He just remarked,

'Listen Shah, we had discussed it only day before, didn't we? I knew it was coming.'

'But sir, they have thrown me out of the state. Sunidhi has at least been transferred to a different branch in the city. I'll be eighteen hours away from my family. Don't know how....'

'I am aware, Shah. All those who have been close to me have been moved out of here and transferred to far off places. I purposely stayed back late in office on Saturday. I had sensed it. As I left office and entered my car, I received a call.... They have made it a practice to order transfers late night on Saturdays.... Sorry Shah, I couldn't do anything for you even though I wanted to. But Shah, it's not only for you. It's been a punishment for me as well. And a painful one... in not having been transferred out of here....' There was deep anguish in his voice.

By this time, everyone in the office had learnt about the transfers. The news had spread like wildfire. Those who were not kindly disposed towards Vikas spoke passionately about Sunidhi's transfer.

'She has been purposely shifted out of this office.'

'But how does it make a difference, only their meeting place has changed.'

These were the people who had blatantly showered praises on Vikas and his leadership qualities, when he was in the good books of the chairman. They were now dumping him only because he had fallen from grace in the eyes of the chairman, for no fault of his.

Vikas's gaze was fixed on his computer screen. He was reading the details of all posting orders issued by the Central Office. Shah listened intently and offered his comments on each and every name. By now, many members of the staff had assembled outside Vikas's cabin, just to get an idea of whatever was going on inside.

'They haven't used our plan at all. I don't know why they call for it at all?' Vikas was giving vent to his annoyance and frustration over the transfer orders. For Shah, his own distress was paramount at this moment. So, he was still trying to bring around Vikas to make an attempt to get his orders reversed.

'Sir they have shifted four officers from our office and given us only three, whereas we had asked for additional two…'

Vikas was quietly looking at Shah as if to tell him that he knew everything…even its root cause. But Shah was unstoppable.

'Sir, even those three who have been posted here are good for nothing… two of them have inquiries against them and the third one is a shirker, he doesn't work at all. He is an office-bearer of the union. Sir, please get my orders deferred for one year. I'll never request you for anything else. I can give an application, if you want. I have never in my service even asked for a posting of my choice.'

Shah was doggedly trying to move Vikas to help him. But it wasn't working, because he was not the only one for Vikas. He had to look after the whole region. His landline phone was continuously ringing. He had switched off his mobile phone. He had instructed Saxena not to transfer any call to him, particularly if it was from the central office. He was told to take down the message.

Finally Vikas broke his silence. Looking at nowhere, he said, 'I know about all three coming to our office. They are being sent here on a purpose. Even the inquiries pending against them may possibly be closed. And that union-guy is being sent here only to create trouble.' Shah felt Vikas was probably thinking aloud.

Meanwhile, many members of the staff had peeped into the cabin. Vikas noticed them, but he neither stopped them from coming in nor asked anyone to come. Confused, they themselves changed their minds and left.

Shah had nothing left to say to Vikas. Right now, his own problem seemed to him to be far more critical than the crisis lying ahead of Vikas. He wanted Vikas to speak to the GM in his presence, as he had done year after year for many officials working under him. Vikas knew that Shah wouldn't leave before he had taken action. So he told him,

'Shah, I'll definitely try for you, though I don't think I can do anything in the present circumstances.' said Vikas.

'Sir, just get me one more year. Both my children...'

'I am aware Shah, I know that. I'll call you later... okay?'

Vikas turned towards the phone. But before he could pick it up, he noticed a mail flash on his computer screen. Vikas read it and looked at Shah in utter helplessness.

'What's it, sir?'

'Read it yourself...'

Vikas turned the computer screen towards Shah.

'It is hereby ordered that all officers under posting should be relieved with immediate effect. Their salary should be drawn from the branch of their posting. The regional managers will be held personally responsible for any lapse.'

Shah seemed to have lost even the last straw.

❖❖❖

24

The recent developments in the office had made Vikas feel utterly helpless. One big blow in his career had totally shaken him off. He felt paralyzed. He hadn't been able to get any of the orders annulled or even modified. Not even Sunidhi's. He felt he was being treated like a slave, for no fault of his. So the only option he had was to compromise with the system or quit. But his dilemma was peculiar. He couldn't quit because he had a family to support. And his conscience and self-esteem wouldn't let him agree for a compromise!

So Vikas started gradually withdrawing from the staff. These days, nobody entered his cabin, nor did he call anyone in. Calls on the landline phone were left to be handled by Saxena. Even those on the mobile phone were taken by him only if unavoidable. He generally kept it on silent mode. Suddenly he saw a call flash on his mobile phone. It was from the Regional Manager, Indore. It rang for a while and when it didn't stop, Vikas picked up the phone.

'Hello Vikas, you take so long to answer a call…? It's Atul Kumar speaking.'

'I know.'

'Then why did you take so long…?'

'Just like that… nothing in particular…'

'Everything alright…?'

'No, not at all… but what's the option?'

'Yes, I know. You have to suffer it… but things will change… don't worry…' said Atul Kumar. He was trying to console Vikas, but very carefully; making sure that he didn't utter a word against the chairman. His own career was at stake.

'I called on a purpose…'

'Okay, tell me…' said Vikas, dispassionately.

'One Amar Kumar is coming to you on transfer…'

'Yes, I know. Has his order been cancelled?' asked Vikas curiously.

'It would have been good for you had it been cancelled. But no…as far as I know, it hasn't.' He still spoke very cautiously.

'Then… what about him?'

'Er, actually I thought I should apprise you about him,' said Atul Kumar. For a moment, Vikas had a mind to tell him that he knew Amar Kumar well, but something stopped him from doing so.

'You'll have to be extremely careful about the man. I have worked with him in Bhopal. He is a bluff-master…an expert in underhand dealings. You can neither befriend him nor afford to antagonize him. He is a really difficult person to handle!'

'You wanted to tell me all this or have you anything in particular?' asked Vikas, losing interest in the general conversation that Atul Kumar was indulging in.

'I want to tell you a lot of things about him. Hope nobody is sitting around you?'

'No, there's nobody here.' Vikas's curiosity seemed to have been aroused by Atul Kumar.

'Okay. Those days I used to sit at the table next to his. Everyone avoided talking to him. But he would impose himself upon all, cracking dirty jokes, giggling loudly and generally indulging in nonsense. He handled the Recovery department. He would call the defaulting debtors and quietly place all kinds of unjustifiable demands on them. When our new RM joined office, he unashamedly took it upon himself to look after his personal chores. In the bargain, he exploited his seeming intimacy with the RM and started looting the office as well as the clients.'

Atul Kumar narrated many stories about the nefarious activities of Amar Kumar. He disclosed how this guy was once caught presenting fake vouchers to draw hefty payments from the office; how he even corrupted the RM by luring him with the latest models of mobile phones and other expensive gifts…and how he could even go to the extent of establishing direct links with the chairman, in case the RM didn't oblige to partake his wicked activities or tried to stall them in any way.

Vikas quietly listened to these stories and wondered how he would deal with such a rogue? What department would he assign to the man? Once again, he felt sorry for not having been able to stand behind his people and protect them from injustice…not even Sunidhi! All those who were loyal to him had been shunted out of his office. And what had been allotted to him, in turn, was no better than a gang of scoundrels and good-for-nothing people.

❖❖❖

25

Vikas relieved all officials under transfer, including Sunidhi, on the date fixed by the central office. He didn't even wait for their substitutes to arrive and bid a highly emotional farewell to all his trusted lieutenants. He felt bad that he hadn't even bothered to see to their personal problems or convenience. Their farewell function was kept on the same day. It was a difficult moment for him, but he faced it bravely.

Vikas was now a totally changed person. He had lost interest in everything. He felt impatient and frustrated with all and spoke very little in the office. His staff had begun suspecting that it would be his turn next to be transferred and Vikas too, lived in anxious despair. His behaviour at home was no different. Preeti took good care of him. She tried her best to make him feel comfortable but she too was often left feeling frustrated. It was easy to understand Vikas but very difficult to make him understand.

Feeling despondent, Vikas had started spending more time in front of the TV, watching shows like Animal Planet, Discovery and National Geographic. Sometimes he even watched news channels. But he preferred reading newspapers than watching news on television as he felt the reliability of the latter was always suspect. Besides, he hated the repetitive and pointless political discussions on TV. They drove him mad. He had already given up watching feature films, though he still had some lingering fascination for black-and-white films and the film songs of that era.

In order to relieve himself of the pressure of work, he started going out for walks in the evening. Preeti sometimes accompanied him. After a few days, he realized that he was never there with her even though she walked with him. He seemed to have turned completely listless, had lost interest in his daughter's studies, in socialization with relatives, even mundane responsibilities like shopping for vegetables.... So far his routine had been to go home late, play with his daughter, have dinner, make a couple of phone calls, feel exhausted, retire to bed and have a sound sleep. He did feel exhausted even now, but hardly got a good sleep.

Soon, he found a way to lighten this mental burden which was taking a toll on his physical health. His house was situated very close to the university campus. The surroundings were beautiful, which, he thought, could enliven his spirits and offer him solace. Every day, while returning from office, he stopped by the university gate, parked his car, put on his walking shoes and a T-shirt and allowed himself to relax freely in the lap of nature. Its desolate roads, thick bushes and wooded areas, lovely flora and fauna and the age-old oak trees drew him close and provided solace. He walked into the far-off nooks and corners of the campus, all alone. One day it struck him that mere walking might not help him much. So he started jogging. Now he felt much more relaxed. It even helped him control his sugar level. He had already crossed forty-five; he needed to take care of his health.

One day when he was jogging, he spotted a female figure, which captured his imagination. She was jogging along the adjoining road. There were thick bushes separating the two roads. Even the gap between the two wasn't negligible. For once, he almost thought of calling out to her, but he didn't. Instead, he started running in the direction the figure was moving. He tried his best to catch it, but the bushes in between kept disturbing him. For a moment, he even feared that he might lose it. So he decided to take a plunge into the thickly entwined bushes to reach the adjoining road. Many bushes were thorny and hurt him, but he didn't care. When he reached the other side, he found the figure wasn't there. It had disappeared. He felt sorry for himself, as he was sure... it was Sunidhi.

Whosoever it was, it had rekindled his feelings for Sunidhi. He kept imagining how beautiful she looked in the dreamy twilight, jogging in a track suit. She had even trimmed her hair which dangled on her broad shoulders and made her look most attractive. The motion of her body was rhythmic, her feet taking steady and measured steps in good running shoes. She looked straight ahead, her head held high, her fists firmly clinched, her arms moved elegantly. It must have been Sunidhi, Vikas was quite convinced. For a moment, he had an urge to dial her number on his mobile. But he realized he wasn't carrying it. He was in the habit of leaving it behind in the car, at the start of a walk. And for the first time ever, he regretted doing so.

It became a daily routine for Vikas to go to the university, on his way back home. But he never saw that figure again. He often wondered whether he could contact Sunidhi on the phone, but he continued to postpone it. Sunidhi still worked in a branch under his regional jurisdiction. He didn't want his adversaries to get an opportunity to scandalize him and her! But the more he tried to wish it away, the more she kept coming back to his thoughts. She had penetrated deep into his consciousness. Sometimes he felt that he was now going to the university only to find her…!

Today, he parked his car inside the main gate of the university, as usual. As you entered the campus, the main road branched into two… each running like an arm of an ellipse, joining near the main building. In between the roads, there were thickly wooded patches, with thorny bushes and open spaces interspersed with buildings of various departments. Vikas always took the road bearing left. Jogging for a complete round, measuring a couple of kilometres on this road, he used to leave for home.

Vikas was passing through a dismal phase of life. His office had been taken over by a bunch of extremely undesirable people; competition in the banking sector was at its peak; there was always a pressure from the chairman's office; the sword of the uncertainty of his own transfer constantly hung over his head; the chances for his promotion had turned bleak; his daughter's education was a great worry and most importantly his tarnished image in the eyes of the 'public' bothered him a lot.

His mind went back to his childhood days, when he had chanced upon a set of rather weird cartoon pictures in a magazine called *Kalyan*. A man was running in a forest to save himself from a chasing lion, when he accidently fell into a dry well. He saw a huge snake crawling in the bottom of the well whereas the lion still stood above. He hit upon a wall in the well which had a peepul tree growing in it. He clung to a withered branch of the tree and soon discovered that some black and white mice were gnawing at the branch. Ho looked up and suddenly, a drop of honey fell from the top the well and landed directly on his lips. He licked the honey drop and became oblivious of all his problems.

Today, when Vikas entered the university for jogging, he changed his route and took the road bearing right. He was still thinking about the man hanging inside the well when, all of a sudden, he hit upon the figure he had noticed a few days ago. Taking extremely measured steps and in perfect harmony with the surroundings and itself, the figure jogged along the side of the road, approaching him from the opposite direction. Vikas couldn't believe his eyes. He felt the celestial drop of honey was about to fall on his lips... it was Sunidhi. She was running with complete ease, her eyes focused on the road ahead, totally unmindful of the surroundings. He suspended his walk and stood still wherever he was... looking at her without winking a lid of his eyes... As she came closer, he noticed how light and agile she looked compared to the past. She had always looked pretty, but it was a different level of prettiness he saw today. He couldn't take his eyes off her. Only when he feared she might go by without looking at him, he raised his hand to wave at her....

Sunidhi looked at him in utter disbelief and slowed her pace. She too was pleasantly surprised. As usual, she clinched both her fists. It was unbelievable! Dreamy twilight. Abysmal fog inside. Endless stress on the mind. Two pairs of feet got together to run the route, every day...!

❖❖❖

26

Sunidhi used to come to the university on a bicycle every morning. She tied it to an electric pole, near the main gate, to safeguard it against any theft and set on her walk.

Sunidhi was highly organised in life. Be it her bicycle or clothes or pen or purse or card or anything else...be it her personal relations with people or her work or daily routine, she did everything very methodically. So, she wore a track-suit while going for a walk. Sunidhi chose elegant colours for her clothes, nothing ostentatious caught her fancy. She had a great fancy for the university campus. Its tall trees, densely growing bushes, desolate roads–particularly in the wee hours of the morning–aroused her passion. The beautifully well-kept sprawling lawns in front of the main building, with a splendid variety of blooms in the early wintry mornings, the ancient tall trees fusing with the adjoining ones in an act of complete surrender, the endless beds of white flowers blooming under the trees resembling the Milky Way, infused her spirits with wild energy. White was her favourite colour, also her choice for bed linen..

Having noticed Sunidhi sitting engrossed in her thoughts, Vikas felt very disenchanted. He didn't want to disturb her trance. So, he watched her from a distance. After some time, it became impossible for him to restrain himself and he slowly advanced towards her. As he approached her, Sunidhi woke up from her stupor and looked at him.

'Oh, sir, you... when did you come?'

'Don't call me "sir". You looked so beautiful... lost in your thoughts...' said Vikas coming closer to her.

Sunidhi wanted to get up from the lawn. Vikas offered her his hand, even though she didn't need any support to rise. She lovingly held his hand, gave him a broad beautiful smile, her face radiating like the morning-sun and got up. Her palms were so warm that Vikas felt a strange current run through his body. He looked into her eyes and asked,

'How are you?'

Sunidhi wondered at the question and chose to convey the answer only through her dreamy eyes: she was not only good but much better after seeing him.

They aimlessly wandered in the area for a while and soon landed in a secluded place. The sun was about to rise. Its light had started brightening the sky. The early morning-walkers had also started to pass by. While Vikas and Sunidhi walked lost in each other's thoughts, their hands touched and brought them back. Sunidhi looked at Vikas for a moment. Her beautiful smile set out on a long excursion. Now they landed inside the thickly entwined bushes, holding each other's hand. As it wasn't easy to wade through the bushes, their hands only pined for an uninterrupted joy of being together.

It was winter. The warmth of the early morning sun gave a cosy feel. Dew drops on the unkempt leaves of grass shone like pearls. They both wished the time to freeze! A strange unknown power controlled their motion. They walked in perfect unison, as if playing to a musical strain. Moments, one could have sacrificed the whole life for…!

They didn't realize that they had already reached the main gate. So soon…! Sunidhi asked herself. She saw her bike tied to the electric pole and felt as if it scoffed at her. Still looking at Vikas, she opened its chain but wondered about the chain inside her heart which had been tied so strongly to Vikas. Vikas looked at his watch. Sunidhi was looking elsewhere. An unknown, unforeseen, wave of time flashed through her mind and she stood there completely overwhelmed….!

'Should we go outside and have a juice...?' Vikas's voice brought her back from her trance.

'Sure...' she said without thinking.

All kinds of juices were sold at this time outside the main gate. Carrot, spinach, beet, bitter-gourd, lemon, watermelon...! There was a tea-stall too. People usually preferred carrot juice after a walk. Both of them also had carrot juice, without sugar and ice. He liked it that way and Sunidhi preferred to by Vikas's choice.

'Did we get late today?' remarked Vikas, finishing his juice quickly. He looked at his watch again. Sunidhi noticed a slight nervousness in his demeanour and understood that it was the office syndrome.

'Okay, then...' he said and settled down on his bike. He didn't start it though.

Sunidhi looked at him and yearned for the time to freeze! He looked so smart and young in casual sporty clothes and walking shoes that he could easily pass for a man at least fifteen years younger. Sunidhi experienced a strange and searing rupture inside her, when Vikas had said, 'Okay, then....' She hadn't said anything in response... just stood there, bewitched. The juice stall was surrounded with customers. It was time for people to come out after the walk. Vikas started his bike and waved at Sunidhi. She also waved back at him... half-heartedly.

Sunidhi watched Vikas going away. When he had reached the turning, he stopped his bike and looked back. He saw Sunidhi still standing there. To her utter surprise, he turned his bike around to come back to her. He had never done it before. He came up to her, said, 'Bye, good day...' and was gone. This time he didn't look back. He only waved his hand on reaching the turning. Sunidhi liked Vikas doing what he had done today. He had really grown younger by ten-fifteen years, she thought! It filled her with a strange energy. She collected her bicycle from the stand and cycled home.

❖❖❖

27

Today, Vikas came to the university quite early. He parked his bike near the main gate and walked inside. He noticed that Sunidhi's bicycle was not there. He thought he would just loiter around till she came. He walked a bit and returned to see if the bicycle was there. On any other day, he could have easily noticed it from a distance. But today, it was extremely foggy and he had to come really close to the pole to see it.

Vikas waited for a while and then gave up. He took the road in the other direction. Sunidhi and her thoughts were soon left behind. His mind was preoccupied with official matters. The audacity on Amar Kumar's part was still agitating his mind.

'Amar Kumar ji, I have a feeling that these bills, for the entertainment of the auditors, are highly exorbitant...'

'Sir, you can check with the hotel, if you like...' Vikas vividly remembered the curt reply given by Amar Kumar. He didn't miss the bitterness it carried and the indignation that was writ large on his face as if to say, 'I'll see... how you don't pass the bill!'

Vikas signed the bill even without examining it and Amar Kumar left his cabin. But Vikas sensed that it was just a spark of an impending inferno, the first baby-step in the long journey of deceits and intrigues Amar Kumar was intending to embark upon!

Vikas remembered that while coming out of the office, he had noticed a notorious Union leader sitting with Amar Kumar. They talked in whispers, but when they laughed, their guffaws echoed in the entire hall. People interpreted them in their own way. He had heard one such guffaw when he had come out of his cabin. But he had ignored it and quietly walked out pretending that he hadn't even heard it. Now that he was walking in the university, he felt those guffaws were probably made to deride him!

Soon, he had almost become oblivious of Sunidhi. His whole consciousness seemed to have been over-powered by the anxieties of office matters. He tried to throw them out of his mind, but to no avail. He had good relations with the general manager. He had even assured him 'to do something', but hadn't done anything. And Amar Kumar had started consolidating his position in the office. Vikas even wished that he was transferred from here. But the system didn't work that way. You didn't get a transfer when you wished for it but definitely got it when you didn't want! And getting a good posting was like asking for the moon unless you had a godfather in the department to look after your interest. He knew he had none.

Vikas didn't know why his mind was totally pre-occupied with office matters, today. The number of his confidantes in the office had been brought down almost to naught. And he knew that no office could accomplish its goals unless it had a sincere and dedicated workforce dedicated and respectful to the seniors. He also knew that no amount of pressure created on workers or punishments for a lapse in work could convert an unwilling employee into a motivated one. Vikas had always taken up his job with utmost sincerity and worked with full dedication. All these years, he had led his staff by his own example and won many laurels for the office. But the recent transfer orders had left him with only a bunch of rogues, none of whom could be trusted for any important job. Even Sunidhi wasn't there. The very thought of Sunidhi brought the taste of honey to his parched mouth, though it didn't last long and was soon vilified by the bitterness embodied in Amar Kumar.

He slowed down his pace. The fog had almost cleared by now. He walked past the electric pole twice, but didn't see the bicycle parked there. Then he went ahead and settled himself on a small culvert. His mind, most annoyingly, kept going back to

Amar Kumar. He remembered seeing Patel sitting with him. He was showing him a building plan, which Amar Kumar was trying to understand. It didn't take him long to realize that Patel was not merely a stooge of Sampat Lal, but also a shrewd and seasoned middleman. These days he never came to meet Vikas. He met Amar Kumar and went back. He knew who could be more useful to him.

A few days later, intimation was received from the head office that some committees were being formed at the regional level to effectively deal with the cases of hiring of premises, grants of loans and recoveries. They had to examine proposals pertaining to these matters and forward their recommendations to the central office. Strangely, Amar Kumar was never found to be there on any such committee. He precluded himself on one pretext or another so that he may not be seen to be involved in any of the proposals, even though he maneuvered almost every committee to recommend whatever he liked, exerting the pressure of his proximity with the Chairman.

Vikas often felt that he was losing his effectiveness and effulgence in the office. Things were slipping out of his hands like sand. In most matters, his position was no better than that of a spectator. It pained him but he couldn't do anything about it. The situation was not likely to change as long as the present chairman held office. He had a choice to quit his job. But he couldn't do that, he had a family to support. It was, therefore, in his best interest to pull on as long as he could.

He recalled that a few months ago, he had gone on LFC to Andaman & Nicobar Islands. In his absence, his charge had been temporarily given to Joshi, who was Chief Manager. During this time, the Committee recommended a proposal for hiring new premises. It went under Joshi's signature. As was customary in the bank, papers of important cases were kept aside to be seen by the regular incumbent on his return. So, when Vikas came back, he looked at this proposal and was shocked to see it. He questioned why such big premises as 7000 square feet had been recommended for hiring, that too at such an exorbitant rent as Rs 350/- per square foot, that is 24 lakh per month? Had anyone even thought for a moment about its impact on the profits of the region? Joshi was speechless. All he said was, 'The head office wanted it to be forwarded urgently lest the Reserve Bank forfeited the license for the branch. They called me every day. Even the Chairman personally spoke to me once. He conveyed his displeasure at the delay. So we reduced the rent from Rs 375/- to Rs. 350/- and forwarded the proposal. Incremental clause was kept at 5 per cent per annum with the rent being revised every five years.'

Vikas hoped that the head office would definitely raise queries and call for his views on the proposal. But nothing of the sort happened. The proposal was sanctioned in less than a week at the rent of Rs. 325/-!

Vikas immediately understood the game. The Chairman must have taken at least 25 lakh from the landlord. He remained upset for many days. The act of forming a committee, the insistence on submission of the proposal when he was on leave, the issue of immediate sanction...everything fell in place. But what could he do? Who could he talk to? He didn't know...and it upset him all the more. Then, for more than three months, there wasn't even a semblance of urgency in opening the branch. Such a hefty rent was paid for keeping a highly commercial space vacant...not even a signboard of the bank was put up there! It all reflected so poorly on the bank's reputation. But nobody was bothered about that and it pained Vikas all the more!

Now, the sun was almost over his head. It was eight o'clock. He didn't realize that he had been sitting there...on a small shabby culvert for so long. It was winter and it felt cosy in the sunlight...but sitting on a culvert for so long was awkward! If an acquaintance had spotted him how would he be assessed? The regional manager of such a big bank sitting on a culvert...wouldn't that appear embarrassing and awkward? Quickly he got up and looked around. Not a single soul had noticed him. Everyone was enjoying his own leisure.

Vikas looked at the electric pole. The bicycle wasn't there. He wanted to call Sunidhi. But he soon realized that he wasn't carrying his mobile. He had left it behind at home while coming out for a walk. Today he didn't have juice or tea. He straightaway went up to his bike. Passing by the other bikes parked there, he stopped near one. It belonged to someone working in his bank, as it wore the bank's parking sticker!

'Good that Sunidhi didn't come today,' he thought.

When he reached home, Preeti accosted him, 'Why are you so late today…not going to the office? And do see your mobile… people have been calling you.'

Vikas picked up his mobile. There were two missed calls. One from an unknown number and the other one from Sunidhi!

❖❖❖

28

Vikas had always been keen and punctual to attend office. But today he got late. These days he didn't enjoy working; his team in the office had been disintegrated and the work culture had drastically changed. Honesty was hardly valued as a virtue…and there were no possibilities of any improvement.

As he entered his cabin, he found a newspaper lying on his table. He picked it up and was shocked to read the headline: 'Scam in New Bharat Bank'. He urgently called Kulkarni, the Planning Officer and started reading the news in detail. It was about their branch on Pt Nehru Road, managed by a fairly young and smart lady officer. How could such a scam happen in her branch, he wondered. He asked Kulkarni how the newspaper had reached his table?

'Sir, someone has placed five copies on my table too. Even outside the office, a hawker was selling it with full gusto', replied Kulkarni.

'There must be someone behind it. What do you say...?' Vikas wanted to go into the depth of the matter.

'Sir, I don't think Soumya can do anything like this. She has very little experience…and doesn't know much about banking, but she cannot indulge in such a scam…something is definitely wrong.'

Of those recently posted in his office on transfer, Kulkarni was probably the only one whom Vikas trusted. He was active, alert and good at work. Like Vikas, he also hated Amar Kumar. But he also knew that the Chairman wasn't favourably disposed towards Vikas. So he expressed his loyalty to him only with a bit of caution.

'But you have been regularly receiving the statements from all branches. Did such an overdraft ever come to your notice...?'

'No...Sir.'

'Why...?' Vikas was keen to know all the facts of the case. This was the first scam of this kind to be reported from a branch in his region and it could tarnish his reputation. Soon, there was a call from the GM (Vigilance) in the head office.

'What's going on in your region, Vikas? The Chairman raised this issue in the morning meeting today.'

'But how did he come to know about it so soon?'

'Somebody faxed him a copy of the newspaper cutting', told the GM. 'The Chairman wants a report urgently. If necessary, the Branch Manager may have to be placed under suspension.'

'Let's not do things in haste. I am going to the branch right away', replied Vikas. 'I'd like to properly investigate the matter before taking any action. It wouldn't be correct to react only on the basis of news in the papers. In any case, I'll send you a detailed report by the evening.'

'Do it fast....you know how the Chairman is?'

'Yes....I'm aware'. That's all that Vikas could say and the phone was hung up.

Vikas quickly set out for the Pt Nehru Road branch along with Kulkarni. As he entered the car, his mobile phone rang. It was Sunidhi. He didn't take the call and put the phone on mute.

'So, what do you know about Soumya Sharma?' asked Vikas. Before reaching her branch, he wanted to equip himself with as much information about her as possible. She headed one of the bigger branches in the city!

'Sir, I don't think there's any reason to doubt Soumya's integrity or intentions. But I have learnt a few personal things about her, which I may share with you, if you please?'

'Yes, please do.'

'Sir, Soumya was very friendly with this client. She is single. Her brother is studying and her father has been ailing since long. She has been looking after the family and chosen to remain single, at almost thirty-six. This client is an engineer. He belongs to a good family. People in her branch say that she had developed an emotional bonding with this client. And that's how it happened.' Kulkarni closely watched Vikas's reactions.

'But it's the bank, which has been put to loss. We might recover the funds, but our image has been sullied. In the present days of cut-throat competition, we issue advertisements worth lakhs of rupees. Still they don't build up our image as much as one such incident can malign.' The bitterness in his voice was very palpable.

There was a message received on his mobile phone: 'Is everything alright?' It was from Sunidhi. Vikas quietly sent a reply back: 'Yes, everything is alright. I'll call you later.'

Kulkarni noticed it and thought Vikas was corresponding with someone in the head office. By now they had almost reached Soumya's branch. Vikas's anxiety was growing. He said in a harsh tone,

'But what was the builder's modus-operandi in this case? How did the amount go beyond one crore?'

'Sir, Soumya Sharma had gone on ten days' leave. Suhas Patwardhan took over the charge.' Kulkarni was trying to narrate it in detail, when Vikas interrupted him and said, 'I know!' He wasn't interested in petty details. Kulkarni felt that the boss' mood had soured after receiving the message on phone. He was aware of Vikas's equation with the head office.

'Sir, this was just an adjustment.'

Vikas gave him a dirty look as if to say, 'Don't teach me banking...tell me about the case'. But Vikas didn't say anything. He knew that taunting Kulkarni at this point would only block further information coming out of him. And it wasn't easy to resolve such matters without full information. Vikas looked at his watch. It was a sufficient hint to Kulkarni that he neither had time nor inclination to hear irrelevant details in the matter. So Kulkarni cut his story short and resumed,

'Sir, these cheques for one crore and twenty lakhs were presented when the other manager was holding the charge. There were three cheques: two for fifty lakhs each and one for twenty lakhs. There was no money in the builder's account. There never used to be. Soumya used to retain such cheques in her drawer and clear them towards the end of the month, when the builder deposited money in his account. Till then, it used to be overdraft.'

Vikas had understood the game. He had called Soumya back from leave and also called the builder in the branch. The builder had deposited the amount of the overdraft before Vikas reached the branch. Vikas verified the details and felt that things were under control. But an irregularity had been committed, all the same.

'But how did it reach the press?' Vikas asked Soumya.

'A journalist had applied for a home loan in our branch and wasn't able to get it. He hadn't submitted any documents. Moreover, his income didn't qualify him for the loan amount. He had been in touch with some disgruntled employees of the branch. So when these cheques came in during my absence, they broke the news through this journalist. But the bank has actually made profit from this overdraft.' Soumya was innocently trying to score a point.

'Profit or loss will be seen later...for the present, a major lapse has occurred...rules have been flouted...so an inquiry will have to be ordered.' Vikas said curtly. They had let builder go. He could have turned hostile. Soumya was given a good chiding. She became emotional, broke down and pleaded that she hadn't done anything for a personal gain. Vikas's silence and the rummaging examination of the documents, registers and the computer were a sufficient indication to her that any emotional involvement in the handling of the financial matters of a bank could always land one in serious trouble.

Next morning, Vikas sent a two-line fax to the head office,

'The amount involved in the overdraft at the Pt Nehru Road branch has been recovered. An inquiry has been ordered and the branch manager Soumya Sharma has been transferred.'

Soumya came to meet Vikas in his office in the afternoon. As she sat down in his cabin, she greeted Vikas with folded hands as if to say, 'Please save me, Sir.' Then she said, 'I have committed a mistake... please pardon me.'

Vikas looked at Soumya very carefully. He had the knack of getting right inside people's heart, by merely looking into their eyes. He could instantly make out whether they were innocent or guilty.

Vikas rang the call-bell. 'Chandresh Kulkarni!' The peon went out. Soon there was a knock at the door. Kulakarni was there with his pen and pad. Vikas beckoned him to take a seat.

Vikas had started avoiding sitting alone with a female employee ever since his name had been linked with Sunidhi. He told Kulakarni,

'Please note all that she says.' Soumya started making a statement. She told them that she had not done anything for a personal gain. Even otherwise, the bank had not been put to any loss. She admitted her mistake and requested for help!

Vikas had full realization of Soumya's situation. But all he could say was, 'I can't say anything at this stage. I have, in fact, been asked to place you under suspension. I have only ordered your transfer. I'll see to it that it doesn't affect your career. But I may not be able to save you from a minor punishment. Okay?' So saying, Vikas started reading a file lying in front of him.

Kulkarni and Soumya looked at each other. They had taken the hint to leave. Soumya rose first. She once again folded her hands before Vikas, and silently expressed her request, 'Please do help me out...Sir.'

❖❖❖

29

These days Vikas seriously felt that he was getting trapped. The rising incidence of scams taking place in the branches under his region, was highly disconcerting. As if somebody was playing dirty tricks on him. Many in the office thought that it was the effect of a *saadhe-sati*, the negative phase of the cycle of Saturn. It could be pacified only through yajna and pooja. Some others suggested that they should have a Satya-Narayan pooja in the office. But Vikas didn't believe in the supernatural and didn't want to get involved in any such thing. He knew that it was the result of his not having towed the line...for not having followed the Chairman's autocratic diktats. His aura was diminishing day by day. Many times he wished a transfer out of this region...but wishes were not horses!

Kulkarni knocked at the door. Vikas noticed that along with his pad, he also held a big envelope in his hand. It was from the head office. He recognized it from its colour. For a moment he felt it was another trouble!

'All the best Sir!' Said Kulkarni, handing over the envelope.

'What's it about...? Vikas asked inquisitively.

'Sir, must be the forms for promotion.'

'How do you know?' asked Vikas, taking the envelope.

'Sir, it's from the personnel department...bears their stamp. Promotion process for DGM, GM level is starting soon,' remarked Kulkarni objectively.

Vikas opened the envelope. It actually contained forms to be submitted for the promotions. He passed on the papers to Kulkarni and said, 'Please fill in the basic information as per my service record. Make all entries with a pencil. Don't forget to get a xerox done first....'

'I'll do that Sir. You start preparing for the interview. Leave everything else to me, I'll handle....'

Vikas smiled and retorted, 'Your preparation doesn't matter. The head office would have already done theirs... anyway...you kindly take care of these forms.'

Kulkarni knew what was going on in Vikas's mind. He picked up the forms and left the cabin.

As he left, Vikas realized that Kulakarni had all qualities possessed by Saxena. He too could be trusted and relied upon. He felt assured that something positive could also happen in his life. Thinking this, he pressed the call-bell.

'Sir...' the peon asked Vikas.

'Tea...'

'Yes sir', said the peon and left. He was glad to see Vikas in a good mood after a long time.

❖❖❖

30

Vikas had now started sitting late in the office. He built up fresh teams of trusted officials with the aim of enthusing confidence and vitality in the office. But he found it difficult to control Amar Kumar. He created divides amongst employees, brandished his connections with the chairman to intimidate people and openly indulged in shady deeds, adding to the challenge Vikas faced. As a result, he left office very late.

At home, Preeti and Garima used to anxiously wait for him. Preeti never asked him anything about the office. It wasn't her nature to interfere. Moreover, she knew that if there was anything serious, Vikas would himself share it with her. Garima used to be busy with her home-work. She had made it a habit to consult Preeti about her problems than Vikas.

While coming back from office, Vikas used to be lost in his thoughts and never even talk to the driver. Once home, he would have dinner and watch some TV before going to the bed. Generally he watched news. It only showed news about scams taking place all over the country…scams involving public funds of hundreds and thousands of crores. 'Where would such greed lead our people to', he wondered. Sometimes he felt that TV channels had turned into scam channels. And rightfully so, there was corruption…corruption all the way...and everywhere. Even the reporting of news hadn't escaped its onslaught. It had even clouded the field of cricket. Instead of sixers, what we watched were fixers, money laundering, terror funds etc.

Communication at home had become fragmented. Preeti devoted most of her time to Garima's studies. She would often peep into the bedroom to see if Vikas had slept. She would cover him with a sheet to make him comfortable and switch off the radio, producing jarring sounds as Vikas's favourite programme 'Bela ke Phool' would have just ended. He would in fact be awake, watching Preeti with closed eyes and even feel her pass by his side. But he never passionately pulled her by the hand, as he used to do in the past!

Preeti would close the door from outside and go to Garima's room. She would set things right and then flip channels on the TV searching for a good movie. She returned to her bedroom late in the night, thinking that Vikas would be sound asleep by now. She wasn't interested any more in bodily pleasures nor expected any amorous advances from Vikas. And he understood it quite well. Somewhere the ties had snapped.

As for Vikas, he would be lying in bed, but his mind would still be wandering in the office! He knew it had to be changed. He knew that if it continued, it would spoil his health and destroy his ability to take decisions. He used to advise others to avoid such a lifestyle, but now, he wasn't himself able to get out of it.

While lying alone in the bed, Vikas would often start thinking about Sunidhi. He hadn't talked to her nor seen her in ages. He hadn't even been going to the university and had started putting on weight. But what could he do… he didn't find time even to call her. She must also be thinking about him, but hesitating to call. The very thought of Sunidhi put his anxieties to rest and he fell asleep. He didn't even know when Preeti entered the room and lay down by him. He ran barefoot on the golden sands of his dreams. There was the sea on one side and lofty Nilgiri trees on the other. It was evening. He wanted to open his eyes to see which place it was? Then something told him that it was Kovalam beach.

Dreams are made of strange stuff! When pleasant, they become fleeting and lend wings to time… and when dreadful, they haunt you all time. You can neither scream nor run away from them. When they show promise, you wish them to come true… and when they are ghastly, you start fearing as to what if they actually came true…?

Vikas and Sunidhi came to the airport from their respective places. After checking in, they started waiting for the security-check. Sunidhi took out two apples from her bag and gave one to Vikas. He took it but said, 'Don't feel like eating so early in the morning!'

'Eat it when you feel like…,' said Sunidhi looking at Vikas. Her beautiful dreamy eyes allured him to the myth of apple-eating. Vikas felt it deep inside his heart and wanted to ask her, 'Why two …why not one in two halves?' But Vikas didn't say anything. He looked at the apple in a mysterious way and giving it back to Sunidhi, he said, 'You keep it in your bag. The security people might take it for a bomb if it's found on me. It wouldn't be so in your case.'

Sunidhi stared at him. Vikas had this ability to say very interesting things in a simple way. She admired his wit. In the plane, she sat next to the window. Vikas sat next to her and most of the time, looked out of the window.

'Would you like to sit this side?' asked Sunidhi, pointing towards the window.

'No…' replied Vikas.

'But you are constantly looking outside the window.'

'That's just an excuse. I actually want to get deep inside you…' Vikas mouthed his heart's desire.

'You don't need an excuse to do that!' said Sunidhi blushing. Her cheeks had turned a flaming red. Vikas felt he was drowning in the deep sea of her eyes. Even without bothering to swim across, he enjoyed floating on the waves which constantly swelled and fell. Sunidhi noticed it and lowered her eyes.

Vikas turned his gaze away from Sunidhi to look outside the window. Beautiful rays of the rising sun had bedecked the dawn with ornaments of gold. He wanted to feel Sunidhi inside out. She too was lost somewhere. The streams down below flowed like the molten rocks. Soon a mystical streak of golden light flashed in front of his eyes. He didn't quite understand what it was. But Sunidhi knew about it. So she enjoyed watching a strong and smart Vikas failing to realize and sitting astonished.

So, she deliberately flashed that golden streak of light again. This time Vikas's reaction was much softer than before. He carefully followed the streak and discovered that it was nothing but a reflection of the sunlight on the diamond in Sunidhi's ring. As she realized that Vikas had seen through the trick, she chuckled loudly like an innocent child.

'Softly', said Vikas lubricating her laughter with his love. He pointed towards the passenger sitting next to him. Sunidhi took her lips almost over his ears and whispered, 'He is fast asleep.' Whispering was just an excuse for getting so close to him. Then she let her head coolly rest over his shoulder. She stayed there for a while. Then she again looked at Vikas with all the love in her eyes and started rotating her diamond ring in the direction of the sunrays. Vikas placed his hand over her fingers. The swaying and shining rays of the golden light got entrapped in their palms. Blocking the rays was only an excuse...Vikas actually wanted to plant the sun on Sunidhi's soft and supple palms. And Sunidhi too didn't pull her hand out....

In the evening they went to the sea shore. The sun was making waves at the other end of the sea. Sunidhi spread her arms wide open and suddenly they froze where they were. She had seen a huge tree lying uprooted by the tsunami. What surprised her was the fact that it had not dried up! Its roots had found fresh ground and discovered their lungs in the soil. She looked at it intently and contemplated how adversities disturbed our life many a times and moved on, leaving us crestfallen and hopeless. But this tree had a different story to tell. It had endured adversity and successfully come out of it with a sense of romance. She leaned over the tree and caressed its newly sprung leaves with her beautiful nimble fingers. Immediately, a gust of wind blew from nowhere and made the leaves rustle and clash with each other as if to applaud the joy of Sunidhi's touch.

Sunidhi really admired the struggle of this tree. Like Gautam Budha, it lay there in a semi-reclining posture, engrossed in meditation. She circled around it to absorb more and more of it. And Vikas wished he could permanently absorb in his heart, the sight of Sunidhi lost in a novel contemplation.

'What are you looking at?' asked Vikas.

'Beauty!' replied Sunidhi. She had already completed a circle around the tree.

'Beauty…? Where is it?'

'Everywhere…we just need an eye to see it…'

Vikas liked her philosophy of life. He repeatedly looked at her, from head to toe. How cheerful and pretty she looked in a black salwar-kurta and a black stole embellished with white embroidery. The tides in the sea seemed to reflect the joy she was experiencing inside her. Her pearl-white necklace crystalized her entire persona. Vikas wanted to say something, but felt speechless in front of her dreamy and bewitching figure of gold. And Sunidhi felt a strange romance in Vikas's silent but impassioned presence. She too felt him deep inside her heart and soaked him with the waves of her ocean-like eyes.

'Princess of Kovalam…!' That's all Vikas was able to utter.

'Hmmm…' mumbled Sunidhi in response. She covered her eyes with her beautiful hands as if to wrap up her bashfulness behind her long, nimble fingers and supple, strong palms. Vikas noticed that her footprints had dug deep into the white sand. He wondered if they would have emerged on the other side of the earth. Numerous images and similes flashed in Vikas's mind for Sunidhi. And the eternal woman embodied in Sunidhi of the twenty-first century, joyfully experienced this novel lexicon around the beautiful fingers of her feet!

Then they held each other's hand and started walking bare-foot on the wet sand. Their fingers tightened. The sea swelled up to their feet and returned effacing the marks it had made earlier. The froth it left behind, merrily frolicked around their feet. The crimson-red sun quietly stood in front of the vast horizon as if to swear a witness to the fall of the evening. A silent companionship and an intimate dialogue ensued between the fingers... and the feet listened to it totally spell-bound!

Vikas noticed how hordes of skimpily-clad foreigners were sunbathing on the white sand. The sun was going down, but their desire to bask in its rays hadn't waned. Poor dusky young boys, hawking to sell gowns, often lost sight of their calling, suspended their hawking activity and focused their gaze at the dazzling sight of countless bare female bodies lying prone on the sand, engrossed in reading books or the swarms of beautiful wet bodies of young girls, rising from the salty sea like mermaids! Such seemly sights for them were no less than a potent ointment for their wounds caused by abject poverty and hunger.

When Vikas and Sunidhi walked past such sights, the grip of their palms got stronger. The sea waves slowly rolled up towards the shore. It was time for high tide. Vikas and Sunidhi walked in knee-deep waters...totally oblivious of everything else in the world, even themselves! It was total solitude and total affinity. Suddenly, a strong current of water hit them and they fell down on the sand. They wondered if it was the force of the current or the commotion rising inside their hearts, which had done the trick! The waves greeted them with a garland of froth and receded into the sea. They lay there like that for quite some time. Soon another wave came rushing to embrace them. Quickly they got up and ran towards the shore. At the far end, Vikas threw himself down on the sand and pulled Sunidhi to fall upon him. Seeing them play pranks on each other like small kids, a white woman lying nearby put her book aside and gave them a hearty smile. The sun had set since long, but its aura still pervaded the atmosphere.

Soon they felt tired and sleepy. Vikas wondered if it was reality or a dream...he, lying on the wet sands by the side of Sunidhi... like foreign tourists... both in their swim-suits...! They had had lot of fun and were now lying calmly on the sea shore. Sunidhi had closed her eyes and Vikas had covered his face with a book. Both were probably lost in their own dreams.

Suddenly, Vikas felt someone remove the book from his face, right at noon, exposing his eyes to the sharp prickly rays of the sun. With half-opened eyes, he saw Preeti pulling open the big curtains in his bedroom, letting the sunlight directly fall on his bed. He shook his head, rubbed his eyes and discovered that nobody was lying by his side. He heard someone ask,

'No office today? It's eight-thirty…' It was Preeti.

Bewildered, Vikas fondly recollected what he had seen in the dream last night. Preeti came up to him. Handing over the newspaper to him, she said,

'I'll get your tea…!

❖❖❖

31

It had now become a routine for Vikas and Sunidhi to jog together for miles, in the mornings as well as evenings. Running under the shady trees, they lost the sense of distance and time. Sunidhi served as a catalyst in keeping him fit in spite of his age. If he ever felt breathless, she looked at him in a way that instantly pumped in energy in his body. She inspired him by teasing him with clinched fists and challenging him to catch her. He put all his might in the feet and soon caught her by the hand. Panting joyfully, they would both settle down on the railing of a bus stop and stay there for hours. Vikas had now overcome his fear of being seen with her. Even Sunidhi had stopped bothering about it. She felt totally mesmerized in his company.

They walked again on this lonely road in the evenings. Only an odd bike or rickshaw passed by them, that too occasionally. They talked very little, but exchanged a lot of feelings and emotions. They had even stopped discussing official matters. Day by day, Sunidhi was getting prettier. Just looking at her, Vikas would be relieved of all the burden he carried in his head. There was a strange chemistry between the two. No arguments… no complaints for coming late. On the other hand, they relished the pleasure of waiting for each other. Then spending hours sitting on the bus stop railing was fun! It used to get dark. They often went to the nearby restaurant and had their dinner together. Vikas often got late reaching home. And so did Sunidhi, reaching her hostel.

In the heart of his hearts, Vikas wished Sunidhi to go a long way in her career and get many promotions. He wanted to see her at the top of the banking hierarchy. So, one day he asked her,

'Why don't you take the next exam?'

'I am taking it. I have cleared the first stage of Banking Certificate… I have even earned two increments!'

'Great, you achieved so much in a year…and I didn't even know. But it's good…what else are you planning to do?'

'I am doing MBA from IGNOU', said Sunidhi. Seeing her eyes sparkle with confidence, Vikas warmly pressed her hand with love and complimented her,

'Good! You are smart! You are great! You proved me wrong in assuming that you had given in to your personal problems…I am proud of you'. Vikas had become emotional.

'It's all because of you. Had you not supported me, I would have given up long ago. Now I have started understanding my life. I have realized that I can face it…'

'I have some very good books for your next banking exam. I'll get them tomorrow.' Vikas wished that she cleared the next exams at the earliest.

'Sure. It will be great help', said Sunidhi, feeling obliged.

'Let's celebrate your success.'

'Sure. Where would you like to go?'

'When the Queen is here, one must go to the Kings only!' said Vikas, thoughtlessly. Kings was a popular restaurant in the locality. But how did he hit upon the epithet of 'Queen', he didn't know. He soon recalled that he had addressed her as the 'Princess of Kovalam' in his dream the other day.

Vikas's act of addressing Sunidhi as 'Queen' filled her with a rush of romance. Her cheeks turned a flaming red in a joyful embarrassment. She clung to his arm and prompted by an unknown emotion, she rested her head on his shoulder…exactly like she had done in his dream, when travelling in an aeroplane. Vikas was surprised at such an early realization of his dream and wondered if joys too needed a shoulder to rest their head upon.

After a few days, when they had finished walking and were sitting at the bus stop, Vikas told Sunidhi that he had brought some books for her. He noticed she didn't react, though she seemed eager to speak. He turned towards her and looked at her face. Sunidhi turned her head the other way and asked,

'Vikas, what according to you is love?'

Vikas wasn't ready for it. And he had never thought about assigning any meaning to love. He pondered over it for a moment and replied,

'Feelings...'

'That's all?'

'Feelings are not a small matter!'

'No...they are not, but I think, there should be something more to it', said Sunidhi.

'I think, looking after, respecting...and providing support to each other.' Vikas spoke like a philosopher. And soon he asked the same question to Sunidhi, 'And what is love for you...?'

'It was I who asked the question. You were supposed to only give a reply and not start cross-questioning. Even if you have to do that, you shouldn't be asking the same question at least.'

Vikas felt that Sunidhi had, in a very short time, matured to be able enough to give such decisive answers. He liked her talking to him not in the capacity of a boss, but as her equal.

'What happened?'

'What...?'

'You turned serious...?'

'Not at all Sunidhi, I was thinking how much you have changed. I can see a very strong and self-confident Sunidhi emerge from a shy, self-conscious...introvert girl.'

Sunidhi knew that Vikas was not indulging in flattery. He actually meant whatever he had said.

'It's the world which has made me matured....taught me everything...I know.' There was agony and sarcasm in her voice. Vikas knew what she was talking about. He wanted to lighten the gravity of the situation and asked her,

'When is your next exam?'

'Next month...,' replied Sunidhi.

'Let's have an advance party for that...my treat!' said Vikas.

It didn't take long for Sunidhi to understand that Vikas had realized what was going on in her mind. His offer for a party was just an excuse to lighten up her mood. This, probably, was love...in realist truest sense...!

❖❖❖

32

These days, Vikas was having terrible nights. He had equally terrible days in the office, where he just did fire-fighting the whole day, handling intrigues and rumour-mongering. And as if that was not enough, the head office had completely let him down. He was pulled up daily for one thing or the other. He felt very insecure...and very lonely. He had nobody to talk his mind to. If he discussed anything with anyone, the news would spread all around like jungle fire. He couldn't go on leave as his adversaries could use that opportunity to do mischief, mess up his office affairs and further complicate his life.

These days, Vikas didn't feel comfortable even at home. Preeti devoted most of her time to Garima. At night, she came to their bedroom only when Vikas had gone to sleep. Even when he was awake and wanted to make love to her, her response would be cold and most disheartening. So, even in bed, he was left alone. He often thought she had lost interest in sex. She was growing peevish, day by day. She was probably heading towards menopause, though she never spoke about it. They had actually never been so candid and open with each other as to discuss such matters freely.

Evil manoeuvrings at office and total disregard at home had pushed Vikas into a situation where he found himself to be standing in the midst of a burning desert. If there was any oasis for him it was Sunidhi. He wasn't even able to decipher if his love for Sunidhi had pushed Preeti away from him or it was Preeti's indifference which was bringing him closer to Sunidhi! Or it was neither of the two and it was he who was abdicating his social obligations for the love of Sunidhi. He would think about these things and keep tossing in bed, but sleep wouldn't oblige him. Many times, he even thought of taking sleeping-pills, but he feared it might in the long run, become an addiction.

It would only be in the wee hours of morning that he would fall asleep. But then, he wouldn't be left alone by Sunidhi's dreams. They had by now, become synonymous to his sleep. Even when he wasn't asleep, for long hours at night, he dreamt about her with open eyes. Her large watery eyes, her luscious lips, her dark black silky hair ruled over his imagination. He saw her sitting by his side, removing her rings and got lost looking at those shapely…sprightly fingers. He hadn't seen any woman with such adorable feet as hers. When she removed her ear-rings, she became conscious of his gaze. Her ears turned red. He longed to feel them with his fingers but feared they might get burnt. When she got up from his side, he was so enamoured that he felt if a heart didn't throb looking at her gorgeous slim body and her elegant gait, it must be a piece of stone.

The dreams Vikas saw with open eyes often brought his past alive in front of him like a film reel.

The hotel phone was ringing. He wondered why and how, he had been waiting for it. But he wasn't able to talk. He had only said 'Hello', when it got disconnected. It was eleven o'clock in the night. He had had a busy day and was feeling dead tired. There was only one balm which could have helped him overcome his fatigue, loneliness, insomnia or every other malaise. Sometimes he took it with open eyes and sometimes with closed.

Suddenly, the door bell rang. Vikas hurriedly got up to open the door. It was Sunidhi. He rubbed his eyes to make sure it wasn't a dream? But then he thought, why get bogged down by this thought… why not enjoy the flamboyant mist he felt all around him. The surprise and joy of the moment were overwhelming!

'You? Here! At this time..?'

'Why? Alone in a hotel in Mumbai? Isn't it surprising?'

Vikas was totally confounded. He even forgot to ask her to come inside and sit. He only looked at her, as if he had never seen her before! Finally, Sunidhi offered her hand. They came inside and settled down on the sofa. It was so small that it could hardly accommodate two persons. So, Vikas got up and sat in a chair near the writing table.

'Why?' asked Sunidhi.

'There, I couldn't see you properly…' Vikas had not seen such a wonderful sight even in his dreams, as was present before him in reality.

'Will you have tea?' He was trying to sound normal.

'You think I have come so far to have tea with you', said Sunidhi, playfully. She was being informal as ever.

'But how did you come to know that I was staying here… at Suba Palace!' Vikas was really intrigued as to how Sunidhi had found out about him and reached there?

'You forgot something my dear… I often find out your hotel's name while talking to you. And Google makes it so easy to find any location. I first checked with the hotel if you had booked it. Then I also booked a room here, online. I enquired about your room from the reception. Luckily I got a room on this floor! '

Sunidhi looked at Vikas as if to question him, 'Don't you find it necessary to ask me why I took so much trouble to…or what name we should give to this meeting of ours…', and she continued to quietly look at him. Vikas too quietly stared at her.

'Don't you have anything to say?', asked Sunidhi shaking him out of his stupor.

'I have a lot… but don't know where to start?'

'I know, you have nothing', she tried to provoke him.

'Let's listen to some music. Masti plays very good songs at night.' He switched on the TV, before Sunidhi could say anything. He had last been watching Masti channel. So it was there again. It was playing really good songs of the 1970s and

'80s. When they had nothing to say, the songs would fill in the gap. Even otherwise, all these songs were only echoing the voice of their heart: '*ye nayan darey-darey…ye jaam bharey-bahrey…*'

Then Sunidhi rose abruptly.

'*Achha to hum chalte hain…!* I just wanted to see you…'

'But stay for a little while…!' said Vikas, casually.

'Okay, I'll stay…!' She flopped down on the sofa again.

Vikas hadn't expected this coming from Sunidhi. They were meeting at a strange place…at a late hour in the night and that too, when Sunidhi was all alone.

Vikas had never imagined that Sunidhi could have such remarkable guts and such a romantic disposition.

Then there was silence…both intently watched songs on the TV. In between their eyes met for a moment. Then Sunidhi got up and moved towards the door.

How fascinating she looks when she walks in a saree…! thought Vikas to himself, following her to the door. Suddenly, she covered her back with the loose end of her saree. Oh…!

She turned back. Vikas stood there right in front of her. She stopped for a moment.

'Stay…' said Vikas. He opened the door to see if anybody was there. It was unlikely that anybody would be out in the corridor at twelve midnight. He beckoned Sunidhi to come out. They stood outside Room 206. Sunidhi had to go to Room 208.

Sunidhi took tiny steps and reached her room.

She waved her hand to say 'bye' to Vikas. He too responded likewise.

His phone rang after about ten minutes.

'Hello'! It was Sunidhi.

'Hello', said Vikas very eagerly.

'What were you doing?' Sunidhi asked as usual.

'Nothing…', replied Vikas.

'I wish you had said...you were waiting for me!'

'That's true, I was thinking only about you.'

'You just keep thinking. It's just I who calls you. Even comes down to meet you...travelling hundreds of miles... comes to meet you in the middle of the night. And you just keep thinking!' As she spoke, her voice and her tone grew mellow. It had a message for Vikas, which was not lost on him.

They kept talking for a long time. There was hardly any sense or meaning in whatever they spoke about. But the peels of such senseless conversations do often carry a fruit inside which one is never tired of eating!

'Shall we only keep talking on phone? What will the hotel guys think?' asked Sunidhi.

'You think the hotel guys would be awake at this time? And how would they know about it?' Vikas wanted to continue talking.

'It's not like that, my dear! It shows on the board, which room number is in conversation with which room number.'

'You know a lot about it...' remarked Vikas out of curiosity.

'They can even hear us, if they want... and everyone likes to hear such conversations.'

'Let's close it in that case.'

'Good night!' said Vikas.

'Good night!' said Sunidhi and hung up.

It was not even ten minutes that Vikas dialled Room 208.

'Hello!' Sunidhi's voice was as fresh as ever.

'Good night', said Vikas mischievously.

'Good surprise...good night!' Both put their receivers down.

In about ten more minutes, Vikas's phone rang. It was two o'clock in the night. Both of them were still awake.

'Hello! Tell me...!' said Vikas, even without waiting to hear from other side. He knew it would be Sunidhi.

'Not asleep…!' It was Sunidhi, with her sweet, tempting and intoxicating voice. 'Come over..!' There was an invitation for Vikas.

'Right now?'

'Then... when else? Come over. The door is open.'

'Really?'

'Of course…please come!' Sunidhi's 'please' conveyed a lot of impatience.

Vikas was in his night suit. He picked up the room key and came out of the room. He gently closed the door behind and tiptoed up to Room 208. The door was open. She was probably standing at the door itself. She gave him an intimate smile and softly shut the door.

The TV was showing the same Masti channel. The night was fleeting. This time they both sat on the sofa. Vikas's hand stretched across to the other end of the sofa and touched Sunidhi's head. For once he thought it would be courteous to pull it back. But soon he realized that Sunidhi was herself rubbing her head against his arm. So he also let his hand rest wherever it was.

Soon, they were both in a state of inebriation, though conscious at the same time. They kept watching the Masti songs sitting on the sofa. The clock was approaching four in the morning... Vikas looked at his watch.

'Feeling sleepy?' asked Sunidhi, coyly.

'Who can feel sleepy in your company? But I should be leaving now,' replied Vikas.

'What time is your meeting in the morning?'

'Ten o'clock.'

'Okay… have some sleep…', said Sunidhi.

'What's your plan? You have to go somewhere?'

'No… I just came to see you. My programme is over. I'll go back by the nine o'clock train in the morning', said Sunidhi getting a bit nervous.

'You too take some rest…' said Vikas.

'How can I rest now?' asked Sunidhi, turning her face away.

Vikas got up from the sofa. Advancing towards the door, he felt Sunidhi was consciously not following him. Perhaps she wanted to but she wasn't. He was surprised and stopped short of the door. He turned back and moved towards her. He shook hands with her. Then he held her face in his hands. Sunidhi instantly closed her eyes. There was a look of complete trust on her face. She was care-free. Vikas felt his palms were burning. Sunidhi's face turned softer. Her lips quivered. She was speechless.

Vikas kissed her forehead.

Sunidhi opened her eyes. Complete trust was writ large in them. Then she moved ahead towards the door, opened it and looked out in the corridor. When she was satisfied that there was nobody there, she beckoned Vikas to come out. And as he left, she closed the door behind him.

Vikas hesitantly walked a bit towards his room, but immediately turned. This time, he didn't ring the bell. He gently knocked. Sunidhi opened the door and felt a strange commotion lovingly enter the room.

Vikas suddenly held her hand in his and rubbed it warmly.

'Good morning!' he said and moved on.

He heard Sunidhi saying, 'Good morning, I like it.'

❖❖❖

33

As suggested by some colleagues, Vikas organized a get-together of the staff of all branches in his region. The occasion was Diwali, a holiday. All employees were invited for tea and snacks. Men mostly came in kurta-pajama whereas women were dressed in beautiful sarees. It was a good gathering. Ravi Shankar's sitar was played in the background. Such a function was being held after a long time and was the need of the hour.

Vikas also came in white kurta-pajama. He personally welcomed all guests and their families. Garima and Preeti were also present.

Some old members of the staff who had seen Sunidhi work with Vikas, were busy whispering in each other's ears, as they were seen together once again. Sunidhi looked awesome. She was in high spirits, freely circulating amongst all the guests. But every now and then she returned to the spot where Vikas and Preeti stood. Her excitement wasn't hidden from anyone, particularly Preeti, who could hardly take her eyes off Sunidhi. And there was no way that Sunidhi could guard her actions and emotions from the prying eyes of a woman. Still, she tried to be with Preeti, most of the time, because Vikas would also be there.

Love is always an interesting subject for people to talk about, particularly for those who relished peeping into other people's lives. Then, there are rumours which spread like wild fire. Many of those present at the party believed that Sunidhi and Vikas had a joint bank account. Some even thought that they had a flat in Goa which was in the joint name of Vikas and Sunidhi!

Not-to-be-bothered by such gossip, Vikas tried his best to redeem his image. He devoted maximum time to his employees and major clients in the town.

The programme was a success and achieved the desired result. Sunidhi took leave and left. On their way back home, Preeti didn't talk to Vikas. He understood her state of mind. So far she had only had some apprehensions about him. Now, there were a lot many developments which disturbed her. In spite of Vikas attending to his family obligations to perfection, Preeti had a niggling doubt about his commitment and sincerity.

Vikas's dilemma was no longer hidden from Preeti. But she was made of different mettle. She didn't believe in blowing things up. Whenever she found herself in a problem, she looked inwards and tackled it quietly. Indulging in unnecessary arguments, claims, counter-claims, winning and losing battles wasn't her nature. But when you were hurt, your demeanor gave you away. And Preeti wasn't even trying to carefully hide her emotions from public gaze.

One day Vikas realized that he hadn't been fair to Preeti. Being all the time mentally occupied with the thoughts of Sunidhi had more or less alienated him from her. He had even lost the desire to have sex with her. He felt a bit scared of himself. Such a reckless way of life had never been a part of him. He shouldn't have been so dispassionate towards his family. The only rationale he could think of was the support he had received from Sunidhi during his difficult times.

So he took an important decision; he should have a house of his own, where Preeti should be the co-owner. He took this decision without informing Preeti. But he made the contract of the house final only with her consent. It was bought in Preeti's name. He had successfully crossed one stage of uncertainty. Now he lived in his own house and EMI was being paid from his salary. More importantly, now he felt less guilty of having done any injustice to Preeti.

❖❖❖

34

'So, what have you decided?' asked Vikas.

'Divorce', replied Sunidhi, apathetically.

'And what after that...?' Sunidhi was startled at this question coming from Vikas. She intently looked at him to read his eyes, but didn't find any such thing there as she had imagined.

'Haven't given it thought...it will easily take two to three years!' She again looked at him. He was busy fondling the leaves of grass.

'It's time you thought about that too, Sunidhi,' he remarked without looking at her and added, 'Anyway, how are you liking your hostel?'

'It's good...much better than living the life of captivity'

'Is it even better than living in your mom's house?'

'Sure. I felt suffocated there. Here, I feel independent and free. I have decided to do further studies. I have already taken the bank exams. Now I want to do CA. By the time divorce comes through, I would hopefully be a CA.'

'That's nice!' Vikas admired her self-confidence and the way she expressed it. He had always wished to see her becoming self-dependent and taking her own decisions.

'Sunidhi...!'

'Hmmm..!' reacted Sunidhi. The way she babbled 'Hmmm' and looked coyly at Vikas, it completely electrified him. He gathered himself and added,

'I am glad to see you become so strong from within. From the time you joined my bank till now, when you are working in a different branch, I can see a sea change in you…'

'It's all because of you…' said Sunidhi. She noticed a dry straw lying over the green leaves of grass. She picked it up and flung it far away.

'Sunidhi you should try to get your divorce expedited', advised Vikas.

'Yes, I too want it to be over soon.'

'What do you mean by 'I too'…?'

'I mean…I want it to be over soon', said Sunidhi, quickly correcting herself. But she couldn't help adding, 'I want to live with you…I can talk to Preeti about it. If it's not in your house, let it be anywhere else. I'm not going to get married. You occupy such a special place in my heart that I cannot even think about any other man coming into my life. If you think it's not possible for you, I'm prepared to live by myself…all alone….' When she said this, her head had already taken repose on Vikas's shoulder.

Vikas was caught off guard and bewildered. He had never anticipated anything like this. He had always felt romantically inclined towards her, but never thought that she could go that far. He was nonplussed and didn't know what to say. Seeing him in this condition, Sunidhi said,

'I'll never stand in between you and your family. Your daughter will be like my daughter. I think Preeti will understand my feelings', Sunidhi held Vikas's hand in hers.

Vikas was speechless. How would Preeti take it? What would he tell his daughter! …No, no, no…it wasn't right.

They were silent for a while.

Very soon, Sunidhi realized that she had broached the subject at a wrong time. She had wanted to say it since long, but she had never been able to muster the courage to do so. Now, when Vikas had himself raised the issue of her divorce, she thought it was an appropriate time for her to open her heart before him. She hadn't thought that her plans were too bold and sudden for him. All his feelings of romance and chivalry had been blown into smithereens and vanished in thin air. What remained was just a feeling of respect for her. But that wouldn't be enough for her to live a whole life. She could see that Vikas was highly disturbed. But she didn't want to let go of this opportunity to discuss it threadbare. So she continued to speak.

'I know, your family is and should be your first priority. Hence, I am fine with whatever you say. I can live my life alone. I have no love lost for the institution of marriage. I don't want to take that risk again. I have just one desire left in my life....'

She looked at Vikas and mustering all her courage, said, 'I want to bear your child...that's all. I know I'll be able to take care of the child. I'll never bother you for it...I'll stay away, all alone...though you'll be welcome to visit me whenever you wish to....' She blurted it all out and stared at Vikas eagerly. He was dumbstruck. There was complete silence for a while. Then as if to break the ice, she continued, 'I don't want to get married. I am disgusted with the very word.'

'A child out of wedlock...?'

'So what...isn't it possible? I am capable...and strong enough to face the world.'

Sunidhi realized that she was now being too vehement about her wish for a child, whereas what she had actually wished to have was a good lifelong relationship with Vikas.

'What would you say if they asked the father's name in the school?'

'It's not obligatory these days, to disclose the father's name. You can give the mother's name instead.' She seemed to have come fully prepared.

'But the world is not so kind...Sunidhi. You are pitted against so much opposition and criticism already; you'll start regretting your decision very soon. Besides, you have a wonderful life ahead. You are so beautiful, so educated and so well-employed that you'll easily get a good match.' Vikas was talking like an elder, indulging in a bit of counselling.

'You must understand that I am already hurt with the way I was married off and the type of man I got for myself. Then I luckily came in contact with the complete man that you are. I have been so deeply influenced by your personality that I'd only be looking for you in a man I meet. No, I don't want to take this risk again. I am scared...I'll be totally broken...if it happened again!'

'Fair enough. I can understand your point about marriage. But what's this craze about having a child from me?' asked Vikas, trying to avoid the issue.

'I want to imbibe and develop your image inside me. I want to feel like a complete woman by becoming a mother...I have no other interest...no claim. And I need no support or protection.' Sunidhi further simplified the matter.

'Well, it's true, Sunidhi...that I have been attracted towards you. I feel good in your company. I have even started loving you. But it's basically our circumstances which have brought me to this pass. I fully respect your feelings, but I cannot bring an illegitimate child into this world. And I cannot let Garima suffer because of my apathy for Preeti. I just can't do it. We are friends...we love each other but it wouldn't be fair for us to upset the lives of our beloved ones. In fact, I have been contemplating to suggest to you to get married again as soon as possible. I think, that would be the right and the best thing to do...and also the most practical one.'

In the bottom of her heart, Sunidhi knew that Vikas was right. But she couldn't help it. The way he had paved his way into her life, first as a boss, then a well-wisher, then a friend and finally a sweetheart, he had convinced her that he was the perfect man for her. The vines inside her heart craved to permanently cling to the tree that he was. But she often found her arms to be too short to take the trunk of this tree into their fold. And every time she tried to climb it, its smoothness just pushed her down.

Both of them remained silent for quite some time. Then Vikas dropped Sunidhi at her hostel. There was a turmoil built up within both of them. They shook hands but felt the usual warmth missing in the touch. Sunidhi quietly departed with her eyes downcast.

Vikas felt that he had deeply hurt her today. He had, in fact, completely disappointed her. But what other option did he have? Sunidhi's proposal had shaken his consciousness and conscience. All the romance in him had vanished. He felt as if he was staggering. He wondered how on earth Sunidhi had conceived this idea! What exactly had prompted her to be so bold; were those words and actions her own or had they been prompted by the circumstances of her life? She appeared to be capable of challenging the whole world! Each word that she spoke displayed her confidence and resolve. Vikas was now fully convinced that if a woman so desired, she could merrily sacrifice everything she had for the sake of her love. She could break all shackles in the world. She could spend her whole life living alone. She could end all confusion and uncertainty in her life, protect herself from the vicious Ravanas of the world and surrender herself to her love. That was the power of a woman...her intrinsic character! Today, what he saw in Sunidhi, was a much more beautiful and determined person than he had seen so far.

Sunidhi found it difficult to sleep the whole night. She kept tossing in bed, recalling whatever Vikas had said that evening. For once, she felt happy to think that he had outrightly rejected her proposal. Decisions taken in an emotional frenzy often proved to be misleading and could lead to future repentence. She was extremely impressed with his foresight and sense of judgment. These were his qualities, which enamoured her.

'I am fifteen years older than you, Sunidhi.'

'So what...?'

'I'll grow old much sooner than you will.'

'That doesn't matter...'

Sunidhi kept thinking about their conversation.

Vikas had not let himself get drifted with the current of his emotions. Rather, he had offered her a sensible piece of advice which further enhanced Preeti's admiration for him.

'Sunidhi,' Vikas had told her, 'I respect your feelings. But this is not a practical suggestion. It can even ruin your career. We may feel that the world has changed...and we are a lot more liberal in our outlook, but the society we live in, still continues to be retrograde and orthodox, particularly when it comes to matters of the heart. Such a decision can, therefore, never get you any happiness and satisfaction. Even if it made you feel complete, it would be disastrous for the child. It will live a life of trauma and be considered a social outcast. Even at school, he'll feel totally lost and forlorn. I admire your confidence and thank you for reposing such a trust in me. But I'll advise you not to nurture such an idea in your mind. Somebody can take undue advantage of it and ruin you....

Sunidhi realized Vikas had truly saved her today from going astray. Their hands were cold when they parted, but his carried the firmness of trust, whereas hers were laden with worries. She felt greatly drawn towards him. She also felt very light and relieved after having given vent to her pent-up feelings. She felt she had discovered a way to get out of the quagmire of worries she had all along been stuck in. Even if she had failed to 'get' Vikas, she had become completely 'his'.

❖❖❖

35

In every bank office, there comes a time when only the most important works are looked after, because everyone's mind is glued somewhere else. That time had come...the time for promotions and transfers to take place. The list for promotions to the posts of AGM, DGM and GM was already out and flashing on the computers.

Vikas had all along had a feeling that the chances of his promotion were very bleak this time. He knew it ever since he had appeared for the interview. The Chairman had very rudely grilled him with questions pertaining to those branches of banking, which he had never dealt with. These ranged from International to Agricultural banking. He hadn't asked even a single question about the work Vikas had been doing. Even the tone and tenor for asking the questions were terrible. Vikas had felt suffocated. Every question was like a big blow aimed to hurt him. He had a mind to leave it mid-way and come out. The Chairman hadn't let any other member ask any question. Vikas had felt like a mouse trapped inside the cat's paws, where the cat derived pleasure in gnawing at it, instead of killing it.

Vikas's name was not there in the list for promotions to the post of DGM. Soon, there was another e-mail from the Head Office. It was about the transfers of Regional Managers. Vikas had been transferred to Aurangabad.

As per bank records, Aurangabad was not considered a good region. It had too many cases of bad loans and there was a lot of political interference. The staff was highly Union-oriented. Three Regional Managers had been transferred there in the last four years. Having given up on the chances of promotion during this year, Vikas had anticipated a transfer, but a transfer to

Aurangabad was no less than a punishment. The Chairman had posted a regional manager of his choice in place of Vikas, so that he could easily get all his works done. Moreover, the new incumbent was coming on promotion. So he would even otherwise be more pliable for the Chairman.

Vikas handed over the charge of his office and joined at Aurangabad. His farewell party was a bag of mixed feelings. Some staff members were happy whereas some others were not. But most of them were excited in welcoming the new incumbent. No wonder...people worshipped the rising sun and Vikas was passing through a bad phase of an eclipse. They even avoided talking to him. Only Sunidhi called. She even wanted to come and see him. But Vikas refused.

Vikas's reputation of being an honest, impartial and dedicated officer had reached Aurangabad, even before he joined there. He had another good quality. On transfer, he never took time to relinquish office and quickly proceed to the new place. And thereafter, he neither visited the place nor showed any interest in its activities. The staff at the Aurangabad office was quite inquisitive about him. Some senior officers had come to the airport to receive him. His stay had been arranged in Gymkhana Club, which was no less than a five-star hotel.

Vikas's first day in the new office was very hectic. He had set upon himself the task to improve it through hard-work and trust. He might have been sent there to rot, but he wanted to convert it into an opportunity. He had shed all malice for the Chairman and taken it up as a challenge. Anyone else in his place would have surely gone mad cursing his stars, playing a victim card and losing all interest in work. But Vikas was different. He decided to put in extra effort, regain the reputation of the office and leave his mark.

It had been a week that Vikas had landed in Aurangabad. And all this time he had just been working. He came to office even on Saturday. It showed results. The staff was fully cooperative. His meetings with the clients went off well. He assured them to find a way to deal with bad loans. Preeti and Garima called in between to enquire about his well-being.

On Sunday, Vikas decided to visit the Ajanta caves. He hadn't been there before. He took a local driver, who served as a guide and gave him all information about the area. Vikas was all alone, but he felt Sunidhi's presence in every cave he visited,. He often thought of calling her, but he didn't. He didn't want to disturb her. In the main cave in Ajanta, where Buddha lay with his eyes closed and a serene smile on his countenance, he felt Sunidhi looked over his shoulders and held him so passionately that his whole body was charged with romance. Many a times, separation produced a feeling of intimacy. Sunidhi wasn't there with him, but he felt her presence every moment. Once he felt that he was a piece of stone and Sunidhi was working on him with a chisel. He wasn't Buddha and he didn't want to become his statue either. Instead, he wanted to feel the sculptor and caress her beautiful hands. He experienced a strange craving inside him and started smiling. Instantly he felt he had realized the truth and was slowly becoming a Buddha. He came out of the cave and seated himself on a stone. The place offered a beautiful panoramic view of the Ajanta region. He became highly emotional. He didn't know how long he kept sitting there ...meditating, may be? Then he noticed, most of the people were going back. He also got up and started following them, as if in a stupor.

On his way back, he visited the Ellora caves and viharas. He was astonished to see the Kailash temple. It was a marvel of a monolithic architecture. It was probably the only instance in the world, where a mountain had been cut from top to bottom, with so many beautiful temples, huge columns and exquisite figures being carved along the way. He wondered at the excellent planning, complete dedication and unique craftsmanship of the sculptors, which had gone into its making. But he noticed Sunidhi in all those lovely figures. He had never realized that she had penetrated so deep into the recesses of his consciousness that she had become inseparable from him. He didn't know when he sat in the car, reached the club and called for coffee! But his conversation with Sunidhi came live the moment he sipped his coffee. He remained lost in her thoughts. He didn't know for how long he kept swimming in the pool. Today he had risen above the quagmire of problems he faced in his old office.

After dinner, he sat in front of the TV. He was staying in a large suite in the club. There was a lobby in front which had a TV. There was a TV inside the bedroom too, but he sat in the lobby and kept surfing the news channels. It was the same set of news being telecast on all channels, though in different forms. Corruption, CBI, orders of the High Court and the Supreme Court.... It could be any party in the government, but there was no difference in the matter of corruption. He had seen it entering his bank too. He felt everybody was in a mad race to acquire wealth, by all means, fair or foul. The rich wanted to become richer. Starting with a small *patwari*, every engineer, minister, IAS officer was involved in corruption, even his Chairman. He felt bored with such news. He switched off the TV and proceeded to his bedroom to sleep.

After the whole day's travel, Vikas was so tired that he could have immediately gone to sleep...but sleep eluded him. Tossing in bed, he switched on the TV and tuned on the 'Masti' channel. It was Sunidhi's favourite music channel. At ten o'clock at night, it played romantic songs of the 1970s and 1980s. Listening to the favourite songs of your favourite stars has its own charm. The song being played right then was '*Is mod se jaate hain*' from the film *Aandhi*; Vikas had always liked this song. He loved the way the heroine walked in this song. Shot on a moonlit night, in the midst of maple trees...it looked enchanting and passionate that Vikas would often imagine himself featuring in the song. Many other songs were played thereafter, but none of them could beat the mood created by the number from *Aandhi*.

Vikas didn't know how long he watched the TV. He thought of Sunidhi and dozed off. She had fully captured his imagination, whether in sleep or wake. Very early in his sleep, he saw a dream. He was knocking at the door of Sunidhi's room.

She opened it and quietly let him in. While doing so, she would always get a bit conscious of getting swayed by him. And he always felt that he had carved a place for himself in the deepest recesses of her heart. But the physical union had always eluded them. She was fully aware of his self-control. Still her sixth sense always remained alert. Hesitantly, he entered the inner room which was the bedroom and sat down in a chair. Sunidhi cautiously lay herself on the king-size bed and beckoned him to come to her. Hesitantly, he got up and placed himself by her side. Both clicked close-up pictures of each other on their mobiles. Suddenly Vikas asked Sunidhi,

'What if I do anything wrong at this time?'

'How can you do anything wrong without my permission?' replied Sunidhi, moving closer to him.

She was so close, but yet so far! For a moment, Vikas felt depressed, but soon he collected himself and said,

'You are right...nothing without your permission. We'll have a good relationship only when we don't commit a mistake even by mistake. Good that you made me aware of it...bodily pleasure is momentary, but mental pleasure is everlasting.

Sunidhi didn't reply. But her silence evinced her trust for Vikas.

Both kept lying next to each other for God knows how long, with their fingers clasped together...losing count of minutes and hours.

It was about two o'clock in the night when they were conscious of the late hour. Vikas said, 'I'll be leaving now...'

'Why don't you sleep here? Go in the morning.'

'What shall I do sleeping here? You don't even let me make a mistake...!'

'Again...a mistake? What will you get out of it...regret, may be? Forget about everything and go to sleep....'

Sunidhi was very clear in her thoughts.

She came right up to the door to bid adieu to Vikas. He wasn't staying back. He had a great liking for her fingers and whenever she waved her hand to say 'bye', he used to get lost in them. When he returned to his room, he was still thinking about Sunidhi.

Vikas's dream was broken by the sound of the doorbell. He woke up and found the Masti channel still playing on the TV. He looked at his watch. It was six o'clock in the morning. He was in his room in the Gymkhana Club and Sunidhi was nowhere to be seen! He switched off the TV, came out in the lobby and sat in the sofa, holding the newspaper and the thermos flask of tea; the waiter had just left. His mind was still occupied by Sunidhi's thoughts. She wished to have a child from him, even without marriage, but wouldn't allow him to make love to her, even in a dream! It was the other way round for Vikas. He held high moral values in real life, but wished to sleep with her and make love in his dreams! He wondered at this strange dichotomy in his life and smiled. He was reminded of the gentle smile on the Buddha's face in the Ajanta cave.

Vikas sipped his tea reading the newspaper. It was Monday morning. He had already started thinking about his work schedule for the day. Soon, he was out in the lush green lawn, taking a leisurely walk and planning the day's activities. He walked there till the beautiful, bright rays of the sun surrounded his persona. He experienced a strange rustle within. He felt as if a new identity was taking birth inside him. A completely new person...addressing human relations with full objectivity. He remembered his last night's dream. Now, he felt that Sunidhi existed more inside his mind as an idea than a figure of flesh and blood. She looked even more beautiful in his imagination. This revelation was lending plenty of mental strength to him. He felt new layers of consciousness opening up inside him...layers which acted as mirrors and reflected images. One such image was that of Sunidhi's. A Sunidhi, whose permission was no longer required for making love with her. When an image penetrates so deeply into your heart, you attain the state of '*adwait*'. Sitting on the threshold of this wonderful state, Vikas penned down his emotions in the form of words and soon realized that he had created a poem! He read it a couple of times:

Hidden from the prying public eye,
Blooms a *semul* flower in wilderness;
When the inner dialogue opens its last window,
The *kalpavriksha* of many inert sagas,
Gets joggled by a mystical world;
Then words start gushing, meanings float,
Desires spring, causing a cosmic clamour;
Emotions get vocal like in a dream.
The heart drops dazed on your palms!
Then the *semul* cotton tells the pillow to
Come out of itself....it's time for the dawn...!

❖❖❖

36

As she woke up today, Sunidhi received a call from Niyati informing about her arrival by the evening train. She had since then been eagerly waiting to see her.

It was good that she has taken a flat on rent. She would have found it difficult to keep her childhood friend in the hostel. They were meeting today after a gap of fifteen years. So much had happened in her life since then. They'd have so much to talk about, which could last hours…!

It was Saturday and Sunidhi had left her office at three. These days, she cooked food at home. She had furnished her flat quite well and could easily accommodate a guest or two. She was receiving her first guest tonight and that too, a dear old friend!

It was evening. Sunidhi came out in the balcony and sat in a chair. She did it daily. Watching people and vehicles move around had become a favourite pastime. She looked at her watch. It was time for Niyati's train. She called her on the mobile. 'Hi, dear, I have arrived in your city…shall be there soon…!

'Come over and give me a call if there's a problem…' Once again, Sunidhi told her about a landmark near the house to easily locate it. She started strolling in the balcony itself. One thing she liked about metro cities was the non-intrusive nature of their inhabitants. Nobody really bothered to know who lived next door, what was the size of his family, his nature, his profession? It gave you a sense of freedom and privacy, though it entailed a complete alertness on your part as you would be virtually living alone. For simply this reason, she had once thought of keeping a like-minded partner in the house, but she didn't. It could have disturbed her studies and curbed her independence. And she was determined to complete her CA at the earliest.

Sunidhi's mind was never empty. She was always engaged in thoughts and as a result she was able to clear all the banking exams in a short time. She had not only earned four extra increments, but also made herself eligible for promotions.

Thinking about promotions, she was reminded of Vikas and suddenly realized that her heart was heavy. She had always cared more for his problems than her own. Then she thought about Niyati. She ought to have reached by now. She bent forward over the balcony-railing to look below. As she did that, the door-bell rang. She ran to open the door.

'I was looking down for you.'

'Must be somebody else in your mind', Niyati pulled her leg. They hugged each other. Niyati put her bag on the floor and said,

'How nice! We'll have a gala time.'

'Sure... I have been waiting since long.'

They were silent for a little while. Then Niyati went to the washroom. By the time she came out, Sunidhi had already made coffee.

'How nice...you made it so quickly! We could have made it together.'

'Take..' said Sunidhi, passing coffee to her.

'So...how are you, Sunidhi?'

'It's all right now...' said Sunidhi, lowering her eyes.

'All right, my foot... You are all alone till now...?'

'You know that... my marriage is almost ruined.'

'Why almost...? It's completely ruined. Nandini told me everything. But why haven't you thought about the next course of action?'

'Just like that…'

'It didn't click…or you didn't try? By the way, you are looking much prettier than before! But you should always remember, a woman's bloom is like that of a flower. The more beautiful it gets, the lesser it lasts. So, it's better to give your heart away before that.'

'But…'

'But…what? You haven't been able to find anyone? If you haven't, then you never will.'

'Let me complete my CA…'

'Damn your CA… it can happen even later.'

'Okay, I'll surely think about that. Tell me something about yourself…' said Sunidhi, trying to change the topic.

'Sunidhi, you know about my marriage. My father never wanted me to get married, in the first place. I was a milch cow… the bread-earner for the entire family. He was retired…both my brothers were good-for-nothing. Only Mom understood my condition. But she was too weak. She felt helpless before Dad and could never stand up against him. Our relatives and family friends suggested and brought in many matches for me, but Dad would always put them off.' Niyati's anguish was evident on her face.

'The world is like that…' said Sunidhi but she stopped short of criticizing her friend's father and saying anything.

'It's okay, Sunidhi, Nandini has told me everything about you. But I still feel that you should think of making a fresh start…' Sunidhi only nodded in agreement.

Niyati was very aggressive about her past. She wanted to blurt out everything. Sunidhi too was interested in listening.

'I found a boy on the net. But he turned out to be a total fraud. Soon I learnt that he wasn't doing much. He was a rogue, had an eye on my salary. So I became cautious…and soon got rid of him. But my people came to know about this. They felt scared… particularly Mom. She brought Dad around, but by then I had grown past the marriageable age. To begin with, I was never pretty like you....' Niyati suddenly stopped. There was a strange expression on her face.

'Then...?' Sunidhi couldn't help asking.

'Well...they fixed my marriage with a boy suggested by a distant relative...and somehow... I got married.' The dark and ugly shadow of this marriage could be seen so clearly on her face.

'But why didn't this one last?' Sunidhi's curiosity was at its peak. Nandini's warning to her to be careful resounded in her mind but Sunidhi couldn't stop. Nandini had turned sombre and Sunidhi hadn't had the courage to probe her any further. But tonight, Niyati was baring her heart to Sunidhi on her own and exposing all that Nandini had stopped short of saying.

'To tell you the truth, Sunidhi, if the marriage had lasted, I wouldn't have. He was a dangerous man. He had kept all of us in the dark. It was his second marriage. His first wife had left him feeling oppressed. He was a drunkard... and very short-tempered. He used to pocket all my salary every month. I wasn't able to send anything home and felt extremely sorry for that. It's disgusting even talking about him. Every day, he came home drunk and fought with me for money. He was foul-mouthed. He abused me if I reacted. Not only that...he even beat me black and blue. When he grew tired and knew that I was totally shattered...he forced me to have sex with him. Let's leave it there...it was like an awful dream. Thank god, I didn't have a child from him...' Niyati guzzled the coffee left in the cup. She had tears in her eyes.

'But I had learnt that you were living in a joint family...?' asked Sunidhi, hesitantly.

'Yes, it was a joint family. One day I shared my grief with my mother-in-law. I thought she would understand my problems, being a woman. Their house had very small rooms. Whatever you said in one room was easily heard in the adjoining one. He used to shout at me so loudly... beat me so badly… but nobody ever came to my help. On the other hand, my mother-in-law started advising me, 'He is like that only. You better learn to live with him…tolerate him… accept him as he is.'

The shadows of the night had already engulfed the evening. But both of them had been so engrossed in their talk that they had not even noticed it. Sunidhi rose and switched on the lights. When she looked at Niyati, she saw that her eyes were tearful. She sat down by her side, patted her on the back and said, 'Cool down Niyati…it's all behind you, now… you should forget about it…'

Sunidhi had said it coolly, but thinking about what Niyati had gone through, she felt shivers run down her spine. She had a weird feeling of relief that it hadn't been so bad in her case…that life had not been so cruel to her!

Niyati gathered herself and said, 'I was saved only because I didn't have a child from him.'

Niyati repeated her words with added emphasis. Sunidhi wondered how strange the ways of the Almighty were! Niyati was happy for not having had a child from her husband whereas Sunidhi yearned to have a child from her love. And both were right from their own perspectives.

Now Sunidhi didn't have the courage to ask Niyati anything about her life. Niyati's eyes were swollen. But still she wanted to further open up her heart. So Sunidhi deliberately avoided looking at the watch.

'Those days, Sunidhi, I would have swollen eyes like this. I had lost interest in work, food…everything. One day, James asked me in the office, 'Do you have any problem? You always look so stressed out.'

'I didn't want to tell him anything, but my eyes betrayed me. I couldn't restrain myself and told him everything.'

Sunidhi was listening with bated breath. Niyati continued,

'James didn't say anything that day. But he was in a rage. I had hardly known him but I could see there no guile in his conduct. Then one day he advised me to leave my husband. He only took me to a lawyer for legal advice. Then he met my husband along with the lawyer and police and forced him to divorce me. My husband took some time to agree but finally divorced me. I got rid of him with great difficulty. James came into my life like God...'

'When everything was over and I was a free girl, I proposed to James to marry me. He said, he'd talk to his mother and let me know...'

'Next day, he took me to meet his mother. They lived in a one-bedroom flat. His mother was very affectionate and liberal...she accepted me with all my gory past. We had a court marriage. He is a Christian and I am a Hindu...but there has never been a problem on that account. He celebrates Hindu festivals with full fervor. Yes, Sunidhi, he came into my life like God. I don't know what love is... but I take it as a triumph of human values over adversity.'

'Life is strange...Niyati. But now is everything fine?'

'Yes, everything is fine. I have a seven–year-old son. James' mother is even more loving than mine. My son is so sweet. I breathe in a free and fair environment...live like a free bird. James and his mother don't object to my freedom of movement. See, how I have come to you for two days. In fact, James also wanted to come, but Gaurav would have been left alone. Yes, Gaurav... James only gave him this name.'

Now Niyati seemed to be somewhat relaxed. She looked at her watch. It was past nine.

'Oh my God, I just forgot about our food. I had planned to cook something with you. I had brought everything we needed. But now, we'll go out. There's a very nice place here...Vaishali. We'll go eat there.' Niyati liked Sunidhi's proposal.

In a little while, they were at Vaishali. It was fully crowded because it was Saturday night. There were many couples with their kids. They waited for some time to get a table. Both of them were lost in thoughts. Sunidhi was thinking about herself after listening to Niyati's tale of woes. And Niyati thought that she had done well in sharing her tale of woes with a good friend. She now felt purged and light. After a long silence, she told Sunidhi, 'Think about yourself.'

Sunidhi gave her a smile and nodded.

Then they talked about Nandini. They both liked her immensely and felt highly excited and emotional discussing her bold lifestyle and carefree nature.

❖❖❖

37

In the last eight months, Vikas had worked extremely hard to set his office in order. He had motivated his staff to work with full dedication. The clients had started co-operating. In between, he visited Pune to meet his family. Even though he longed to meet Sunidhi, he always avoided doing so. She too never pressed for it.

Now, Vikas had started developing a favourable disposition towards Aurangabad. He had realized that there were good and bad people everywhere. But if you were clean and led them by your own example, you always achieved results. His integrity came in handy. His region had started showing profits. As the Chairman had written it off and never really bothered about it, Vikas got the freedom to work without any pressure and interference.

One day, he received a call from Saumya. She was the one who had once been appointed by him as PRO in his office. She was middle-aged plain looking lady with a daughter; however she had a wonderful personality. What impressed Vikas most was her jovial nature and her free and frank behaviour.

He remembered when she had come to see him in response to an advertisement for the post of PRO. At that time, she was working as a clerk in a government office. It was a permanent job, but it didn't interest her. She found it too mundane and without any challenge. Moreover, it didn't promise any future. Vikas remembered how talkative she was. Even without any provocation on his part she had told him everything about herself.

'My father left us when I was a kid. We belong to a South Indian family. We don't have any relatives in the town. When we moved in here, we came in contact with a Marwari living next door and I was hurriedly married to him. I had hoped to study further, but everything came to a halt. Then I got the job of a clerk in a government office. It was close to our house. So they allowed me to accept the offer. I have been working there since. When I saw your advertisement, I thought it would be a good change for me.'

Vikas had advised her to apply for the post.

'Hello, Vikas ji…?'

'Speaking...'

'Saumya here…!'

'Oh, Saumya, heard from you after such a long time. I thought you had forgotten me!' Vikas was being formal.

'I can never forget you in my life.'

'Why, what have I done...?' Vikas replied casually.

'I'll tell you later…first you tell me if you are properly settled there? Hope the chairman is not troubling you now! How's the staff? But you are an expert in handling people…are you alone or with family…or…?' She had a hearty laugh and stopped.

'They have wrongly named you Saumya…it should have been Mrs Unstoppable. You have asked me so many questions, all at one go! You haven't changed at all.'

'How can one change at this age…and why pray?'

'That's well said. Why change? How is your daughter? Must be a grown up girl now?

'Grown up? She has taken the exams for XIth grade. She's a big girl now. You wouldn't recognize her if you saw her…so big.'

'That sounds good! You must educate her well. Let her do all that you couldn't do.'

Vikas knew that Saumya's daughter was a bright student. Her father wasn't too inclined to educate her much. But Soumya wished to continue with her studies. So he once spoke to her husband and advised him to let his daughter receive good education. He had fortunately agreed to Vikas's advice.

Saumya was fond of Vikas. She always talked to him very plainly. She was even aware of his relationship with Sunidhi. But she didn't look at it the way other people did, though she liked to tease him about it, once in a while. She enjoyed watching Vikas blush in embarrassment. Talking about her daughter, Soumya told Vikas,

'She says I'm scared of going in front of Vikas uncle.'

'But why? Do I look so terrible…?'

'She says you can read a person's mind when he comes in front of you…that's why she is scared of coming before you.'

'Well, even if I can do that…why feel scared?'

'You can ask her…and for that you'll have to come to our house. When you come here next time, do visit us…'

'Sure…'

'Okay…then. See you later.' So saying, she disconnected the phone.

Vikas put the phone down and started thinking how garrulous Saumya was. And how pure at heart! She never tried to conceal anything and always wore her heart on her sleeve. Humour and candour were her assets. That's what he liked about her. Such qualities made you a good marketing person. It was basically for these qualities that Vikas had requested the interview committee to include her in his marketing team.

Once appointed, Saumya had soon carved a place for herself in the office. Her good work showed up and Vikas was happy for having put a competent person in a place she rightfully deserved.

One day Saumya was about to leave his cabin after completing her work when Vikas's mobile phone rang. He looked at the number flashing on the mobile and then at Saumya. Out of decency, she asked him, ‘May I leave?’

Vikas was confused for a moment but signalled her to stay. So, she sat there and watched Vikas’s expressions while he talked on phone, only in monosyllables. She was smart enough to guess whose call it could be and Vikas too had sensed that she had guessed who the caller was. Saumya had smiled for a moment and lowered her gaze, but while doing so she had noticed Vikas biting his lips. None of them talked about it. Vikas had always believed that all relations must be kept shrouded under a fine veil. Silence reigned for a while.

‘May I ask something?’ Saumya had finally broken the ice.

‘Sure…’ Vikas realised she would ask something concerned with the office.

‘It’s not about the office. Take it as a personal question…’

‘What’s it?’ asked Vikas looking at his watch.

‘I don’t know how you will take it…but I’m sure, you’ll not mind it.’ Saumya was trying to build firm ground before broaching the subject.

‘Such a long introduction?’

‘Yes, it’s required…’

‘Okay, ask…whatever you want to ask’ said Vikas as if he had sensed that Saumya was probably going to ask something about Sunidhi. Very few rumour mongers in office circles had the courage to directly bring up the topic. But Saumya had guts! She was very outspoken and could have asked anything. And nobody could tell her a lie. So Vikas was also ready, by now.

‘What according to you is love?’ she asked very softly.

‘I didn’t quite understand, sorry!’ Vikas mumbled in a perplexed voice.

‘There’s nothing to understand. I am not asking about anybody specifically…generally what do you think it is?’

'I haven't thought about it much, but love would mean caring, security… from someone or someone's emotional security.'

'Not romance?' was Saumya's next question.

'Romance is the beginning. It's superficial. You have to go beyond it to…' he broke off mid sentence.

'But Saumya… why did you ask me this question today? Anyhow, I have told you what I feel. Now you tell me, what do you have to say?' Vikas redirected her question back to her.

'What can I say…life has never given me the opportunity to know what love is. When I came of age, I was already knee-deep in responsibilities…and what could you expect from this Marwari… love for him was just profit and loss… day in and day out. I wasted my life in this rigmarole only… never developed any feelings for any finer things in life… and now there is no chance at all…!' Saumya had stated her position very emotionally.

'Well…I hadn't asked about your personal life…like you didn't ask about mine. I just wanted to know your views.' Vikas was trying to bring the situation back to normal. He had realized that Saumya was really distraught while talking about love.

Saumya brooded for a while and responded–

'Actually when a friendship starts growing intense, it turns into love. Then, even if it crosses the threshold of the body, it shouldn't really matter. Because true love is boundless, it doesn't entertain any conditions and doesn't impose any restrictions.

'Your thoughts are too deep and strong like you…but your experience has been so arid…why so?'

'Because this realization dawned upon me only when I had already lost everything. Such emotions had absolutely no place in the calculus of my Marwari. I may sound very open and modern to you, but I am fully aware of the limitations of a marriage and I have full regard for them. Many times these are against my philosophy and my desires, but it doesn't matter, this alone is the safe and dependable option in the long race that life offers. That kind of love was not in store for me…but it doesn't matter…everyone is not entitled to everything in life.' Saumya spoke like a philosopher.

Vikas had realized that there was still a sensitive heart inside Saumya's seemingly superficial façade…even though she had long ago mortgaged and left it behind to move forward in life. She had only told him once that she fully understood her responsibility towards her family. She had had a rebel inside her, even resentment…but now she also nurtured a strong desire to live a decent life. Now she didn't want to cause any hurt to a husband, who had, in their earlier days, helped her family to come out of their financial crisis.

Vikas was now convinced that Saumya's parents had given her an apt name. She was so cool, tolerant and caring about her family and believed in following traditions. At the same time, she had a person inside her who was modern, skillful and polished.

Vikas had a lot of respect for Saumya. He was happy to have received a call from her. He wished to meet her next time he visited her town… finally he got busy at work.

❖❖❖

38

It had been raining the whole day, today. Vikas listened to ghazals sung by Jagjit Singh. These days, he didn't like watching TV as much as he liked listening to the radio or playing CDs. He had always been fond of Jagjit Singh's singing. It had an uncanny quality which lifted your spirits and transported you to an altogether different world. His all-time favourite number was *Woh kaaghaz ki kashti...woh baarish ka paani....* He wondered at the power of imagination! The soft rhythmic sound of raindrops fell on the thatched roof of his balcony adding to the romance of the evening. He increased the volume of the CD player and came out in the balcony.

This residential accommodation had been given to him by the bank. It was situated in highly idyllic surroundings. Sitting in the balcony, you could have a wonderful view of lovely woods, spread as far as you could see. He lived here all alone. It was Saturday evening. Today, the woods weren't fully visible from the balcony. A thick white blanket of hailstorm had shrouded everything around. The winds lay quiet and resting. It looked like white pearls were falling from the sky with a rustle... absolutely fine, flashing pearls...producing an enchanting rustle! Vikas went inside the room to make a drink for himself. He wasn't a regular drinker. Black Label was his favourite brand. He poured the drink and brought it out in the balcony.

As he sipped his drink, he felt it had also been raining inside his soul. He tried to look across the white veil of the raindrops and felt he had seen a familiar figure in the far off woods. It was beckoning him to come towards it...! He shook his head and whispered, 'No, it's not possible.' He had just taken a few sips of his drink. Then was it an illusion? He couldn't believe his eyes. He took a few more sips and felt that figure had now put on eyes and lips and cheeks and smiles and was talking to him. But the sound of the raindrops came between that voice and his ears, though he had by now recognized the figure. It was none other than Sunidhi.

For quite a long time, Vikas and Sunidhi had been thinking of undertaking a long rail journey together. So they decided to go to Shimla. Rail tickets were booked from Delhi to Chandigarh. From there, they had to travel by road. Vikas had taken a flight to Delhi from Aurangabad and Sunidhi from Pune. They met at Delhi railway station at the appointed time. They were travelling to Chandigarh by the Shatabdi Express. It was a pleasant journey of four hours. They decided to first occupy their respective seats and then move together by requesting a co-passenger to exchange a seat. They had intentionally not booked the tickets together.

When they reached the station, they were surprised to see that their reservation was in the same compartment. They entered and discovered that even their seats were together. How was such a coincidence possible? They were completely taken aback. At the same time, they felt extremely happy. Smiling, they looked at each other and wondered at this strange coincidence and stroke of luck. Soon the train left the station. It was truly a pleasant journey. If you looked out of the window, you could see endless stretches of lush green fields spread on both sides of the track. It appeared to be quite windy. Moreover, it had started to rain. The crops in the fields seemed to be dancing in glee. Inside the train, Vikas was looking at Sunidhi's beautiful feet. It was a winter morning. The passengers had woken up rather early to catch the train. Most of them had already gone to sleep. Those who were awake were busy reading the newspaper. Vikas and Sunidhi had no sleep in their eyes. And how and why could they be reading a newspaper in such a romantic setting? They were still quietly wondering at this beautiful coincidence, which had made them sit together. The compartment was absolutely full. Yet, they had a strange feeling of isolation. There were so many people around them, but all were strangers. There was not even a single familiar face. They really felt isolated. They were absolutely quiet but a dialogue unfolded inside. They didn't utter a word, but they both heard so much being said! On top of that, there was this strange coincidence. God was really great!

Then something weird happened. Both of them got up from their seats, went out of the compartment and stood near the door. Probably the AC inside was too cold. It felt so much better outside. They opened the door. A wet draught of wind blew into the bogey and almost drenched them. They instantly hugged each other. There was an awesome view outside... twinkling drops of drizzling rain gently showered their love on the green leaves. It was pure romance, inside their hearts reciprocated outside in nature.

The measured sound churned out by the wheels of the speeding train seemed to echo the feelings of their heart, to say, 'How beautiful it is!' Yes, it was really beautiful for Vikas because Sunidhi was there! When they had come out of the compartment, they had held the steel bars on their respective sides for support but, Vikas didn't know when he had left the one on his side and clung on to the one held by Sunidhi, that too just over her hand! Sunidhi was thrilled for a moment. She felt as if the drizzle had changed its direction with the wind. But she soon realized that it wasn't the cold drizzle, but the warm energy emanating from Vikas's palms, which had caused the thrill.

Suddenly they both felt that someone was standing behind them. So they turned back to see, but there was nobody. Vikas had lifted his hand from the bar. A gush of heavy rain entered the bogey and almost drenched them again. They moved behind, closed the door and returned to their seats. They were lost in thoughts and quiet. Only their eyes conversed with each other's...conveyed what they felt in their hearts...and indulged in an unending dialogue.

After a little while, Vikas realized that he was holding Sunidhi's hand in his and their fingers had almost fused. A queer energy oozed out of their palms. They felt as if something in their hands had started to burn and melt. The lines in their hands were possibly dissolving!

Sunidhi used to claim that she professed a sound knowledge of palmistry. So she held Vikas's hand in hers and started reading it seriously. She reflected on each and every line and then softly murmured something. Then she stared at him with her big, beautiful eyes and carried out some calculations inside her mind. As for Vikas, he felt extremely honored in placing his fate in her hands, like an open book. He had absolutely no anxiety to know his future. He was immensely happy with the present moment. Sunidhi placed her hand along with Vikas's and out of sheer curiosity started comparing the lines in both hands. She was pleasantly surprised to note that they appeared very similar. But it held no surprise for Vikas. He knew that they had to be similar because they had just been cast by the energy jointly generated by their palms.

They were engaged in this mute discourse endlessly. The train moved fast, but time had come to a halt for them. Vikas felt something touching his feet. He bent forward to check and found that it was Sunidhi's foot. He didn't say anything…neither did Sunidhi shift her foot. Vikas glanced at her. She probably wanted to apologise but before she could, Vikas conveyed his acceptance and possibly…pleasure. Sunidhi blushed and drowned her face in the cusp of her hands. Hiding her crimson cheeks with her hands, she glanced at Vikas through the gaps between her long nimble fingers. It seemed to Vikas as if the sun was peeping out at the damp earth through small fissures in the clouds after a spell of heavy rain. Sunshine after the rains always feels pleasant. He felt similar joy simply looking at the beautiful eyes peeping through the fingers. His head buzzed and swayed with pleasure…. And Sunidhi's eyes beckoned and spoke– watching covertly could never be enough.

The train moved at a thunderous speed, piercing through the clouds. Vikas could actually feel the clouds entering the train. Nothing was visible. He wanted to extend his hands to grope in the dark. But no…! His hand hit the glass. He picked it up to see what it was. There were no clouds. Nor was Sunidhi around. Outside the balcony, it still poured heavily.

Vikas had finished his second drink.

❖❖❖

39

Today, the phone had been constantly ringing since early morning. Preeti would normally call at about seven. Vikas was normally up by that time. But today when she called, Vikas noticed it was already 7.30 am. He picked up the phone.

'Had your tea?' asked Preeti.

'No…woke up late today', answered Vikas, yawning.

'Why…what happened? Another late night party…? Well, it's good to promote your business, but not at the cost of your health. Are you feeling alright?' Preeti wasn't giving Vikas any chance to say anything.

'No…I am fine?'

'No? Why did you say no…in the beginning?

'No, my dear…everything is fine. Don't you worry.'

His mobile had started ringing.

'I'll call you later….' Vikas had already connected the call on his mobile. Preeti always preferred to call him on the landline. She had a reason for doing so. On the mobile, you never knew where the person was… and whether it was convenient for him to take your call or not.

Vikas had finished talking on the mobile. It was a call from a 'valued customer'. He wanted his credit limit to be increased. He claimed to know the Chairman very closely and did good business. The bank benefitted from his account. Even otherwise, he had never caused any embarrassment for Vikas. The only complaint about him was that he always called Vikas on the mobile. But his manners and his way of talking were so nice that Vikas didn't like to put him off. Apart from business matters, he also always enquired about the well-being of Vikas's family. Although he had never met Preeti and Garima, yet he always asked about them by name. He addressed Garima as his own daughter.

As Vikas put the mobile phone down, he realized that today he had forgotten to ask Preeti about Garima. Then he decided to first have a cup of tea as he was feeling a bit out of sorts. It had been a strange night, last night. All those memories and...he had probably taken an extra drink. He wasn't used to it. But it was all right. He didn't mind taking a little liberty once a while. Now, he wouldn't touch a drink for a few days.

Vikas had kept a tea-maker at home. He was fond of 'dip-dip' tea-bag tea. While he was making tea, the phone started ringing again. He noticed who it was from. It was Kulkarni, a trade union leader. Vikas had saved his number in his phone. For a moment, he wondered whether he should ignore the call. On second thoughts, he picked it up. There was no problem. Kulkarni was talking about the transfer of an officer. Vikas had made a policy not to pick up any quarrel with the union guys. They were the ones who generally generated and propagated rumours and controversies about officers. He knew how to handle them tactfully. But receiving their calls in the early hours of the morning usually spoiled your day. Then there was no respite from the phone calls and he couldn't talk to Garima. He thought of calling her several times but there were the milkman and the newspaper-wala, and then the house-maid and the whole lot of morning chores. He couldn't call Garima. Then the driver arrived. The files lay on the table in an unopened bundle. Today, the driver was saved of the hassle of collecting papers and arranging the files, as he did every day. So he picked up the bundle of files and the briefcase and went out.

It was probably the first time that Vikas had not cleared the files he had brought home. It disturbed him. He looked at his watch. It was nine o'clock. He wanted to rush to the bathroom when the phone rang again. He first thought of ignoring it but he was curious to know who it was.

It was Sunidhi. He immediately picked the call.

'Hello…' Sunidhi appeared to be quite excited.

How sweet was her voice! All his giddyness was gone. He felt light and fresh. The irritation caused by the constant ringing of the phone, the pain of having to attend unwanted calls, the paucity of time at his disposal, everything was behind him.

'Hi…' He answered with equal excitement.

'A great and good news…!'

'Tell me fast!' He was genuinely curious.

'Don't rush…I want you to make a guess…tell me what could it be...come on,' said Sunidhi, playfully.

'Your brother's got a job?'

'That can't be such great news. That would just be news.'

'…Er…your sister's marriage…?'

'Wrong!' Sunidhi exclaimed and realized that it wouldn't probably be possible for Vikas to guess what the news could be.

Vikas guessed that it could be the finalization of her divorce case in the court. But he didn't want to say it. It wasn't a comfortable subject for Sunidhi. So he was confused.

'Now tell me… don't pose riddles…'

'Lost it? You'll be stunned to hear it.

'Now, it's getting too much, Sunidhi. Okay, I've lost it… Even otherwise, now it's your time to win and shine in life. I just keep waiting to hear good news from you.'

Sunidhi also realized the gravity of the matter and felt that she was unnecessarily troubling Vikas. She didn't know where he was and in what condition. He could have been busy…or in a thick soup. However, she brushed aside these thoughts and happily resumed her talk.

'Will need a grand party,'

'Agreed', committed Vikas, even without knowing what it was.

'I have cleared my CA!' Sunidhi's happiness knew no bounds. It was obvious from the way she spoke. Vikas too was extremely happy. He had, for a long time now, been advising her to take up further studies. She had listened to him and acted upon his advice. She had achieved what even he had tried but failed.

'I am so proud of you, Sunidhi. You are really great. Now nobody can stop you from achieving your dreams. Your determination and hard work have yielded results.'

'.....'

'What happened? Why are you not saying anything? Are you there...!' Vikas felt that Sunidhi had become serious. He could hear her heaving...even feel it. It seemed like her voice had choked... she was unable to speak. Past sorrows often cloud over happy moments, even when it's raining joys.

'Come on, Sunidhi... you have done it. You have won over the hard times. Why are you not saying anything? Hope you are listening!'

'Yes, I am listening. I have broken this news to you first.'

'I know...I should have been there with you, today...'

'You are there with me. You just turn around and... you'll see me there, right in front of you. You are always there with me.' Sunidhi said it all in one breath. Vikas knew how deep her love for him was. Lightly, he said,

'Will you come to Aurangabad to treat me or should I come over to you?'

'If I go there, you'll waste all your time in blushing. You think I don't know you? Moreover, you'll have to throw the party. It's your success; I had merely taken the exams.' Sunidhi had regained her excitement.

'All right...as you say. I'll be there. Congratulations once again.' The conversation was drawing to its natural end.

'I'll not say thanks...I'll wait for you. Bye...' Sunidhi disconnected the phone.

Vikas realized that Sunidhi possessed an indomitable spirit, ability and sharpness. She had scored a victory even under the most adverse circumstances. He had himself wished to do CA. But he always missed it by a few marks.

Vikas's trust in Sunidhi had grown triplefold. Her presence, her feelings, her way of talking and her sensibility possessed his heart. He neither had his breakfast nor got ready to go. He continued to sit and bask in the glory of the emotional togetherness they shared last night. His reveries were broken only by the doorbell. He walked up to the door to open it.

'Uff...' he exclaimed, upon finding the driver waiting there. He looked at his watch. It was 9.45 am.

The driver saw that Vikas wasn't ready yet. Politely he asked, 'Sir, are we going somewhere else?

'No... you just wait downstairs... I'll be there soon.' The driver started climbing down the stairs.

Come what may, Vikas used to generally leave for office at a quarter past nine. Today, he was already half an hour late and he wasn't ready yet. If he ever left late, it was only when he had an appointment to visit some other branch. But all rules had been broken today.

When success opens its doors on you, joy takes up a large chunk of your time. Such time generally belongs to the intimate ones. Everyone has to prepare himself for such a time. When it comes, everything else gets deferred.

Vikas was overwhelmed by Sunidhi's success. Then he paused for a moment to really decipher whether it was Sunidhi or her success.... He felt it was both.

❖❖❖

40

Sunidhi had shared the news of her clearing the CA only with Vikas. She hadn't talked about it with anyone in the bank. She knew it wouldn't make them happy. It would rather cause heartburn and make them jealous and envious...and provide them a fresh opportunity to censure her again for her unsuccessful marriage. At a very young age, Sunidhi had realized that people were always keen to express their consolation on your failures, even when they didn't have any sympathies with you, but they invariably felt grieved at your success. It wasn't easy for them to digest it. They always indulged in nit-picking your failures to down-play your success and achievements. Sunidhi knew she had to go a long way. So she hadn't spoken about this with anyone.

One day, Sujay Kumar, the branch manager called Sunidhi on the intercom and asked her to come to his cabin and meet him at around four. He was a gentleman and a successful and popular manager. Normally, he didn't call anyone in his cabin but issued directions through the intercom. He would even come out to discuss important matters with the staff. He called for staff-meetings only when unavoidable. Today, going against his usual practice, he had called Sunidhi to come into his cabin. Sunidhi wondered what the matter could be!

The manager's cabin had glass walls. Whatever was discussed in it couldn't be heard outside, whereas anybody sitting outside could see what was going on there. The banking hours were already over. The staff was busy finishing their work, mostly on their computers. Some even chatted with each other. When Sunidhi entered the manager's cabin, it caused quite a flutter in the office.

'Congratulations...' said Sujay Kumar to Sunidhi, as she entered the cabin.

'For what, sir?' asked Sunidhi, surprised.

'You think, if you don't tell us, we wouldn't know...?'

Sujay Kumar, beckoned her to take a seat. He opened a magazine he was already holding in his hands. It was *Bharat Jyoti*, the house journal of the bank. He forwarded it towards Sunidhi.

'I have just now received this copy from the head office. I was flipping its pages, when I noticed the name of our branch mentioned on the top of a page. Instantly, I went through the full news. Accept my congrats on your clearing the CA.'

Sunidhi took the magazine from Sujay Kumar and wondered who could have got it published or informed them about it? Vikas? Yes, it had to be Vikas. She read the news, looked up at Sujay Kumar and reciprocated with a simple, 'Thanks!'

'Mere thanks won't do...you'll have to throw a party...' said Sujay very innocently.

'Sure, sir...' Sunidhi felt Sujay Kumar resembled Vikas in many ways. He shared many of his traits.

'It's a big achievement, Sunidhi...it will not only help you keep pace and personally grow in service, but also be an asset for the bank ...keep it up!'

Sunidhi accepted the genuine appreciation with humility. Then she saw all her colleagues entering the cabin. Sujay Kumar had asked them to come. He broke the news to the staff and felicitated Sunidhi by presenting her a book titled, 'Seven Secrets of Success'. He always kept some books and pens with him for gifting.

By the time the staff had finished greeting Sunidhi, it was already late afternoon. She left office a little early that day. Around seven thirty, she rang up Vikas.

'You sent the news about my CA to *Bharat Jyoti*?'

'Yes. People should know who you are and what you have achieved...'

'But you should have informed me, at least...' Sunidhi spoke without any intent. She could overhear some people talking to Vikas.

'Are you busy....?' asked Sunidhi.

'Yes. I am in a meeting with branch managers...'

'Okay, I'll call you later...take care.' Sunidhi disconnected the phone.

Next day, everybody in the bank knew about Sunidhi's achievement. She ordered coffee and samosas for all. They congratulated her once again. But their outlook towards her seemed to have changed already. A CA working in a bank was considered special. During lunch break, many of her old associates didn't feel comfortable in talking to her. Several of them seemed to have suddenly developed a strange sense of respect for her. Some of them had already turned jealous. Many others had started planting rumours. Sunidhi had expected all this. But it pained her to see it actually happen. Sometimes, even an achievement in life became a burden for you. But it was all a part of the game.

Sunidhi had, many times, wondered whether it was the deadly charm of her beautiful body or her intellectual acumen which played a major role in the journey of her life. If she ever placed more credence on her efficiency and skills, she soon realized that she owed her success more to her physical charms. Yet, for the development of her personality, she liked to give equal importance to both. But she was fully aware of the fact that in a society dominated by males, a woman's physical charms did open up many possibilities for her.

Sunidhi had, by now, become quite an expert at handling any kind of tricky situation. She could easily see through the greed of elderly men in the corporate sector and foil the tricks played by them in order to throw their weight around. Her efficiency, knowledge and wisdom had strengthened her self-confidence. If she ever feared anything, it was the fear of her underestimating the slipperiness of the moss she was treading upon, though she treaded very cautiously. She could differentiate between the entreaties of Rama and Ravana.

Sunidhi received many phone calls and letters congratulating her. Even the regional manager, who had replaced Vikas sent his greetings and the HR in the head office sent her a letter. She shared all these developments with Vikas. He would tell her, 'It's all due to the news in the bank journal. The promotion season is very close. This news will definitely help you in that segment.'

Sunidhi always believed that Vikas had a great contribution in bringing her to the level where she presently was. He had instilled confidence in her which not only helped her achieve success in life but also resolve her personal problems. But for him, she wouldn't have sailed through the strong currents in the stream...she wouldn't have known where the swamps were...she wouldn't have scaled lofty heights...she wouldn't have even thought of taking divorce. Vikas had acted as her true friend, advisor and mentor. He had taught her to act with reason and behave sensibly... enabled her to take her decisions. Hence, whenever she sent him a greeting card, she addressed him as, 'My dear friend, philosopher and guide Vikas...'

In just three years, Sunidhi was promoted as a manager. When Vikas congratulated her, she told him that it was all because of him. But she also said that she would have felt happier if it had been his promotion.

And it was not just a formality.

One day Sunidhi called Vikas to tell him that the court had finally accepted her divorce. Her voice was totally objective. It was a very important event of her life, but both were silent on it. Sunidhi coolly conveyed the information and Vikas quietly listened. Both spent some moments in silence. A conversation took place inside them. It was another landmark in Sunidhi's mute journey.

❖❖❖

41

Sunidhi's promotion and her CA success were indications enough that she now deserved a better charge than just a branch. She also felt that she needed a bigger canvas to work on. A normal comment made by her regional manager at their last meeting was resounding in her ears, 'Sunidhi, you should now be ready for higher responsibilities.'

The new regional manager, Ajay Bhattacharya had just been promoted. He had taken over from Pradeep Shukla who had replaced Vikas. Shukla couldn't work in the region even for a year. There were numerous complaints against him, from the customers as well as the union. On the chairman's backing, he indulged in a lot of illegal actions for loan recoveries. But when things started going wrong, the chairman quietly withdrew himself and Shukla was left in the lurch. He was transferred to the training college and an inquiry was instituted against him. Even though there was no direct charge against the chairman, everybody knew that Shukla was working at his beck and call. Basking in the glory of the chairman's protection, Shukla had gone overboard and landed himself in trouble.

Amar Kumar, the mastermind in all these cases couldn't be caught on papers, but his involvement in these cases was an open secret. He had, in fact, played key role in pushing Shukla into this mess. But people in the office had no soft corner for Shukla either. He was not a child to have been misled by Amar Kumar. Besides, he had thrown all rules and regulations to the wind to satisfy his greed and mint money for the chairman and himself. He had badly vitiated the office atmosphere. There was fear and mistrust all around. The chairman had so far used

Shukla as a pawn to make money; now he used him as a scapegoat to save his own skin.

Sitting in front of Ajay Bhattacharya, Sunidhi recalled that it was the same cabin, the same set of books and shields on the shelf, the same table and chairs…! All these things had left a permanent imprint on her mind. They had become an eternal part of her memory, because it was here that she had written her joining report. Then, Vikas had bid her farewell from this very office. She could never forget the day when she was feeling utterly helpless but Vikas had held her hand, shown her a ray of hope and filled her with fresh energy and inspiration to live. He taught her so many things and gave her the self-confidence she lacked so badly.

'Welcome on your posting' said Ajay Bhattacharya, putting the phone down.

'Thank you, sir!' replied Sunidhi, feelingly.

'Actually Sunidhi, this office will have to be raised from scratch. You'll have to look after recovery along with accounts. You are a CA, you can handle both the departments well. And you have been posted here before. You understand the working of this office much better than others.' Ajay Bhattacharya was trying to solicit maximum cooperation from Sunidhi.

Sunidhi carefully listened to Ajay Bhattacharya. She could make out that there was sincerity in his voice. She watched him intently. She had met a genuinely good person after a long time. She noticed that he was in his forties, but showed grey in his sideburns. And he had not tried to hide it by dyeing. Bulgarian beard, straight hair parted in the middle, sharp eyes behind thick glasses, confident voice, measured speech, white shirt… extremely natural movement of hands while talking…no ring on any finger… this one was very special for Sunidhi as she had seen all executives wear a ring or two. She liked Ajay Bhattacharya's personality.

Ajay Bhattacharya thoroughly briefed her about her work. He even hinted that she might have to put in an extra effort to improve the work culture of the office. Sunidhi nodded in agreement and came out.

Sunidhi noticed that many things had changed in this office, since she had left. Barring a few clerks, the entire staff was new. Even Amar Kumar had been transferred. The Shukla episode had totally unnerved him. The chairman had also abandoned him. Ajay Bhattacharya took advantage of this situation and quickly got him posted out.

In a few days, Sunidhi was in full control of the office. Some employees, particularly female employees, who had earlier worked with her were still there. They had been making fun of her and taunting her about her alleged relations with Vikas. Now, they were all scared of Sunidhi. She had acquired tremendous self-confidence.

Interviews for departmental promotions were to be held in Sunidhi's office. She had been made the 'in-charge' of this work. She was supposed to make all arrangements. Some senior officers were coming from the head office to conduct the interviews.

All of those to be interviewed were junior officers. Most of them were extremely nervous. However, there was one, tall, slim, jovial and fearless Pankaj Bhatt in a check shirt and jeans, who didn't seem to be under any pressure.. Whenever somebody came out of the interview chamber, others asked him about the kind of questions that were being asked. But Pankaj Bhatt was totally unconcerned. The door of Sunidhi's cabin was open. She was holding all the files of the candidates to be interviewed and sent them in, one-by-one. Pankaj Bhatt constantly strolled in front of Sunidhi's cabin, peeping inside every time he passed in front of it. Her sixth sense gave her some signals about him.

When he was called for interview, Bhatt stopped in front of Sunidhi, stared at her, wished her good morning and went inside. He was soon out of the interview room. There was absolutely no tension on his face. He thanked Sunidhi and asked her which office she was posted in. He also asked her name. He then took a can of coffee and began drinking freely, without a care in this world. After about a month, Pankaj Bhatt stood in front of Sunidhi. He had been promoted and posted in a rural branch away from the city. He had brought her a box of sweets.

'Just a piece will do…give it to the others too', said Sunidhi.

'This is for you. It's not much…' said Pankaj placing the box on her table. Sunidhi thanked him. He expressed his desire to meet the RM. Probably he had some more boxes in his bag. He went inside and came out soon. This time, he sat down in front of Sunidhi and started talking to her.

'Ma'am, I have been posted in a far off village…please do something for me'.

'You should talk to the HR.' With a gesture of her eyes, Sunidhi pointed towards the HR's table. She wanted to get rid of him.

'I'll speak to him as well…but I know that if you talk about me to the RM, my job will be done.'

Sunidhi told him straightaway that she couldn't do much in this matter, but he was still insistent. 'Still…' he said and took her leave. While going out he looked at Sunidhi with eyes that seemed to pierce deep inside her. She noticed that he hadn't stopped to meet the HR, but turned back to look at her once again before he left the office.

After he had left, Sunidhi for a moment thought that it could be wonderful to live with a man like him…same age, overflowing with confidence and energy, free and frank… impressive personality, nice gait. No…no, she got scared of herself. It was for the first time after her divorce that Sunidhi had felt the need for a life-partner. All this time, her mind had been preoccupied by worries, Vikas, the CA exam and promotions. She gave herself a jerk and tried to focus her attention on an advertisement published in the *Times of India*, for the post of 'Senior Executive'. It had a special mention of priority being given to those possessing a CA degree!

Was this advertisement just for Sunidhi?

❖❖❖

42

'Portico' was a very nice hotel on the outskirts of the city. It was also a favourite joint of Vikas and Sunidhi. It was here that they had first met. She had almost broken down narrating the tale of her woes and felt very light and relieved thereafter! It was here that he had, many times, inspired her to bravely face the challenges of life and keep moving ahead. Portico was witness to the budding idea of Sunidhi pursuing CA; and also the proposal gradually taking roots. It was here that Vikas had given her a lot of reading material useful for CA. And here that she sat today, waiting to meet Vikas after a long time.

It was already half an hour past the time fixed for their meeting, but Vikas was nowhere in sight. She wondered what could have happened. He was always very punctual. For a moment she thought of calling him up on his mobile, but she didn't. The waiter had already approached her a couple of times to note down her orders. It was a relatively quiet place to meet. It had a beautiful garden and idyllic settings. It played Jagjit Singh's *ghazal*s in the background. But Sunidhi grew restive. The long wait made her anxious and impatient. Then she recalled that Vikas was visiting his family after a fairly long time and could, therefore, have been held up at home. Then she got lost in the lyric, '*Tum itna jo muskura rahe ho…*'

Suddenly Sunidhi felt there was somebody standing in front of her. She looked up and saw…Vikas. She stood up immediately. For a moment she was absolutely nonplussed. She didn't know how to receive him. Should she shake hands or greet him folding them? Then she quietly extended her hand towards him.

'Sorry, I got late', said Vikas. For a moment, he stood there spellbound...lost in the marvellous sight of Sunidhi rising in her seat, looking startled and then offering her hand to him. In his imagination, her beautiful shapely body had sprung out of the chair like a beautiful gazelle, an antelope. He had experienced this feeling after a long time!

They settled in chairs facing each other.

For a long time, they just kept looking at each other, without uttering a word. The background music played another Jagjit Singh number, '*Pyaar ka pehla khat likhne mein vaqt to lagta hai...*' (It takes time to pen down the first love-letter). They both listened to it very intently...reflecting on its beautiful lyrics. It wasn't their first meeting. Nor had they greeted each other for the first time. Yet, this number deeply touched their hearts. It felt fresh like the sweet musty scent of the soil with the first rain of the season.

'Isn't it beautiful...!' remarked Sunidhi.

'Yes, it's very beautiful... and Jagjit Singh's soulful voice makes it really grand', replied Vikas, still looking at Sunidhi like he had never seen her before.

Overwhelmed by his loving gaze, Sunidhi blushed and lowered her eyes. She felt completely fulfilled and asked Vikas,

'The lyricist has probably penned down his own experience of writing this letter...?'

'I don't' know. But do you know who the poet is?'

'No!'

'It's Hasti Mal Hasti...,' said Vikas.

Sitting in the sprawling lawns of Portico, no other couple would have indulged in conversation such as this. The shrubs around the lawn had been dimly lit up with colourful lights which flickered like the glow-worms. The background music added to the romance. All guests were lost in their own world.

Carrying his pad and pen, the waiter came up to their table once again to take the order. He looked at Sunidhi, as she had come before Vikas. Even otherwise, if a man and a woman sat in front of you, you would always tend to first look at the woman. Sunidhi was quick to place the order.

'Give us a clear soup first...one by two...'. Then she looked at Vikas to confirm, 'Is that all right?'

'Sure, it's fine...', Vikas was glad to see Sunidhi taking the lead. Now she appeared to be absolutely fit to hold command. In their earlier days, she used to be very shy and reluctant to place an order in a hotel. She went through the menu, when Vikas said,

'Keep the menu card aside...to begin with, please accept my congratulations. I am not sure what kind of treat I should ask for!' So saying, he moved his hand out towards hers.

Sunidhi didn't extend her hand. Instead, she stood up and occupied the chair lying next to Vikas. Smiling, she tightly held his hand in hers and uttered, 'Congratulations, received from close quarters give more happiness'. Ever since entering the Portico, Vikas had felt that his hands were freezing cold. But now, a warm current of energy ran through his body.

Then they briefly talked about their old associates... and the work they were presently doing. But it all finished too soon.

'So, what else...?' Vikas seemed to be interested in asking something particular.

'All's well... How are Garima and Preeti ji?'

'They are fine...now it's time to pay attention to Garima's studies...'. These days, Vikas didn't feel any hesitation in discussing his family affairs with Sunidhi as he used to feel earlier.

'So, what's next...now?'

'You tell me...what should it be...?'

'You know what I am asking...'

'I know...but I haven't thought anything about that.'

'Then do it fast. You know very well that time is fleeting', said Vikas very affectionately. Sunidhi looked into his eyes, as if expecting to see something particular.

Sunidhi knew that Vikas had a crush on her. She was still his 'heart-throb'. He loved her from the core of his heart. But he never let himself get carried away by his emotions. There were limitations in their relationship but absolutely no hypocrisy. Many times, they did feel the compulsions of the body, but exercised full restraint and always held themselves back. But Vikas had now started feeling that Sunidhi should get married and settle down in life. He knew that left to herself, she would have spent her entire life living alone and loving him. But he wanted her to get married.

'Do you know something...?'

'Yes, I know!'

'What...what do you know...?'

'Nothing... I was only joking' Vikas was in a playful mood.

'You know, this year, I coordinated the interviews.'

'Wonderful. Must have done well'

'It's not that...I mean there's something else. There was a guy at the interviews...Pankaj Bhatt....a Romeo of sorts!'

'And you had a crush on him...?'

'Shut up!'

'Then what?' Vikas was growing impatient.

'I met him at the interviews. He started trolling me. He brought sweets for me on his promotion. He even spoke sweetly. Every month or two, he used to find an excuse and come to meet me along with a gift. One day he invited me for his birthday party and offered me a lift. I'm not sure how and why I agreed. He drove a big Skoda car. He opened the door for me and let me in. I sat in the front seat. The car smelt nice. And I don't know how but strangely enough he played Jagjit Singh's *ghazal*s on the car deck. Most of the time, he spoke about himself. He said he lived alone, his father was general manager at a big company and his mother was an advocate. He said he had a bungalow in an upscale neighbourhood. I was surprised at myself for having accepted his invitation. He looked nice, rich and garrulous. He seemed to possess all knowledge about women. I was really carried away for a while. Very soon we were in the porch of hotel Pride. There was valet parking and he handed over the keys in style. The way he carried himself at the hotel, it was quite clear that he must have been their regular visitor.

'A small table in the extreme corner of Durbar Hall was already booked for us. There were no signs of any birthday party there. Just the two of us… and nobody else. I felt ill at ease. But I kept listening to him and didn't create a fuss. From the very beginning, his intentions appeared to be quite dubious. Somehow, we had dinner. He paid the cheque by card. After ten-fifteen minutes he asked if I would have coffee, which I declined.

'Now, what he said to me was really an eye-opener. He came very close to me and said, "Sunidhi, you are beautiful…you have a good job…you are highly qualified…I don't want to know why your marriage didn't work out…I have full sympathy with you, though. I have wanted to talk to you since long. So, I chose to do so on my birthday. Don't get me wrong please…"

'By then I was left wondering if it really was his birthday... He appeared to be a complete sham. I never wanted to have a husband like him. The paltry salary we draw from the bank can't support the lavish lifestyle he boasts of. There definitely was something very dubious about him.

'Then he looked at me and asked, "….where are you lost…?" He must have thought I had already started dreaming about the grand life I was going to spend with him! He said, "We'll live in a rented house for some time. I haven't yet availed the housing loan. Later, we'll move into our own house."

'Then he took out an expensive flashy mobile phone from his trouser pocket and said, "Will call you later". He seemed to disconnect the phone and press some keys. I became apprehensive as to what he was going to do next. I had a hunch that he had put his phone on recording mode. However, I was mostly quiet. Had it been some other woman in my place, she would have either been highly impressed by his pranks or felt slighted and quit. I too would have quit, but for my *sanskars*, which held me back from being rude.

'He asked me about my opinion on marriage. I kept silent. "Oh, you don't seem to have thought about it yet...even I am not in a hurry. But you must be feeling its need sometimes!" Having said this he stared at me inquisitively...as if to ascertain whether my silence conveyed my consent but I maintained my silence. He picked up his mobile and put it in his pocket. Then he took out his ring from his finger and started playing with it. He kept rotating it on the table. Once or twice I made gestures indicating my desire to leave. But every time, he pleaded me to stay just for another minute. I was completely fed up by then and cursed myself for having come with him! People sitting around were busy drinking and making merry. It was awfully loud and filthy. Nobody seemed to be interested in anyone else. He too had asked me for a drink, to begin with. But I had opted for the soup. Now I could feel that he was badly missing his drink looking at the others.

I looked at my watch. He took the hint and straightaway came to the point. "What do you say about a live-in relationship? I'll take excellent care of you. I'll never enquire about your past..." I lost my cool and was mad with rage. I felt my body was burning. He thought I was scared. Quickly he added, 'I promise...don't you worry at all, you won't be pregnant...that much precaution I will take..."

'This was indeed too much for me to digest. I couldn't take it anymore. Without a word, I stood up in a flurry and left. He followed me shouting, "Please listen to me... please listen to me..." I walked so fast that he had to virtually run to catch up with me. I didn't stop till I came out on the main road, took a rickshaw and left. I had never felt so wretched and humiliated in life; not even while leaving my in-laws' or parents' house. I had never despised myself so much. I couldn't sleep that night. I tossed and turned miserably in bed, feeling feverish. I couldn't go to office the next day.

'One thought continued to nag me; since I wore the tag of being 'divorced', people thought I was easily available!'

Sunidhi kept her head on Vikas's shoulder and burst into tears. For a moment, Vikas didn't know what to do. He gently held her hand and tried to calm her. He looked around. The lawn was crowded...but all were busy with themselves. He regretted having raised this topic. At the same time, he was happy that he had done so because it had given her a chance to blurt out her pent-up feelings. Who else could she have shared them with? Slowly she stopped sobbing and became normal. She looked at Vikas and said 'Sorry'.

'It's okay', Vikas consoled her.

Her eyes were still red. Vikas was absolutely quiet. But his fingers were conversing with hers!

They had finished their dinner. Neither of them had imagined that the celebration of her achievements would end up in this manner!

'Look, Sunidhi...just listen to me...it's time you made up your mind for a second marriage...!' Vikas reiterated the reality.

Sunidhi didn't reply. She stared at him like a wounded deer. Many kinds of emotions swelled up in her eyes, but got crushed by the eternal feeling of her intimacy with him. Vikas patted her head a couple of times and said, 'Come on, Sunidhi...!'

The waiter had come to clear the table and take further orders. This time Sunidhi was silent. Vikas said, 'Two coffee... sugar separate.'

Sunidhi had by now completely returned to her normal self.

Vikas looked at her. She closed her eyes and very gently placed her head on his shoulder once again. Vikas told her very affectionately,

'Sunidhi, you are now an absolutely free person. All your problems are over. You should think of making a fresh beginning in your life. I'll be very happy to see you married, but I can't see you in pain.'

Sunidhi didn't say anything in response. But she knew for sure that there was a lot of sincerity in whatever Vikas said. She gave him a glance full of love.

'Look Sunidhi, your sister will get married shortly and settle down in life. Your brother too will find his way and move on. Your parents too will be gone with the passage of time. Why do you want to ruin your life for their sake? Love, no doubt, is supreme in life, but you need a support as well. Besides, we have our bodily needs. So long as you are alone, evil eyes will keep devouring you. You need a companion in flesh and blood... mere romance is not enough. You need a man with a good heart and brains. You're young, you can get everything.' Vikas had probably said all.

Sunidhi wasn't able to say anything. She just kept looking at Vikas...his words were like honey to her ears. But where could she find somebody like him? She compared every man to Vikas and found them lacking in similar qualities.

Sunidhi was quite calm now. The storm had passed. She had not only paid heed to what Vikas said, but also taken it to heart. It was obvious from her smile.

They finished their coffee and left the hotel.

'How did you come?' It was Sunidhi who asked tonight.

'I took a cab,' answered Vikas.

'Come on, I'll give you a lift tonight...so far you have only been doing it,' said Sunidhi, with love.

'That's a nice proposition. When did you learn driving?'

'Six months ago.'

'Which car have you bought?'

'I-10...'

'It's a good car. Now you should always travel in your car', said Vikas. He knew how risky it was to drive a two-wheeler in Pune.

'I have been using it ever since I bought it.'

'That's obvious from your confident driving,' said Vikas looking at her.

Sunidhi always accepted a compliment with a smile. And Vikas was madly in love with her smile.

'O my God, we have reached my house so soon,' said Vikas, as the car stopped in front of his house.

'That's exactly what I used to feel, whenever you dropped me home,' Sunidhi remarked in a normal, calm voice.

She applied the break, held Vikas's hand and gently placed her head on his shoulder. Vikas softly rubbed her forehead and said, 'Think over what I have said.'

Vikas climbed out of the car and it slowly drove away.

❖❖❖

43

After reaching home, Sunidhi sat on her sofa for quite some time. She lived alone. While studying long hours for her CA, she had picked up the habit of drinking coffee at night. Tonight, she didn't have to study for anything. Yet she had a strong desire to drink coffee. It was already past eleven, but coffee was a bad addiction.

Her mind kept travelling back to Vikas and his advice tonight. There was nothing wrong with his advice. She couldn't be living alone forever. Besides, a good looking woman living alone was always easy prey for depraved men. For that matter no woman was safe in this male-dominated world. She was wronged and sexually abused every day, on roads, in cars, buses…and made headlines in the national dailies. She was invariably the centre of heated debates on TV channels; she rocked public bodies from panchayats to the Parliament. But what was the result? Absolutely nothing. Men continued to be the beast that they have always been and she continued to suffer as ever. Even many of those holding senior positions in our legislative bodies, the law-makers of our country faced charges of atrocities against women. Women were not safe anywhere…in offices, universities, institutions private or public, nowhere.

She had come across men even in her own family and close relations who, given a chance, wouldn't have taken a minute to violate her modesty. Even at work, she had faced many such wolves in the garb of sheep. If she had so far survived them all, it was only because of the firmness of her nature and a bit of good fortune. But there were men like Vikas as well who, in spite of having immense opportunity to take advantage of her, had never exploited it. He had even declined such an offer made by Sunidhi. Tonight, she felt even more drawn towards him. Tonight, she in fact wondered at her own self for having made such an offer to him! She knew she had always been emotional, but how could she go to that extent! However it was also true that her emotional weakness had brought her so close to Vikas. She continued talking to herself even when she went to bed.

When she woke up next morning, she noticed it was quite late. She had left all the lights and fans on while going to sleep last night. Her thoughts had not come to rest when she had hit the bed. She had continued to wonder where she could find a man like Vikas. She had found herself caught in a strange dilemma. There could only be one Vikas and nobody like him. The loud doorbell interrupted her thoughts.

She came out of her trance and went to open the door, wondering who it could be so early in the morning! The washerman, newspaperman with the bill or…? The bell rang again. She opened the door. Her parents and Sudha stood outside. She let them in warmly and made them comfortable. This was their first visit to her flat. All three of them seemed to be lost in their thoughts. Sunidhi pulled up a chair and sat down. Suddenly her gaze fell on the clock. It was quarter to nine.

'Is it time for you to go to the office?' It was her father.

'It's okay… I'll make some tea…!' Sunidhi got up to go to the kitchen.

Her mother and Sudha also followed her to the kitchen. Sunidhi didn't know what to talk about. She started making tea.

'Let me make it…', offered her mother.

Sudha kept staring at her.

Babu-ji picked up the newspaper from the table and started reading it.

They had tea together. They were meeting after a fairly long time. For a minute she thought she wouldn't go to office today. That way she could take them out for lunch. She knew there were hardly any vegetables at home. She had a hunch that they had come for a specific purpose, but hesitated talking about it. She recalled how they all had refused to welcome her in their house when she had left her in-laws' place and wanted to stay with them.

Sudha had shown maximum resistance. Quoting the reasons of privacy, she had objected to sharing the room with her. Then she realized that it wasn't the right time to think about all that. But she was helpless. Some events of your life left an indelible imprint on your mind. Certain memories just didn't leave you alone. Many such memories were flashing on the screen of her mind. Even her guests seemed to be lost somewhere.

'Sunidhi, we have brought you a good news', said her mother, finally breaking the ice. Sudha was still lost somewhere. Sunidhi looked at her and immediately guessed as to what the news was!

'Sudha's marriage has been fixed.' Sunidhi had rightly guessed it.

'Yes, the boy is an officer in an oil company. He gets good salary. The family is also good...!' The mother was sharing all details even without Sunidhi's asking for it. She heard it half-heartedly. She felt hurt and wondered as to why had they not bothered to check all such details in her case? Or they probably did... she didn't really know. But she knew it was no use now to cry over spilt milk. Living too much in the past, only crippled your present growth. Had she always been thinking of such things, she wouldn't have reached where she presently was. But what could have brought them to her house today... surely not this news alone? It could have easily been conveyed on phone.

When she had finally left her in-laws' house, nobody had come forward to her help. On the other hand, they had ill-treated her... short of hurling abuses, they had done everything they could. She had lived in their house like an outcast. They had distanced themselves from her because it could have created hurdles in Sudha's marriage. And now she was getting married. Sunidhi felt suffocated with the calculus of these relationships.

'Congratulations, Sudha!' Said Sunidhi, coming out of her stupor.

Sudha was unable to say anything.

'Thanks Sunidhi,' said Babuji, 'we have already made all preparations. We have even thought about whatever is to be given…' he paused a little and then continued, 'We are falling short of some funds to arrange her jewellery…'

'How much…?' asked Sunidhi nonchalantly. She probably had a hunch that they had come to ask for financial help.

Her Babuji and mother were stumped at the promptness of her reply. They looked at each other, hesitated a bit and then her mother came out, 'Just about five lakhs…' Sunidhi was stunned to hear that. Ever since her coming of age, she had been supporting the family. She had taken up many small-time jobs and provided them necessary succour. But nobody had ever shown any gratefulness. And now they were expecting her to shell out such a huge amount. How could they do that? Where would she get it from? She thought over it for a minute and explained her position,

'Babuji, I don't have that kind of money…but I'll definitely contribute my bit….' Then she looked at Sudha.

Her mother was quick to ask, 'Sunidhi, if you could tell us how much you would be able to contribute…we'll try to arrange for the rest from somewhere else.'

'I can try to arrange up to three…I'll perhaps have to take a loan', said Sunidhi.

They looked at each other. Sunidhi felt that they were quite happy with her offer. They too had probably expected this amount from her. All four were quiet for some time.

'Excuse me for a minute', said Sunidhi and called her office to inform that she wouldn't be coming today. She took a day's leave. Then she told them that she'd arrange the funds in about two weeks. All three of them seemed to be greatly relieved.

It was about twelve o'clock. They hadn't had any breakfast. Sunidhi hadn't even taken a bath.

'Why don't you guys take some rest? I'll get ready and then take you out for lunch. There's a good hotel nearby. I have taken leave from work.'

Sunidhi realized that the calculus of funds had weighed so heavy on their mind that they hadn't even joyfully talked about their daughter's marriage. Or was it the feeling of guilt for whatever they had done to her in the last three years... that bothered them now? Whatever it was, she felt happy for Sudha. She was going to a good family. When you are caught between remorse for the past deeds and needs of the present, the culprit inside you prefers to remain silent. The otherwise talkative Babuji seemed to be caught in this situation. He had been very fond of Sunidhi ever since her childhood, but failed to stand by her when she faced difficult times. On the other hand, he had abandoned his responsibility and left her alone to aimlessly drift in the vast skies like a forsaken kite, until Vikas came into her life and held her hand.

Sunidhi took out her car and drove them to a hotel for lunch. Babuji felt strange feeling sitting inside the car. It was the first car in their family. Looking at Sunidhi driving the car, he felt extremely sad and sorry for the disturbed life she had had. Similar thoughts ran through her mother's mind whereas Sudha was still lost in the reveries of her future.

Sunidhi wondered at the complicated webs of human relationships and the call of one's social obligations. She could never shirk work or evade responsibility. She was emotional, but not the one to get carried away with emotions. She could endure people's presence in her life, even if it was an unwanted one. She never got depressed by the neglect and injustice meted out to her. She rather preferred to find out solutions to the problems and to convert adversities into opportunities. Even today, Sunidhi made extra efforts to make her family feel comfortable.

Sunidhi had opened a recurring account after her confirmation in the service. She had intended to use her savings as margin money to take home-loan. But it was okay. She withdrew all that she had saved, took a loan from the Credit Society and raised three lakhs to be given to Babuji.

Sudha's marriage went off well. Her room in the house also fell vacant. Her parents hadn't expected so much help from Sunidhi. But when they saw her doing it so willingly, they were extremely touched and once again started worrying about her future. One day, Sunidhi's mother lovingly patted her back and commented, 'We should now think about your marriage. But this time we'll let you select the boy yourself.'

Sunidhi knew her mother said it with sincerity but she didn't respond. They implored her to forget the past differences, come home and start staying with them. But it was difficult for Sunidhi to obviate her past so easily, though she was now in a better position to understand the limitations they had had when she had left their house. She had forgiven them somewhat.

Sunidhi took a decision to live alone.

❖❖❖

44

It was Monday morning. Vikas was astonished to see the headlines in *The Economic Times*. His bank had been named in a scam involving crores of rupees, involving an airlines. The airlines company was running many other businesses too. Many airline companies had suddenly cropped up when the economy was thrown open to private players. It was a profitable business but also carried risks. There was too much competition. Many companies couldn't sustain and just went under.

The governing body of the bank had raised many concerns on advancing loans to this company. Yet they were sanctioned an exorbitant credit limit by the chairman. He was very shrewd. He not only had full knowledge of the strengths and weaknesses of the bank directors, but also fully exploited it to his benefit. He generally held board meetings at hill stations. He would have held them abroad, if only the bank had some branches outside India. Still, he used to freely allow foreign travel to the directors and the general managers on the pretext of attending seminars and trainings. Offering expensive gifts and other perks to the board members were the order of the day. That's how he always succeeded in getting his favourite proposals through. But even he was shaken up by the exposure of the scam in the airlines.

A high-level committee was appointed to enquire into the scam and fix responsibility. As a knee-jerk reaction and to divert people's attention from himself, the Chairman immediately placed a general manager and a deputy GM of the bank under suspension. For many days, the entire establishment of the bank worked in an atmosphere of mistrust and uncertainty. They felt highly demoralized. But the chairman wasn't even bothered. He had powerful connections in the government. He pulled the right strings and got himself shifted to another bank at an equally important position.

❖❖❖

45

Sunidhi was happy that her sister was finally married to a decent boy. They made a nice couple. She was happy even for having been able to help her parents at the time of their need. The wedding went off well. All their relatives attended it. They saw Sunidhi after a long time and were highly impressed by her looks and demeanour. Many of them even asked her father about her (re)marriage. He discussed it with interest but refrained from making any commitment. Her past didn't allow him to do so. He even felt scared to talk to Sunidhi about it, though she knew it very well as to what was going on in her parents' mind.

When Sunidhi joined office after her sister's marriage, she found a strange curiosity amongst her colleagues, but she preferred to ignore it. Soon her assistant brought her an envelope, which bore the stamp of a multinational bank. It didn't take her long to know why her colleagues threw meaningful glances at her. They were probably curious to know what the envelope contained. Sunidhi too was keen to know whether the contents spelt good news or bad, but she didn't want to open the envelope in the office, lest her expression gave her away.

She attended to her work the whole day, though her mind kept flying back to the interview she had taken in a multinational bank. The interview panel was a three-member board. She had fared well and was quite satisfied with her performance. It had been made possible only because of Vikas's help. It was he who led her to the path of success and glory.

The experience of visiting the office of this multinational bank, at Mittal Chambers in Nariman Point, had been no less than visiting a bank abroad. People worked at work-stations, spread over a relatively huge hall. Every station had a computer and a phone; there were no papers and no files. A few colourful slips hung on the side boards. People occupying the work-stations appeared to be officers. There were no peons, no clerks. Women seemed to outnumber men. The interview was held in a conference room. Candidates had been seated just outside the room. Free tea and coffee were available. Even snacks were on offer. Everything spoke of a certain class. The entire premises were air-conditioned, perfumed and quiet. There was a distinct glow on everyone's face...the glow of contentment.

Coming out of the office, Sunidhi had noticed that Mumbai looked so resplendent after sunset. She crossed the Oberoi Towers and the Air India building to reach her hotel. She was enchanted by the human rush on the roads, the waves rocking the sea, the glimmering lights of ships in the distant waters. Countless couples locked in amorous love loitered along the coastline or occupied the benches placed along the sea. She couldn't restrain herself from crossing the road and reaching the seaside. She walked there aimlessly, lost in her own reverie. It was time for high tide in the sea. The water merrily rode the swelling waves smashing the shores. Sunidhi was totally lost in the magic of what she saw, till a violent gush of water hit the seashore and drenched her. And she was immediately reminded of Vikas who had always been so fond of the sea.

Sunidhi walked along the sea-shore to reach Chaupati. Her Bentley hotel had been left far behind. She turned around and saw that the glittering street lights actually shone like the Queen's Necklace. The roaring sea and the screeching sounds of vehicles rushing down the road seemed to be in competition. There were cars of all shapes and sizes–popular international brands interspersed by those with beacon lights beaming on top. Suddenly she started evaluating her performance in the interview. It had gone well and she hoped to be selected.

She reached hotel Bentley. Vikas had recommended it for her stay. It was located on the third floor of a building known as Krishn Mahal. It faced the sea and the popular Wankhede cricket stadium lay behind it. Sunidhi realised she was falling in love with this city. What pomp and show, what hustle and bustle and yet everyone was lost in his own business. Such affluence couldn't probably be seen in any other city. It was truly the financial capital of the country.

Sunidhi changed her clothes, rested for a while and then came out of the hotel to take a walk. She decided she'd eat out. She left the 'D' road and started moving towards Churchgate station. It was 8.30 in the evening. The homebound crowd rushing back after the day's work had thinned. Still it seemed there were a lot of people around.

Tonight Sunidhi felt romantic walking on the Mumbai streets without any constraint or intrusion. She had never tasted such solitude. She had always lived amongst people known to her. Here, she was a total stranger. Nobody knew her but many people just stopped and stared at her when she crossed them. That was the charisma of her personality. She could bewitch even the passers-by.

She saw a sign-board for Gaylord hotel. She entered out of plain curiosity as she had heard the name somewhere. Here it was no big deal to see a lone woman entering a hotel. She occupied a table for two. Soon, a smartly dressed waiter came up to her to take orders. She had hardly completed her sentence ordering Veg clear soup, when her mobile phone rang. It was Vikas. She narrated everything to him. She had her dinner and returned to the hotel. Next day, she came back from Mumbai, feeling absolutely fresh and rejuvenated.

Sunidhi remained awfully busy the whole of next day, though the beautiful memories of her Mumbai visit kept haunting her. In the evening while she was coming down in the lift, she felt like opening the envelope. But by the time she put her hand to it, she had already reached the ground floor. So she rushed to her car and opened it. It was an 'offer letter'.

Sunidhi read the letter at one go. She was amazed to see the package. The salary was three times of what she was currently drawing. Then there were many perks. A house in Mumbai, an offer to take over her loans and other financial liabilities…much much more than she had ever expected.

Sunidhi switched on the car, but didn't know where to go. She switched the car off, picked up her mobile and dialled Vikas's number. She narrated everything to him in breathless excitement. Vikas too seemed to be quite excited when he uttered,

'Congrats…join immediately….'

'But statutory notice, resignation, relieving…?'

'Don't worry about all that…just pay three months' salary and quit. It will be compensated in a month…hurry up.'

'But I have to give a bond for two years… a guarantor is required for that…' said Sunidhi.

'I am there… go ahead…!' replied Vikas.

46

Vikas didn't know why he was feeling so happy today. On the way to office, he never conversed with the driver. Nor did the driver. He just drove the car while Vikas went through the headlines in *The Economic Times*. He used to read full news at home in the evening. But today, the newspaper wasn't catching his eye. Instead, he started talking with the driver.

'Have you had your breakfast?'

'Yes sir', answered the driver politely.

Vikas looked out of the car. He was thinking about Sunidhi. Her joining a foreign bank was a great achievement. It could solve her financial problems and take care of her worries. He felt happy for her and smiled. Then he realized that even his times were changing for the better. His new chairman appeared to be much better than the previous one. He wouldn't have to work under pressure any more. This, perhaps, was another reason for his being happy.

He felt like calling Sunidhi, but soon realized that he had almost reached office. Leaving the car, he experienced a strange energy flowing inside his body. His staff was happy to see him in a cheerful mood. His cabin was daily sprayed with a room-freshener, but its aroma had never smelt so good as today.

He turned his computer on and saw an e-mail flashing on the screen. It had come from the head office. The new chairman had taken over charge. His bio-data and photograph had also been posted. Vikas enlarged his photo and looked at it carefully. It showed all attributes of a perfect gentleman. He had an impressive bio-data...an engineering degree from IIT, Pawai, and a fairly long experience of working in reputed banks. Apart from that, his face described it all. Vikas quickly prepared a nice press release and issued to the local press. He also called a staff-meeting to discuss the possibilities which lay before them under the changed circumstances.

Later in the day, there was a call from the new chairman. He had already acquainted himself with complete data of Vikas's office. He talked for about five minutes and left a good impression on Vikas's mind. Next day, Vikas compiled all press-clippings, got them scanned and sent across to the chairman's office. This act of his was highly appreciated. It was not only the first in the entire circle, but also worthy of praise for the wide coverage and publicity it had earned for the bank. He was informed that the Chairman would even write to him separately.

About a week later, the chairman called a meeting of all regional heads, which was followed by his own visit to Aurangabad. He first met the staff and then the clients. He liked Vikas's nature and appreciated his professional acumen. In his valedictory address, he showered immense praise on the working of the office and the way Vikas handled it. When he was leaving, there was an eerie quiet at the airport. Sitting in the VIP lounge, Vikas hesitatingly asked him, 'Sir, have you been to Ajanta?'

'No...never got the time for it', answered the chairman.

'Sir, you must visit us again along with your family. Ajanta is a very nice place...'

'Yes, I have heard a lot about it. But let me make it clear, I never go on an official tour with my family', said the chairman very dispassionately.

Vikas recalled how he had even declined to accept any gift in the office. He felt embarrassed at his suggestion about taking family along. Right then there was an announcement about his flight to Delhi and they all moved towards security check.

After the chairman's departure, Vikas spent some time with his staff and then returned home. It had been a hectic day and he was extremely tired. He straightaway went to bed and revived the day's memories. He was immensely impressed with the chairman's personality. The glow on his face was a reflection of his inner strength, his adorable character, his honesty and integrity. He wasn't the kind who could easily be impressed by others. He had a knack of judging people impartially and accurately.

❖❖❖

47

Sunidhi joined her new job in Mumbai. Her office was in Maker's Tower. It was a bank office with a difference. It didn't have any public dealings; no counters, no rush of people, no queues and no public complaints. It offered an absolutely quiet and congenial working environment. Everybody was busy in his own work. Everybody, including the ladies, were formally dressed in blazers, trousers and neck-tie. Sunidhi had always liked wearing a saree. She looked so elegant in it! Later, she had started wearing salwar-kameez, to suit the job requirement. And now it was blazer and trousers. Initially, she felt a bit hesitant, but soon got used to it. Women are generally adept at adapting themselves to changing conditions. And Sunidhi was no exception.

Sunidhi's physical charm, her way of handling people and her overall demeanor soon helped her establish her individuality at her new job. Her inimitable grace, dedication and understanding of the work soon contributed to her reaching a pivotal position in all decision-making in the office. She worked so hard and with such zeal that she often lost track of time.

She often compared the work-culture in government banks with that in the private ones. It was so different, particularly in matters of facilities for the staff! Many times she also fondly reflected over the course of her professional journey and realized how wonderful it had been! From a very humble beginning, she had managed to reach such a senior position in a foreign bank. And it had happened only because of Vikas's help and guidance. The very thought of him filled her with a rush of emotions. She had an urge to call him. But she didn't as there was so much work on hand.

Sunidhi usually reached office by 9.30 in the morning. Her official residence in Colaba was just a few minutes' drive from office. She commuted by her own car and had a reserved parking in the building. It was a comfortable living. But once she reached office, she would get awfully busy in work, finding absolutely no time for herself.

There was a knock at the door of her cabin. Sunidhi looked at her watch and then at the calendar lying in front of her. It was time for Punit's appointment. He gently opened the door and stepped inside, murmuring 'good-morning'. Sunidhi beckoned him to take a seat.

'I have gone through your file. It's a good proposal. We'll need some more documents, before we sanction your limit.'

'But ma'am, I don't have time; I have to clear the workers' payment...and there are...' Punit wanted to narrate his problems but Sunidhi cut him short saying,

'You know the market conditions very well. Unless you offer a security, we won't be able to do anything.'

At this time, the peon entered her cabin holding a visiting card. Sunidhi looked at it and told him to send the client in. It was also a hint for Punit to leave. He stood up, saying, 'Okay...' and left.

In the last six months or so, Sunidhi had acquired sufficient knowledge of the rules, regulations and procedures of doing business in this bank. She now behaved like a highly professional executive. She worked under an exceptionally efficient and cultured officer of the rank of Vice President. He operated mostly through phone or e-mail. He called her to his cabin only if it was unavoidable. She had full freedom to work the way she liked...without any pulls and pressures from the top. That was probably the reason she had acquired so much confidence and become an expert at taking the right decisions, in such a short time.

In a few days, Punit submitted the documents required by the bank and got a hefty limit sanctioned. His promptness convinced Sunidhi of his commitment and integrity. She was happy to have helped him. It was the first major case she had handled on her own. So she craved to share the joy of her achievement with someone, but her corporate position made her feel awkward about getting close and casual with most of her colleagues.

At such times, she deeply missed Vikas. Feeling the urge to call him, she dialled his number. She got through after a few attempts but his phone was engaged. Later on, when he did take her call, he told her that he was busy and would call her back. She was upset. All her excitement seemed to fritter away. She wound up her table and left for home, rather early.

She took her car out and drove towards Colaba. Till now, she had always left office quite late. Today, she was out at 6.30. There was still ample daylight. She turned the car around and started driving towards Marine Lines. She had always had a great fascination for the sea. The evening rush had started building up. The sun was about to set. It had already painted the sky copper-red. She wanted to park the car and step out, but couldn't find space. So she kept driving slowly towards Chaupati. Her mind was fixed on the sun. Soon she noticed an empty space and parked her car. She merrily strolled along the seaside for a while and finding an empty parapet, settled down there, watching the beautiful sight of the sun going down into the sea. She felt a strange current run through her body. She had started her journey from practically nowhere and look where she had arrived...!

The shadows of the evening had started lengthening. The rush of people was swelling. One could see innumerable young couples settling down on the parapets, ready to steal each other's love. Many ships, big and small, drifted aimlessly in the distant waters. Closer to the shore, a myriad of boats rowed to and fro, rowed by invisible boatmen. Sunidhi got lost watching one of those. Vikas had not called yet. He must have been stuck in important work. It was he who had skillfully rowed the boat of her life to such a safe, sound and shining shore. Tonight, she was missing him much more than she usually did. She felt very lonely and had a strong urge to call him. But she didn't. When she looked at her past, she felt sad and sorry for having led such a meaningless, hollow and insignificant life. If she hadn't given up, it was only because of Vikas...his immense love and unfailing support. It was he who had kept her moving and ultimately brought her to the stage where she was at present.

Mindlessly driving on the brilliantly lit streets of Mumbai, Sunidhi reached home. Her part-time help was preparing her dinner. It was unusual for her to see Sunidhi back so early. But Sunidhi was on a totally different trip tonight. She gave leave to the maid; flung her bag on the sofa in complete abandon, took a quick shower and made coffee for herself. It was 8.30 and Vikas had still not called. Normally he never did this. Must have been really caught up in a mess, she thought. Again she had a mind to call him, but dropped the idea once again. She thought she'd do it later in the night.

In no time she stood in front of a life-size mirror, wearing jeans and a jazzy top. 'Looking smart!' She was startled to hear Vikas say that. She gave herself a naughty smile and left the house. She leisurely walked along the seashore from Radio Club. Tonight, she was completely herself. There was nothing to bother her...no bank, no family, no joy, no sorrow. She had left everything behind. She walked in great style, taking measured and rhythmic steps. Looking at the lively waves rise and fall in the sea, she felt fully drenched from within.

Soon she was in front of Hotel Taj and the Gateway of India. She shuddered to think about the horror which was unleashed by the terrorists. It had not only defaced these monumental buildings but also pierced the hearts of humanity. Why did people indulge in such horrendous activities, she wondered. She saw people taking selfies at the Gateway. She moved towards Regal talkies. On the way she noticed Suba Palace and passionately remembered Vikas. All those sweet memories came alive in her mind and she felt a bit disturbed.

Vikas, Mumbai, terrorists, bullets...she found herself standing in front of hotel Leopold.

She had heard a lot about hotel Leopold cafe. It was a hot-spot for film celebrities. Many strugglers also visited it, hoping to get noticed for film roles. The terrorists had attacked it too. It was a popular joint for foreigners, especially Americans. She didn't realize that she was already inside Leopold!

It was a strange world for her; bursting with the smoke of cigarettes and the smell of beer. Most tables were occupied by couples...lost in their own world. But she was alone. There was a time when she couldn't have gone out alone even for a cup of tea in her hometown. And tonight she was inside Leopold, all by herself. She looked around but couldn't find any empty table. Then she noticed a foreigner woman sitting alone. She mumbled 'Excuse me' and placed herself in front of her. The lady was already high...on quite a few cans of beer and had almost finished a full pack of cigarettes.

This kind of life was new for Sunidhi. It carried a certain romance with it. There was much din and a strong smoky scent in the air. The waiter came to take her order, but she was lost in soaking in the environment. Even Indian women were drinking and smoking ... some even more than the foreigners. Their dresses were highly provocative, exposing more than they concealed. Their body-language projected them like the most blessed creatures on the earth. But not all were like that. Some were sad and sober too. They seemed to drink and smoke only to obviate their sorrow. The waiter came up to her again to take orders.

'One fried rice and veg Manchurian...'

'Madam....drinks?

'Sorry....No drinks!' said Sunidhi softly.

The waiter gave her a weird look. She was probably the only one not having a drink. At such places, the waiters didn't like serving teetotallers because they didn't get hefty tips. Sunidhi felt that people had come there more for drinks than food. Many men, both old and young were eyeing Sunidhi. She too was conscious of their gaze and her sixth sense had already given the signal. But right now she was lost in Vikas's thoughts. Her phone started ringing. She looked at her watch. It was ten o'clock. It wasn't easy to take the phone out of the jeans. She stood up and removed the phone from the pocket, but by then, the call had already been disconnected. She looked at the phone...it was Vikas!

❖❖❖

48

'Hello…' Sunidhi had dialled the call.

'Hello…' replied Vikas, zealously. 'There's so much of noise! Are you watching a movie?'

'No…you'll find it strange. Okay, take a guess as to where I am?' Sunidhi said playfully.

'At a function…?'

'No.'

'At a party…?'

'No.'

'Then where are you?'

'In Leopold Café.'

'What…? What are you doing there…?'

'Nothing much… Remember, you had once told me about its culture. Tonight I was passing by …and I thought I'll just peep in…'

'But…Sunidhi that place isn't good for you…' Vikas seemed to be getting into a serious mode.

'That's not fair…if you go there, it's okay and if I come there, it's not good…?'

'……'

'Anyhow…Today…I had a great desire to talk to you… and when you didn't pick up my phone, I felt lonely and came out.'

'But how did you land up in Leopold?'

'You only advised me once that one should not have any taboos in life!'

'Uff…'

'Anyhow...leave it. I have plenty of things to talk to you about.'

'Okay, tell me why had you called?'

'What do you mean by why I had called you? Do I need a reason to call you?'

'I didn't mean that...' said Vikas, apologetically. He realized that he had never talked to her like this. Then why did he, tonight? Was it because she was sitting in 'Leopold' or the pressure of his work or his attachment to his family or a feeling of estrangement in their relation because of Sunidhi reaching such a high position? He took charge of himself and asked, 'Have you had your dinner?'

'Almost done...'

'Finish it... is anybody with you?'

'No.' Now, Sunidhi also realized that they had unnecessarily allowed their talk to get serious. She said,

'I have finished my food. It's very noisy here. I'll go home and call you. Have you had your dinner? Everything alright...?'

'Yes, all fine. I had a meeting which lasted very long. There were some problems. I'll tell you later...' said Vikas, trying to bring their conversation to a normal level.

'Just give me ten-fifteen minutes, please.' Sunidhi's voice had acquired a particular kind of softness. She knew how to handle a situation. Her flat was just a few minute's walk from 'Leopold', but she took a taxi to reach fast. She couldn't have waited to talk to Vikas. So she called him just as she stepped into her flat.

'Now... tell me...'

'How did you like Leopold?'

'Let's forget it...!'

'Okay... tell me what was so special today...?'

'Today, I sanctioned my first big loan. The boss supported me, but it was my decision. I processed the case. There's a client called Punit. He is in great trouble. It was a bit risky, but I felt that the guy was gentle, he really needed it. He'll do business honestly… the bank too will profit out of it.'

Sunidhi blurted out everything she had wanted to tell Vikas, immediately after sanctioning the limit.

'Hope you've checked the documents carefully and collected guarantees etc…?'

'Of course. I made use of all that I had learnt from you. The boss was happy and so was the client.'

'Great. But Sunidhi, do remember one thing… never take a decision emotionally… particularly when you are dealing with the sanction of a big loan or limit…'

'I know. I've taken care of that.'

'Congratulations…'

'This was my first big case. I was dying to share it with you.'

'Good. Go ahead and do wonders…'

'Only if you are with me…!'

'Sure, I'll always be with you…'

Vikas and Sunidhi talked for a long time about their work, families and Mumbai. These days Sunidhi made it a point to enquire about Preeti and Garima. It was late in the night, but there was no sleep in her eyes. She hadn't even had a proper dinner. That wasn't the place to have it. She had casually gone there to have a look at the place. She made coffee for herself; it was Saturday night, so there was no rush. She switched on the TV and surfed channels, stopping at a channel showing the film *Silsila.* Sunidhi settled down comfortably in the sofa and remained glued to the movie.

She felt strange when she woke up next morning. She had gone to sleep in those tight-fit clothes! Laughing at herself, she was glad that she didn't drink. She switched off the TV…it had been on the whole night. It was perhaps the aftermath of the long chat she had had with Vikas!

She got up and twisted her body. Then she looked out of the window. The sun was already up, radiating energy in the whole world. The boats rowed as usual. The sun-rays merrily glimmering on the sea-waves looked awesome.

The newspaper had been delivered at the door. She picked it up and was startled to look at it. The front page carried a picture of a young girl trying to hide her face. Sunidhi instantly remembered seeing her... smoking and drinking in the company of some highly fashionable boys in 'Leopold'. And the very next morning she was in the news... 'Drunk Driving Takes Toll of Two'. She had been drinking till late in 'Leopold'... and going home she had lost control of her Audi car and trampled two men sleeping on the footpath!

❖❖❖

49

Sunidhi had begun coming to office at 9.30. She had also started feeling comfortable in her grey suit with black high-heel sandals...perfect outfit for a senior female corporate executive! She carried a resolve in her eyes, a rhythm in her gait and a grace in her beautiful body. She'd become so smart that nobody dared cast an evil eye on her or take liberties with her.

Reading newspapers after reaching office was a routine for her. Most of the papers she read, like *The Financial Express, The Economic Times, Business Standard* had direct connection with her job. But they also carried news about the girl in Leopold ...whisky...big cars... accidents. She started thinking about that girl. Why did she have to drink so much? What must have been troubling her! Had she faced too much suffering in life? Would she not now be subjected to an even greater one? Facing the police, harassment and ignominy? Sunidhi's own suffering in life hadn't been any less...but she hadn't surrendered herself to such a life-style! Maybe because of her financial constraints or... her *sanskars* which didn't let her fall on bad habits...!

Knock...knock...she heard somewhere and returned to herself. But she wasn't still back in the newspaper or her office or 'Leopold'. A strange 'no-man's land' she was in. At such times, she just thought of Vikas. She thought of narrating the post-Leopold story to him and get rid of it. She looked at her watch. It was 10 o'clock. She didn't know where he would be? But there was no harm in calling. She picked up her mobile and heard *knock...knock* again. This time she knew it was at the door. With her usually stern voice, she said, 'Yes, come in...!' A figure gently peeped in from behind the glazed glass and entered her cabin.

'Come in, Punit. How are you?' Sunidhi asked, putting down her mobile phone.

'Sorry, I couldn't call you before coming. I'll just take a few minutes of yours,' said Punit, hesitantly.

'It's okay…settled your business?' she asked as a courtesy.

'Yes, it's settling down…only with your help.'

'Now you can gallop…and increase it manifold,' said Sunidhi and wondered since when had she learnt to talk like that?

'I came only to thank you. It's only with your help that it has been possible for me to…' So saying Punit pushed the bag he had brought towards Sunidhi. 'Some *mithai*…please don't refuse…'

'There was no need for this. We only wish your business well. That would be real *mithai* for us', said Sunidhi, pressing the doorbell.

Sudama, the outsourced sub-staff, came inside and stood there respectfully.

'Sudama, please open this box and distribute the sweets to the staff…! But first get us some tea.' Sunidhi thanked Punit through a gesture of her eyes and looked at the box he had brought. 'You brought so much…'. She put a piece in his hand, 'You also have it.' Then she added, 'All the best…' and picked up a piece for herself. She put it on the saucer, shifting the cup of tea lying over it since morning.

Sudama entered again with tea and went out carrying the box of *mithai.* Punit had his tea and was about to go, when Sunidhi thanked him once again.

'Thanks for what…you sent the whole box outside…and didn't even taste it'. There was obvious unhappiness in his tone.

'Oh…I forgot…but I'll surely eat it later,' replied Sunidhi looking at the piece of *mithai* she had kept on the saucer. Then she picked it up and putting it in her mouth, she commented, 'It's very sweet!'

'Thanks!'

Punit got up to go and Sunidhi couldn't help looking at him leave the cabin. He didn't turn around, though Sunidhi waited to say 'bye' to him. The door was closed but Punit's figure could be seen going away, across the glazed glass. His bashful countenance flashed in front of Sunidhi's eyes. She liked the way he talked...his manners and his sartorial sense.

At 4 o'clock in the afternoon, the Joint President of the bank called her inside his chamber.

'How are you doing, Sunidhi?' he asked her.

'I'm fine sir... thank you.'

'Congratulations, Sunidhi. Your appraisal has been excellent. Very few people get such a good one in the first year of their service. You are one of those few.' So saying, he handed her an envelope.

'You have handled the credit department well. All accounts are doing well. Congratulations to you.' His eyes gleamed with appreciation for Sunidhi.

Sunidhi wanted to open the envelope, but hesitated until the boss himself asked her to see what was inside. She opened it and saw it contained a bonus voucher for five lakh rupees and a letter of appreciation. She was still in the boss' cabin, when a message flashed on her mobile confirming the credit of five lakh rupees in her bank account.

'Thanks, sir...' was only she could gratefully utter.

'It's all right. You deserve it.' The Joint President had nice feelings for Sunidhi and she could feel them. The way the bank was looking after her was overwhelming. She felt extremely obliged. She was quite familiar with the boss' nature and his administrative acumen, today he impressed her with his sense of timing as well. They had a hearty talk while sipping coffee. Sunidhi kept feeling that it was her intimacy with Vikas, which had enabled her to see this kind of life. All the credit she had got in life actually belonged to him. She was getting lost in Vikas's thoughts when the Joint President said,

'So, Sunidhi... all the best. Go ahead, my wishes are with you...!'

'Thanks, sir. This is all because of you...' Sunidhi was laden with humility and gratefulness.

They shook hands and the boss came up to the door to see her off. Sunidhi returned to her cabin and opened the envelope again. She had earned a bonus of five lakhs and an increment of twenty-five thousand per month. For a moment, she fell in love with herself. Then a face peeped out of the inner recesses of her heart...Vikas! She picked up her mobile!

❖❖❖

50

Sunidhi had left her past behind and moved on. Now she stood in front of a never-ending ladder. She just had to climb up. There were new steps every day...new possibilities. When you had such a promising future in front of you, you didn't wish to look back at your gloomy past. When success and fame knocked at your door, you automatically had a wide choice of new avenues, new friends and a new world waiting for you.

Even when she passed through the most difficult phase, Sunidhi had firmly kept her feet on the ground. She was always aware of the fact that success and fame were lines drawn on the flowing waters. They disappeared even before they were noticed. And the waters flowed at their pace. Life moved on uninterrupted and unmindful of what happened to you.

Sunidhi's past was shrouded in such a gloom, she didn't like to look back upon it. She dreaded to imagine where she would have been, had Vikas not happened in her life! He came into her life like a myth...and she knew that a myth could never substitute life. Success and fame didn't easily happen in everyone's life. One had, many times, to struggle through the entire length of one's life to achieve them. And for many, they still remained elusive, like a mirage.

Sunidhi had now achieved almost all she had heard about in her childhood stories. Sometimes it even seemed much more than she had even dreamt of. The dazzling glitter of the world she inhabited often made the woman inside her feel forlorn. Riding the waves of success, she often felt alone. Even one's friends and relations had a limitation to go along beyond a certain point.

When you lived in the season of right opportunities, nobody could stop the talent inside you from blossoming. Sunidhi had never deliberately tried to run after opportunities. Nor had she used anyone to achieve success. She let everyone have his or her due. She never even longed for something that was not hers. She only made sincere efforts and moved on. Sometimes she wondered how she had not only survived in a world driven by cheating, deceits and cut-throat competition but also reached such a high position! At the same time, she knew that her success had not come due to her physical charms but for her talent and hard work.

Sitting in the balcony of her flat on the eleventh floor at an upscale residential complex in Colaba, Sunidhi was busy reflecting over her past and her present. Future was still unknown. This part of Mumbai was so beautiful that it just dazzled the common man. Particularly the site of myriad boats calmly floating on the placid waters, their lights and their rhythm and the dark unending sea beyond the boats, produced a unique play of tides and ebbs in her heart. It was eleven o'clock in the night. She was unable to find any solace in the TV programmes, or music, or sleep! She couldn't even go out for a walk so late at night. For some time she strolled in the balcony. Then she lay her hands on Shivaji Sawant's book, *Mrityunjay*. She had read it many times. But tonight, she got lost in it again, trying to resolve the mystery of Kunti's relationship with Karna, against the backdrop of power, dharma and duty.

Whenever she thought about relationships, she felt all kinds of emotions throb in her heart. There was Vikas and her parents, sisters and then...Nandan and Yashodhara... and Alok too...and all her friends.... They all came alive before the eye of her imagination. How long could she continue to nurture those relationships which were not even complete? She found Vikas coming even closer to her. When you couldn't take such a close relationship to the stage of consummation, the void caused thereby hurt you even more. But Vikas had his own family to look after and be with! And he was so dear to her that she wouldn't at any cost let any injustice happen to his family!

Sunidhi realized that a successful single woman's life was like a well-bedecked boat without a boatman. Today she had everything. Her life was replete with worldly comforts. Her beauty was her unique asset. Even her age was on her side. That reminded her of what Vikas had once told her. 'I'll grow old', he had said… 'How long would you live alone? You must find a companion soon.'

'Companion' was a word which always troubled Sunidhi and held a challenge before her. In the thirty-five years of her life, she had never seen a relative become a companion. They always came to her with an interest, a motive or an expectation! Only her relationship with Vikas was absolutely pure and selfless. It had no strings attached to it. That was why he stood so tall and unique when compared to the others. That was why she considered him her companion. And that was why she never found anybody else whom she could accept as a companion. She found herself caught in a strange dilemma.

Punit's was the first case of big financing done by Sunidhi. It had settled his business. His dealings with the banks had also been fair and clean. He had already cleared a major part of the finance. He had even opened some other accounts with the bank and become one of their important customers. He attended all their functions and loved to indulge in long talks with Sunidhi.

Looking at the way he conversed with her, his expressions and his tone, she always felt that he wanted to talk about something not connected with the bank. He had given many such indications. One day he mustered courage and invited Sunidhi for dinner. He made it a point to clarify that it wasn't a business dinner. After joining this bank, Sunidhi had attended many dinners and parties. Here it was considered 'socialising' and a part of the work-culture. Many such parties were thrown by the bank itself. Many press conferences were also held. Attending these dinners therefore wasn't new for Sunidhi. Still, she had some reservations in accepting Punit's invitation.

Punit hadn't fixed any day or time for the dinner. He had left it open for Sunidhi to decide, as per her convenience. She knew it wasn't intended to take any undue advantage of her position in the bank. So when he started repeatedly calling her, she decided upon a convenient date and accepted his invitation. From that day till they met, Punit kept eagerly waiting to meet her, while Sunidhi continued to toy with the idea, undecided as to whether she should go or not go!

She finally decided to go when Vikas, during a routine telephone conversation, suggested that she 'must go', though while saying, he felt something break inside him!

❖❖❖

51

The evening lights in Mumbai made it young and charming. The brightness all around was further enhanced by the powerful beams of the headlamps of big cars on the roads. In such brilliance, Sunidhi too drove her car, though slowly. When you didn't have much anxiety to meet someone, your speed also slowed down. She was going because she had said 'yes', though she never enjoyed parties in big hotels. Tonight she was going to Taj Hotel. Punit had even offered to pick her up, but she preferred to travel by her own car.

As she reached the porch of the hotel, she found Punit already standing there. She left the car for valet parking, looked at her watch and said,

'Sorry, I got a bit late.'

'No problem. I also just came in', said Punit assuredly, warmly welcoming Sunidhi.

Taj Hotel is considered the pride of Mumbai and stands majestically in front of the Gateway of India. A newly constructed skyscraper also stands by its side, but it cannot match the grandeur of the old building. It was recently attacked by terrorists and the whole world saw a corner of the hotel burn in flames. Several flocks of pigeons restlessly hovered around those flames.

Sunidhi had never forgotten those soulful sights seen on TV. They all came alive in front of her eyes as she entered the hotel. Punit started explaining, 'Here, they had fired bullets in this very restaurant.' Nothing was visible now, as everything had been restored to its original condition, yet the spirit of Taj stood badly wounded. And Sunidhi felt it quite deep inside her. She had herself suffered many such attacks at the hands of her own people. Her spirit too stood badly wounded though everything looked normal from outside, camouflaged by her successful career.

'Excuse me!' Punit's voice brought her back on the table. 'Sorry, I disturbed you,' he added.

'It's all right…' said Sunidhi, taking charge of herself. 'See, how beautiful this hotel is!' She exclaimed. 'Tourists come here from all over the world. And the terrorists targeted it, mercilessly killing innocent people, getting killed themselves too, in the process. I often wonder about the master brain behind this. When will it stop?' She paused resignedly and blurted out, 'Sorry!'

Punit had been intently watching Sunidhi. He knew that she was saying all this from her heart. So he took the narrative further ahead and replied,

'Things are worsening day-by-day. And it directly affects our business. Probably that's what our enemies want, to weaken our economy.'

Now it was Sunidhi's turn to watch him.

'It's all due to the weakness of our government', Punit continued. Our leaders are so busy indulging in politics and in making money that they have no time for the country. First they let such disasters take place and then they run ambulances on the roads. They have become utterly selfish and heartless. The common man is fast losing faith in the government…'

A waiter was standing close by to take their order. So the topic of their discussion quickly changed. Punit asked Sunidhi, 'A drink…a small one maybe?'

'No, I don't drink. But you can have if you want…'

'No, I never drink alone. Even otherwise I am not too fond of it. Take it only at a business party. What soup will you have?'

'Veg clear…!'

'Okay.'

They ordered soup and started chatting again.

'See, I gave you this date but I got so busy with work today that I couldn't even go home and change ...', Sunidhi remarked.

'But you look so fresh! And then, beauty needs no ornaments, as they say...' He said it on the spur of the moment but soon realized that Sunidhi might not like such a comment.

Sunidhi quickly changed the topic, 'Tell me about your family and the members. Who all are there in your family?'

'I am alone, all alone. I had differences with my father. He gave me a factory to run. I couldn't handle it well. That's all...' Punit became emotional. Sunidhi felt sorry for having started this topic. Then she asked, 'You didn't marry...?'

'I did. I married and that's how differences cropped up in the family. But all that is history now. I don't want even to think about that...' he almost had tears in his eyes.

There was complete silence for some time. The waiter had served the soup and stood there to take the order for the rest of the meal. Sunidhi picked up the menu and placed the order.

Punit continued from where he had left.

'Nobody was in favour of my marriage with Meghna. Neither of our parents. Still we went ahead and got married. My father has a big business. He wanted me to join him... but when I married Meghna...he was angry. He just gave me a flat and a small unit of the business. He told me to fend for myself. I had not expected much!'

Sunidhi couldn't make out whether he was upset because of his separation from his father or Meghna. He only clarified the matters when he said,

'Meghna was a gorgeous girl, very garrulous and fashionable too, whereas my father always wanted a sober and quiet daughter-in-law. She wanted to become a singer. So she quit her job and started training with a musician every day. Slowly they became very intimate and tuned in afresh with each other. I tried to check her but she didn't listen to me. Finally we divorced.

This was a great setback for me. My business was ruined and I was left a broken man. Later on, I learnt that Meghna had moved to Delhi with the musician and later learnt that the guy was already married...'

By now the dessert had been served. Punit realised that he had been talking a bit too much. He felt sorry and clarified that he hadn't invited her to tell her all this.

'Then for what had you invited me?' asked Sunidhi.

'First, there has been a record profit in my business, the credit for which goes to you...'

'And second...?'

'And it also happens to be my birthday today...'

'Oh...that's very nice. Many happy returns of the day...' said Sunidhi extending her hand towards him to congratulate him. She asked a waiter passing by,

'Excuse me...can we get a cake?'

'Yes, Madam, what size...?'

'For two persons.'

❖❖❖

52

It was Sunday morning. Vikas called Sunidhi at 7.30.

'How did you like Punit?'

'...He is okay, but...'

'But what...? If the intentions are good, everything else can be taken care of with time...'

'......'

'Are you there...?'

'Yes...but his past life is very distressing. He has suffered a lot at the hands of his own people...his close relatives.'

'Oh, that means he has already earned your sympathy? Good...but do what your heart says. Listen to your heart, Sunidhi. As it is, marriage is a coincidence, a compromise, a union... whatever you see today may not be there tomorrow...because we keep changing, our desires, our needs, our expectations all undergo change every day. Our relationship with our life-partner also passes through highs and lows. But marriage is also a responsibility...to understand each other, to support each other. It's a sacrifice, a complete surrender...I feel you are going in the right direction.'

'He asked about me, but I just smiled and changed the topic. Today we didn't discuss any such thing which may lead you to think about marriage.' Sunidhi had explained her position.

'Many times we just have to let things happen. We must always remember that we aren't permanent in this world. Mountains on the earth, rivers, forests, trees, sky, light, are all permanent. The greenery spread all around us, the crops, the flowers are all permanent sights. Sitting at the window of a moving train, we should enjoy their sight as long as we can watch it from the window…'

'How well you explain things. How nicely you talk…only if somebody like you could come into my life. So far I haven't decided anything…nor have I given any hint…'

'Hints are not given, Sunidhi…you get them. From whatever you have told me, I have got enough hint about both of you. But remember one thing…don't take a decision out of sympathy. Think impartially and then decide…And keep your conduct in the bank totally above your personal decisions…do you get me?'

'Yes, I know what you mean. You are absolutely right. I hadn't thought on these lines. But now I'll take care…'

'I'll come to Mumbai very soon and then like to meet this Punit of yours…'

'Sure…but so far nothing is sure…'

Sunidhi had her breakfast and started flipping pages of the newspaper. But there were the same old news, politics…films and sports. She put it down and switched on the TV. This too was stuck in the same old rut. She switched it off. She wasn't at peace. There was no remorse in her heart… nor any desire…but she was restless. Then she thought she ought to leave everything to time…! Sitting in the sofa, she went to sleep. When she woke up, she saw the sea fully covered with a golden sheet of sunshine. She felt light, had coffee and changed her clothes. Then she took out her car and set out. She now felt highly energetic. She entered a big mall on Peder Road and shopped to her heart's content; bought plenty of dresses for herself. Normally she hesitated to buy very expensive clothes. The wants experienced in childhood give rise to a particular mindset. But today she bought some expensive clothes as well. Suddenly she hit upon a T-shirt. It was light blue in colour…very attractive. She felt a rush of romance. It was size 42. She didn't even look at the price-tag and bought it. Vikas always wore size 42. She got it packed in a nice gift wrapper.

Sunidhi decided to eat at the revolving restaurant in hotel Ambassador. She went there and sat at a table near the glass wall. That was the only vacant seat. There were many couples among the customers; only a handful of family groups. Sunidhi was all alone. But the image of Vikas, permanently positioned in the deep recess of her heart gently whispered, 'I am there….!' And Punit also seemed to appear out of nowhere occasionally! She looked at the high-rise buildings of Malabar Hills and let her eyes and senses float in bliss.

Sitting in this restaurant, one could get a panoramic view of Mumbai. Big and small ships floating in the sea looked like glow-worms; the Queen's Necklace and Marine Drive flashed like a dazzling string of beautiful pearls; interesting stories emanating from the lives of wealthy people living in Malabar Hills lent Mumbai the title of *maya-nagari*. Crowds of homeless people jostled together in unauthorised shanties erected along the sea beach, presenting the ugly side of the city's pretty face. Shabbily clad urchins peddled nuts out of vessels tied to their waists, particularly to young lovers sitting in secluded spots. As the restaurant revolved, it offered a complete view of the famous Wankhede stadium. Mumbai local, the life-line of the city, ran to and fro with full force. Sunidhi was wonderstruck looking at the effervescent buoyancy of the city. She picked up her mobile phone, but stopped short of dialling a number!

❖❖❖

53

One day Punit came to Sunidhi's office and sent his visiting card in. It was printed on expensive paper, signifying his affluence. She immediately called him in. He always wore a smile while entering her cabin, but today it was much broader than usual. He wore a brand new suit with a nice necktie. Obviously, he hadn't come for official work. As he sat down, he took out a piece of paper from his briefcase and showed it to Sunidhi. It was about the repayment of his bank loan. When she congratulated him, he replied,

'You'll have to congratulate me for another thing as well.'

'Congratulations…but what is it for?'

'I have bought my own apartment. You have to come for its housewarming.' His joy seemed to know no bounds.

'That's very nice…your business is really flourishing,' said Sunidhi in an appreciative tone.

'Yes, I have made a huge profit in an export deal in Dubai. Much more than I had expected. Your help in time made it possible. Now I may not need bank financing…'

'No, it's because of your hard work and business acumen.'

Sunidhi was extremely delighted to see that her first big loan worth many crores of rupees had been successfully closed. She didn't want to let go of this opportunity and took Punit to her Joint President. She always kept her seniors abreast of her banking achievements. Coming back to her cabin, she said, 'Now you'll have to have coffee with me.'

Sipping coffee, Sunidhi couldn't resist asking him where he had purchased the apartment.

'In a building on the Malabar Hills!'

'Malabar Hills?' She couldn't believe her ears. The other day, she had felt so romantic looking at Malabar Hills at night, from the revolving restaurant of hotel Ambassador. She still remembered that sight vividly. Suppressing her excitement she asked,

'When is the housewarming?'

'I'll let you know very soon...when everything is set.'

The peon entered Sunidhi's cabin, holding a visiting card. Punit stood up to leave; while walking out of the door, he glanced back at her and smiled. Sunidhi remained quite lost in that smile till the peon came in again to remind her about the next visitor.

On the appointed day, Punit sent an Audi car to pick up Sunidhi. She quietly sat in the car thinking how well Punit was doing. Of late, she had even observed a certain decency and grace in his conduct. She didn't know why she had started thinking about him. Then she wondered who could be there at the housewarming... she hadn't even asked him about it.

By the time she reached Marine Drive, it had started raining. Sunidhi liked rains. It always evoked a sense of romance in her. For a moment, she even forgot where she was going. Young couples had already turned their umbrellas into love nests. Raindrops falling on the sea-water looked awesome. Water mixed with water ...and the clouds which had originally arisen from the sea were taking refuge in the sea itself. When she crossed Chaupati, she saw many high-rise buildings kissing the skies. This area was still lush green.

The car stopped inside a big building. Punit stood there waiting for her. He gently opened the door of the car and led her inside. Sunidhi flashed a beautiful smile and started following him. The lift stopped at the twenty-first floor. Sunidhi still wondered who the other guests would be. Punit opened the door with a key and ushered her in. She was dumbfounded. To her utter astonishment, there was nobody else present. It was a big three bedroom flat, tastefully furnished, a chandelier in the living room, fully equipped kitchen. A pooja had been performed in the corner of a bedroom. Sunidhi was bewildered at the absence of people. Punit understood her predicament and said,

'Actually, today I have invited only you. We had a pooja in the morning. My parents had come. Babuji was happy to see the flat and appreciated the way I was growing in my career. He had raised a huge business empire absolutely from scratch and in spite of having everything at my disposal I had wasted my time running after Meghna… But let's talk about nice things tonight. Tell me, you'll have tea, coffee or a cold drink?

He poured a cold drink in two glasses. Sunidhi wasn't still feeling comfortable. Punit's flat was worth a few crores...even his car was no less than a crore… but nobody present at the housewarming! She felt lost and awkward.

'I have invited you here on a purpose…', Punit said softly.

Sunidhi was sitting in a single sofa. Punit sat close to her, and said,

'Please don't misunderstand me. I have already told you everything about myself. I have suffered treachery…and my father's rage as well. I have lived away from my mother. I have had big losses in business…and even gone bankrupt. I have passed through difficult times. Then I realized that I was myself responsible for my predicament. My carelessness…my indolence and my overall dependence on my father had only estranged me from him and my family. I was spoilt. I tried my friends. I tried all my relatives and learnt it the hard way that nobody stands by you if you are a failure. Then one day, I took a resolve to work hard and prove myself. Luckily I met you and received your support. Whatever I am today is all because of you.'

Punit poured it all out in one breath. But he had still not finished and continued,

'I have to tell you something.'

'…….'

'Don't misunderstand me please...and excuse me if you don't like it.

Sunidhi looked inquisitively at him.

'When I saw you for the first time, I was highly impressed by you. At the age of forty, I don't want to unnecessarily indulge in romanticism. Moreover, I am not a young bachelor. But it wasn't just your physical charm which impressed me, but your overall personality. It was a mix of attraction and respect.'

Punit paused for a minute and then continued, 'I hope I'm not saying anything wrong...please stop me if I do...'

Sunidhi heaved a sigh of relief that it wasn't anything of the sort she had feared. She raised her eyes and looked at him. He noticed it and lowered his eyes. Movement of the eyes conveyed a great deal to each other.

'Every time I met you, I felt that your influence was growing on me. It wasn't because you helped me every time, but because you always treated me nicely. That gave me the courage to ask you for a dinner. I have seen lots of bank officials. They always had their own demands. The bank's interest was always secondary for them. But I didn't find such selfishness in you. Whenever I came to you, you helped me. I got new contracts, new business and repaid the loans most honestly. I had taken a vow that till I repaid the loans, I wouldn't talk to you about what I'm about to say tonight.

'I want to say something very seriously. I wouldn't say that I have fallen in love with you, even if it's a one-way love. I want to propose marriage to you. I don't know anything about your personal life. I wouldn't even want to know it. I'll only say that if you don't like my proposal, please tell me without any hesitation. I'll get out of your life and never meet you again...and if we ever meet by chance, we'll only meet as friends.'

'It's too sudden and early for me to say anything. I'll need some time to think about it...some more opportunities to meet and know each other', replied Sunidhi.

'That's not a problem. Take your time…I'll wait.'

Punit walked across and brought a box of sweets. Giving a piece of *barfi* to Sunidhi, he said, 'Have a sweet…for the housewarming. Now I'll tell you why I called just you. I couldn't have said all this in front of other people. But I'll once again ask you to take your time to decide…I'm in no hurry.'

The whole evening, Sunidhi didn't utter a word, but spoke only through her eyes. She had no desire to speak. She simply listened to Punit, looked at him and realised that he was a nice guy. After dinner, Punit dropped her back at her flat. She entered the lift alone. She was left to take her decisions herself, and alone.

❖❖❖

54

Vikas was now the General Manager of his bank, one of the major nationalized banks in the country. His work load and responsibilities had also increased manifold. He had lots of visitors every day, apart from his own officers. There was virtually no time for himself. On top of that, there were always some complications or the other...and there was nobody to share his worries. Now he sadly realized that one was all alone when one reached the top. If there was anybody there, it was your own ambitious self, which still wanted to go higher and refused to stop because stopping, for it, was no less than falling down. But neither the self nor the top ever realized how much they had left behind in being there!

Today, Sunidhi had called twice, but he hadn't been able to talk as he had meetings. And after that he had to attend a dinner. Sometimes he took a few drinks too. By the time he returned home, he felt awfully tired and retired to bed. It was past eleven but he wasn't in deep sleep. So, when his mobile rang, he didn't know if it was a dream or reality. He picked it up and without putting on his glasses, he knew it was...Sunidhi.

'Hello...were you asleep?'

'No, but I was getting ready for it,' said Vikas, yawning.

'Sorry...I called you so late. But I tried a few times earlier too...'

'Yes, I know. I was in a meeting. But I couldn't call you back even after that...extremely sorry.'

'I wanted to talk to you about Punit.'

'Tell me, have you decided anything...?' Vikas was extremely keen to know.

Sunidhi narrated everything about Punit. The Malabar Hills flat, the furniture, the car, and...everything else. Vikas just listened quietly. His reactions carried more of speculation than sound.

'His urge for happiness just shook my consciousness. But just as there was nobody in his house, the same desolation seemed to create a storm inside him. Hello...are you listening...?'

'Yes, I am listening. But what have you decided...?

'I'll tell you later. Before that, there's a surprise for you. You'll be amazed to hear it. Okay, you try and guess, tell me what it can be?'

'You have started liking Punit?'

'No, it's not about Punit...it's something else!'

'Something else or someone else?' There was apprehension in his tone.

'No you are wrong! Why are you stuck with the idea of getting me married? I'll tell you about that when the time comes. Now it's totally different... just take a guess!' The typical thoughtlessness of a young girl was bursting in Sunidhi's words.

'Okay...you tell me...!'

'So, you give up...?'

'That happened a long time ago...'

Sunidhi's hearty laugh only added to Vikas's inquisitiveness.

'Listen, my dear Vikas...Sir. Your own Sunidhi has got a promotion...she is now a Senior Vice President,' said Sunidhi, wishing if only he were there in front of her to appreciate the glitz of achievements in her eyes. Looking into his eyes, she could've also asked him if she had met his expectations or not?

'Many many congrats...!' said Vikas. He was totally at a loss for words. He managed to say, 'Wish you were here with me...to see how I congratulated you...!' He wanted to say much more but his age came in the way.

'You can tell me on the phone! So that I may remind you and take it from you when we meet next,' said Sunidhi playfully.

Vikas felt as if Sunidhi was standing in front of him and had sensed what was going on in his mind.

'Blushing…even on the phone…?' asked Sunidhi.

'What do you think I had said?'

'The same which you had thought…'

'What had I thought…?' asked Vikas very emotionally.

'You are asking me to tell you what you had thought…'

'Yes, I also want to know how well you know me and my mind…'

'You already know that. Okay, tell me when are you coming to Mumbai?'

'Not decided as yet. But I'll surely come soon, even if I have to come there especially for you.'

'Good… Sorry to have kept you awake for so long. Now go to sleep, it's quite late at night.'

Vikas looked at his watch. It was 1.30. He said,

'Okay… goodnight. Congrats once again.'

'That congrats which you propose to give when we meet…?' asked Sunidhi with a pinch of salt. Vikas laughed in his own unique way. Even on the phone, Sunidhi felt that his face had turned red. She said,

'Good night…sleep tight.'

'Good night,' said Vikas and wondered if the phrase 'sleep tight', wasn't an indicator of a changed, self-confident and somewhat dominant Sunidhi? He had seen her as a shy, fearful and reluctant young girl and now, leaving all that behind, she was scaling new heights and giving tough competition to the confident corporate bosses. Still she had retained her pristine innocence. Her progress and position hadn't gone to her head. He really appreciated her talent and capabilities. But had she not met him and succeeded in her efforts, what would have become of her? Where could she have been, had she compromised with her domestic issues and accepted defeat? For a long time, Vikas kept travelling with Sunidhi in the wonderful journey of her growth and forgot that more than half the night had already gone by....like his age!

Something which kept bothering Vikas was Sunidhi's indecision about Punit. In the earlier days, she used to share even the most insignificant details of her life with him. He remembered how he had been motivating her to get married. But now he himself felt insecure by the very thought of her getting married! Was it possible that she would continue her emotional connect with him even after her marriage? If not, then what would happen to him? How would he live the rest of his life? Preeti was now generally busy looking after their daughter. Garima was now a grown up girl with lots of dreams in her eyes. Even though they both cared for Vikas, they could never give him the warmth and energy, the emotional support and succour, which he received from Sunidhi.

When Sunidhi had evaded talking about her marriage today, he had felt completely cut-up. He lay in bed tossing and turning in extreme mental agony. Sleep was nowhere in his eyes and there were no signs of the night coming to an end. He didn't know what was bothering him...love or the scare of being left alone? He hadn't received so much love from anyone in his life. Tonight, he admitted to himself that if he ever lost Sunidhi, it would make his life absolutely lonely and meaningless. In that case...should she not get married at all? No, he would never ever wish that. Was he jealous of Punit? But how could that be? He had not even seen him. But Sunidhi had told him so much about Punit...his riches, his property, his prosperity, his struggle and his success. Sunidhi would get a much better life with him. Punit had clearly told her that he wouldn't come in the way of her career. She'd be very happy with him. What had he given her...and what would he be able to give her?

Vikas's unending monologue was only confounding his confusion. No matter how mentally strong one was, he always fretted inside. Everybody had an unseen desire, a mirage of thirst, a longing for the moon. When he was alone, it badly pricked and provoked him. Vikas's love for Sunidhi had never been just an infatuation for her physical charms. He had never even craved for that. But he too was made of flesh and blood and couldn't have probably been aware of something lurking inside the deep recesses of his heart. Whatever it was, he had emotionally become so attached to Sunidhi that the very thought of losing her ran shivers down his spine. He wondered why hadn't he thought about all this when she had herself proposed to live with him, that too, without causing any disturbance in his family life! His cherished ideals seemed to be at war with his heart's desires. Finally he drifted off to sleep.

It was a grandeur usually seen in the dreams. Johannesburg looked so beautiful from the twenty-first floor. The whole town was visible from there. Nelson Mandella had awakened the people of the third world. Promising South African young faces could be seen ringing bells carrying trays of tea and coffee. There were more women than men doing jobs starting from housekeeping to the reception desks. Men could be seen drinking beer here and there. Vikas didn't know when and why he got entangled in the economic aspects and social conditions of this country. Right then he received a phone call from Sunidhi...staying in the same hotel, 'What are you doing?'

'Nothing much...' replied Vikas, hesitantly. How could he say that he was thinking about the economy of African nations. He was there to attend an International Seminar on banking.

'When will you tell me that you were thinking of me?'

'Do I need to tell you that!' said Vikas, effortlessly.

'Then come over immediately. Let's have coffee together!' Sunidhi put down the intercom.

In a few moments, Vikas stood in front of Sunidhi's room. The door opened even before the doorbell had ended its chime. Sunidhi beheld Vikas from head to foot. He looked so young and fresh in white *kurta-pyjama*. A whiff of intimacy and love overflowed from his eyes. Still, the woman inside her was fully awake and alert. They shook hands and sat down. Nobody said anything for a while. Then she got up and asked Vikas,

'Tea or coffee…?'

'You called me for coffee…"

Sunidhi smiled and went up to the coffee-maker. As long as she stood there, Vikas couldn't take his eyes off her. The contours of her swells and curves looked more beautiful and attractive than ever in pants and a shirt. She knew that she was being watched. A woman's senses gauged such situations in no time. She turned back, holding two cups of coffee and announced,

'Coffee…'

'Thanks!'

Sitting close to the glass window, they sipped coffee and watched the view outside. It was a pleasant evening. All kinds of emotions rose and fell inside Vikas's heart. And Sunidhi wasn't ignorant about it. Vikas came close to her…so close that he could even hear her heart throb. He felt as if he experienced an uncanny vivacity much beyond the confines of both the physical and celestial worlds. In such a calm and quiet evening, Sunidhi's words suddenly shocked him,

'Anything except sex…?'

'……'

Sunidhi looked at Vikas. He was finding it difficult to gulp the bitter saliva in his mouth!

'Sunidhi, did you ever feel that I ever made you feel like that…in spite of our being so intimate…ever placed any demand for that…?' So saying Vikas sat in a chair. He took a sip of his coffee. It tasted bitter…and cold.

The hotel was close to the airport. Soon, they noticed an aeroplane, roaring and piercing the sky. They silently watched its flickering lights slowly disappear in the sky.

Vikas tried hard to come out of his sleep as he had heard a knock at the door. But his eyes just wouldn't open. The room was filled with sunshine. It even pierced his eyes. Before going to sleep, he had set the air-conditioner at 11 degrees. So, early in the morning, he felt extremely cold and covered himself with a quilt. Then he heard a sound like that of the doorbell. Still half-asleep, he got out of the bed and walked toward the door, thinking it must be Sunidhi.

He opened the door. It was the washerman, carrying his suit. The night's dream was over.

He looked at the watch. It was 8.30. He thought that the driver would also have come by now. Then he realized, it was Buddha Purnima, a holiday. He wondered why he was becoming so forgetful...!

❖❖❖

55

There was a familiar knock at the door. Sunidhi looked up …it was Punit, carrying a huge bouquet…a big bunch of blood red roses!

'Many many congratulations!'

'Thanks, thank you very much…why did you take the trouble?'

'It's such a great achievement of yours…I couldn't have conveyed it on phone,' said Punit, looking at Sunidhi with piercing eyes. 'Thanks. Thanks a lot…it's good wishes from all of you.'

Sunidhi pressed the bell and ordered coffee. After the evening of housewarming, Punit had tried a couple of times to call her, but couldn't ever get through. Today, he had come prepared to talk to her about his marriage proposal, but felt embarrassed. Looking at the bunch of flowers he had brought, Sunidhi had sensed what was going on in his mind, but she didn't want to broach the subject. So, she said,

'How's your business doing?'

'Excellent. Your support has set everything right. Now, I am planning to open a branch in Dubai. There are too many restrictions in India. In Dubai, there are none. I am thinking of shifting my operations there.' Punit kept bragging about his achievements and future plans. Sunidhi felt he was trying to impress her, first with flowers and now with the stories of his success.

'Now you don't have any business relations with our bank?' said Sunidhi, in a business-like tone.

'Now I have plenty of funds. Business is going very well. You helped me just in time. But if I still need any help, I'll come to you…'

Sunidhi noticed that Punit's phone constantly rang but he avoided the calls. There was a brief silence after their coffee. Finally Punit broke the ice,

'Congratulations once again…I'll take your leave now.'

'Thanks for everything.' Sunidhi stood up to thank him.

Punit wasn't ready for a sudden parting. He was expecting Sunidhi to shake hands, but she just folded them and said goodbye.

'Bye…we must celebrate this achievement…spare some time for a dinner one day.'

'Sure,' replied Sunidhi. 'I'll call you.'

Before leaving the cabin, Punit looked back at Sunidhi with a lot of expectation in his eyes and blurted out an 'Okay.' Sunidhi felt he was trying to ask her about her thoughts regarding the marriage proposal. After he was gone, she looked at the roses again. Each one of them seemed to narrate Punit's success stories. She wondered whether he had come to congratulate her or impress her with his accomplishments in business? How different was his behaviour! Business, money, contracts, profit, new office… restrictions in India… and opportunities in Dubai…! Sunidhi wondered how some people lived for money alone! She got a message, her boss had called her.

'Congratulations, Sunidhi…your posting orders have come. You have been made the in-charge of South India and posted in Bengaluru. Is it okay… hope you've no problems?

'Not at all, sir. When do I have to leave?'

'You'll have to join at Bengaluru by next week.'

'Okay, sir.'

❖❖❖

56

Once again tonight, Sunidhi had no sleep in her eyes. After a week's time, she was going to miss this seashore, this beautiful city of Mumbai and its sparkling lights. Change alone was eternal in life. There was continuity in it. It never stopped. But one thing which didn't change in her life was Vikas's place in her heart. She saw him everywhere and in everything in her life, her fame, her isolation …her life was desolate without him!

There was a call from Punit, 'I've heard that you have been transferred…!'

'Yes.'

'When are you leaving?'

'Next week.'

'In that case, you'll have to immediately spare an evening for me. I'll keep the whole of my week free…whenever you want, Oberoi or Ambassador…wherever you want.'

Sunidhi knew very well what was going on in Punit's mind.

'I'll wait…'

'Okay…'

'I'll remind you…'

'There's no need for that…'

Sunidhi was now getting bored with his talks. She felt his only interest in her was to make her agree to his marriage proposal. And he was pampering her only for that. But the closer he tried to get to her, the farther she drew herself away from him. Sometimes, she felt he didn't even know how to live well. He only knew how to do business and succeed in it. He had no regard for others' happiness. Even in Sunidhi, he saw a successful business woman more than a life-partner! What he admired in her most was her business sense.

Sunidhi missed Vikas intensely. But she didn't call him. She didn't know where he would be and how busy. She didn't consider it proper to call somebody without purpose. Suddenly she realized that her childlike playfulness was fast giving way to a mellowed solemnity. New assignments and responsibilities always tended to mould us in their own way.

Sunidhi painfully recalled her childhood marred by wants and deprivation, her meaningless marriage held at a time when she yearned to study and the mental agony caused by her marriage. She also recalled how Vikas had entered her grief-stricken life like a messiah, turning the course of her journey towards hope and fulfillment. It was his unfailing support which prodded her to move on...undeterred by all her adversities. He only helped her achieve whatever she had desired...a comfortable life and an excellent job. Today she held a top position in a foreign bank. All her life's events just flashed before her inward eye. Amongst a multitude of faces which appeared before her...the faces of her kith and kin and others...there was only one who had always stood by her, over-riding the compulsions of time, relationships and personal desires. Even when he wasn't physically there, she felt he was there with her...her most valued friend, philosopher and guide...Vikas! He had only enabled her to be what she at present was!

Today, Sunidhi had everything in life...riches, fame, respect, position. Only because of Vikas!

❖❖❖

57

One day, Vikas's life suddenly came under an eclipse. Sometimes, you had to bear the brunt for something you haven't really done. His blind trust in one of his deputy general managers landed him in deep trouble. Chandran was his confidante and in-charge of the department dealing with the advance of loans to small and medium enterprises. He had shown excellent results in the past and earned the chairman's applause not only for himself but also for Vikas. But what emerged from the inspection report, just baffled Vikas. The Chairman knew that it was Chandran's doing, but he couldn't save Vikas from being implicated in the case. Vikas had been betrayed.

Chandran had advanced several loans to one Khurana on a single proposal of the purchase of trucks for his transport company. In a few cases, even the requisite papers had not been obtained. The scam involved almost a hundred crore. Vikas had absolutely no hand in it, but he had burnt his fingers all the same.

When confronted, Chandran had shamelessly stated that it wasn't a big deal…it wasn't going to cause any loss to the bank as the entire loan amount was going to come back. But Vikas wasn't satisfied with his explanation. The environment of corruption prevailing all over the country had always bothered him. It was a pity that even his own office hadn't escaped its onslaught. He ordered Chandran's immediate transfer, but had to himself appear before the inquiry, the head office had ordered against Chandran. Finally he escaped unscathed because the chairman and all others who mattered, knew very well that he was clean and above board. They in fact sympathized with him for having been cheated.

But this incident left Vikas totally shattered. He became highly cautious and extremely short-tempered. He would get irritated even on small matters. He started keeping his mobile switched off. One day when he was literally shouting at some officers, his landline phone rang.

'Hello…' he shouted into the phone.

'Oh, my god…!' It was Sunidhi.

'Sorry,' said Vikas.

'What happened…why are you in such a rage?'

'The fool I blindly trusted stabbed me,' replied Vikas.

'Cool down. You'll spoil your health like this.'

Vikas talked to Sunidhi at length. He felt light and relieved after having shared everything with her. He thanked her for calling. At the same time, he wondered how she always came to know he was in trouble and called immediately! Was it merely a coincidence, telepathy or the bond of love…?

Sunidhi had now reached a stage where she was in a position to offer advice to others. The nervous and timid girl who couldn't utter anything beyond 'Yes sir', 'No, sir', in front of him, was today practically grooming Vikas. He enjoyed listening to her. By now he had fully calmed down. Just to change the subject, Sunidhi added,

'These days everyone wants to grow rich overnight. Even when the common man is starving due to high inflation…our leaders and administrators are busy indulging in scams involving crores. God only knows how many Gates would finally open. Greed is at the root cause of all this, Vikas ji…when the governments tend to get weak, the hyenas get liberty to run away with whatever they can get their jaws in. It's high time we had a change,' she suddenly stopped, realizing she had already been too didactic.

'Nothing can change in our country…they are all alike. Only the colour of their signboards changes, otherwise they are all dealing in the same wares,' replied Vikas.

'But you weren't like this Vikas ji…you have always been a great optimist, a great inspiration for all those who know you…a never-give-up type of person! What has happened to you?'

'Let's talk about something else. Tell me how you have been doing?' Vikas wanted to change the subject. He was delighted to see Sunidhi talk like a highly intelligent and matured person. But he wasn't interested in politics. What he was keen to know was what she had decided about Punit. But he didn't ask her. He wanted her to bring up the subject.

❖❖❖

58

Sunidhi had started liking Bengaluru. She was in-charge of the whole of South India. She remained extremely engaged in work. She had everything except time. She found it difficult even to talk to Vikas, because he too would be awfully busy. Priorities had changed for both of them. Punit called Sunidhi many times in the beginning and bragged every time about his growing business. But she was no longer interested in listening to his mundane talks. So she never called him.

Time passed.

Now even when Sunidhi and Vikas talked to each other, they generally discussed banking and the current affairs rather than their personal matters. Sometimes they felt they were becoming too formal. Still they cared deeply about each other. Even though Vikas was always curious to know about Sunidhi's relationship with Punit, he never enquired about it, nor did she ever offer to talk about it.

Whenever Sunidhi travelled on tour, she always thought of Vikas. Particularly on her foreign trips when she had plenty of time at her disposal. Even now, she kept Meena Kumari's poetry book with her. She had read Ayn Rand's *The Fountainhead* many times, she liked reading it again and again. With her advancing age and changed social circumstances, she discovered many new angles in the book...about power, about systems and the people who ran it.

In her free time, Sunidhi would wonder about her future! Her mind was still oscillating between the anticipation about Punit and Vikas's affinity. Besides protection and respect, what a woman needed most was love. And she had experienced love to its inner-most recesses. She had earned protection and respect on her own strength. She had felt many times that a woman fell in love only once...rest of the times it was only a compromise. That's why nobody could replace Vikas in her heart. She might not be talking to him for weeks or months together, still he was always there in her thoughts.

Sunidhi's relationship with Vikas remained multi-faceted. Having sprouted in sympathy, it passed through the stage of ideological exchanges and finally brought them together on one platform. Acting as an engine of motivation, Vikas pulled her sometimes, pushed her at others but always carried her along. Then, there was that chemistry of youth too, between the two of them, which always flowed through their arteries, but never degenerated into banal bodily pleasures. Drifting aimlessly in the flood of insecurity, Sunidhi desired many times to hang on to his sails. But Vikas's farsightedness not only saved himself from the vortex, but also groomed her. She learnt that not every image of man was like Vikas. She even learnt the trick of being alert, when alone, only from his behaviour. She felt an intellectual, emotional and spiritual connect with him, rooted in love and affection.

In her day-to-day life, Sunidhi experienced a dignified relationship with him. Hardly a day passed when she didn't feel him inside her. He kept constantly drenching her like a cloud of love. Now her career demanded her full time...a career which she wanted to take to the summit, the highest point in her official hierarchy. For this, there was no compromise for her. She had started living this career with full dedication. Only a love, with all the hues of a cloud that kept hovering around her conscious and unconscious self was ... Vikas!

Sunidhi learnt through her struggles that there could be many solutions to our problems. We had only to consider all options. If we protected ourselves from negative thoughts, there was nothing which couldn't be achieved. Circumstances also taught her that insecurity, fear and despair had to be overcome to fight the odds. She felt she had the power to face any problem...whether it was about her work at the bank or anything else in her life. Now she didn't feel the need to depend on anyone...though she couldn't imagine her existence without Vikas.

Punit's image also spontaneously emerged inside her mind. His marriage proposal still haunted her. He was hard-working, enterprising and practical. But he was extremely flamboyant. Such people proved weak in achieving eminence. They only wanted more...and even more. They didn't want to stop and enjoy life. For them, destination alone mattered in life...and not the way which led them there. They didn't even care to know what lay on both sides of the way. Such people were romantic only for a while. They suddenly got detached and transferred all the blame for their infamy to others. Is that what happened with Meghna...Sunidhi had now started thinking about Punit on these lines. Even otherwise, if one idol in the temple was extra-ordinarily majestic, the other automatically faded before it. The images of Vikas and Punit were similarly positioned in her mind.

So, Sunidhi almost stopped thinking about Punit!

The election results had started flashing on TV. The incumbent government was losing badly and the leadership was passing into the hands of a person who had come up from a very humble background, spending his childhood in extreme deprivation. He had struggled hard and people now wanted to hand over the reins of the country in the hands of this common man. Sunidhi was extremely happy. It was a victory for her dreams.

Sunidhi felt things would now change, for sure.

Next day, all newspapers and TV channels were flooded with election results. In this fanfare, one particular news which got buried from the public eye was about the CBI exposing a hawala-case. The names and photos of four persons involved in the scam had also been published. Punit was one of them!

The secret of Punit's riches and glory suddenly opened up before Sunidhi. She was speechless. The election results began to fade before her eyes. Right then, her phone rang. It was Vikas.

'Sunidhi...did you watch the news? Congratulations.'

'For what...?' Sunidhi felt he was mocking her for the news about Punit.

'Your party is forming the government...you always argued with me...now everything is put to rest.'

'Oh... okay...I thought...'

'You thought what...?'

'Nothing...nothing else is special?' Sunidhi wanted to be sure about Punit's news.

'What else would be more special than this...?'

'Yes...right.'

'What's the matter? You don't seem to be happy?'

'I am...I am very happy...' said Sunidhi, nervously.

'Okay, tell me something...I didn't want to ask, but now I can't resist this any longer...what have you decided about Punit?' Vikas asked after mustering all the power at his command.

'Would you like to know...?'

'Of course...'

'Now, I have decided to stay alone!'

❖❖❖